AN ANECDOTAL DEATH

A HARRY BROCK MYSTERY

AN ANECDOTAL DEATH

KINLEY ROBY

FIVE STAR
A part of Gale, Cengage Learning

Farmington Hills, Mich • San Francisco • New York • Waterville, Maine
Meriden, Conn • Mason, Ohio • Chicago

LIBRARY OF CONGRESS CATALOGING-IN-PUBLICATION DATA

Roby, Kinley E.
An anecdotal death : a Harry Brock mystery / Kinley Roby. — First edition.
pages ; cm
ISBN 978-1-4328-3024-3 (hardcover) — ISBN 1-4328-3024-4 (hardcover) — ISBN 978-1-4328-3019-9 (ebook) — 1-4328-3019-8 (ebook)
1. Brock, Harry (Fictitious character : Roby)—Fiction. 2. Private investigators—Florida—Fiction. 3. Gulf Coast (Fla.)—Fiction. I. Title.
PS3618.O3385A85 2015
813'.6—dc23 2014041374

First Edition. First Printing: March 2015
Find us on Facebook– https://www.facebook.com/FiveStarCengage
Visit our website– http://www.gale.cengage.com/fivestar/
Contact Five Star™ Publishing at FiveStar@cengage.com

Printed in the United States of America
1 2 3 4 5 6 7 19 18 17 16 15

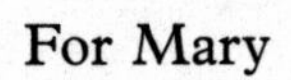

Chapter 1

On a warm, sunny spring morning, following a bad night, Harry was leaning on the railing of the Avola fishing pier, watching a female dolphin and her baby, not more than three feet long, quietly surfacing and diving close to the pier, scarcely rippling the sun-drenched, blue-green water. He was thinking how deceptively peaceful and free from harm they looked when a woman's voice scattered his reflections.

"Mr. Brock?" she asked. "Am I disturbing you?"

He started to say yes, traces of the night still with him, and was glad he hadn't when he turned to look at her. "Not at all," he told her, straightening up from the railing.

She was slightly taller than Harry, wearing a black dress, black shoes, and a wide-brimmed black hat, a black bag slung over one shoulder, and black-framed sunglasses hiding her eyes. The only sign of vitality Harry saw in her funereal turnout was the mass of softly waved, honey-colored hair spilling over her shoulders, lifting and falling in the gentle onshore breeze.

"My name is Meredith Winters," she said in a clear but colorless voice that matched her face, which Harry guessed might be beautiful, placed in another setting. "Are you a private investigator?"

"Yes. How can I help you?" he responded, struck by how isolated she looked among the fishermen—young and old, male and female, scattered along the railings, holding long rods and accompanied by rank-smelling bait pails. And more so from the cheerful crowd of Hispanic visitors from Miami on their annual spring west-coast holiday, streaming past them, the men in shorts and wildly colorful shirts, the women in skin-tight black pedal pushers and flaming tops, all laughing and talking loudly.

Standing stiff and straight as the crowd flowed by, she was a dark rebuke to the revelers and everything else around her. After a long moment of silence, she opened her black bag, took out a card, and passed it to him.

"I'm not sure you can," she said, "but will you call on me tomorrow at three?"

"Let me walk you back to your car," he said. "You can tell me why you want to talk with me."

"No," she said. "Tomorrow . . . or not. I won't blame you if it's *not.*"

She paused to glance at the dolphins and said in a voice carrying such sadness that it wrung Harry's heart, "How lovely, how full of love."

Harry stifled his impulse to tell her that the young dolphin was in danger. A few minutes before her arrival, he had seen a large white-tipped shark cruise past the pair, obviously hunting. He might have, but didn't, tell her that if the mother's attention wandered, even for a few seconds, she would probably lose her baby.

"Yes," Harry said, trying to sound supportive.

Nodding almost imperceptibly, she strode away. Harry watched her go, admiring her straight back and the strength of her long, open strides. Whatever the nature of the burden she carried, she bore it like a warrior.

When she vanished into the crowd, Harry found he had lost interest in the pier and walked back to the parking lot. Recent rains had muddied the dirt roads, bone dry all winter, and the sides of his silver SUV wore the results. But it was Meredith Winters who occupied his thoughts, and curiosity about her took him to his friend Jim Snyder, captain of the Tequesta County Sheriff's Department.

Jim's office looked as if it had been furnished out of a low-end, secondhand office furniture shop because it had. Like that of many county activities, the sheriff's department's budget had been running on empty for years. From the worn and cracked algae-green floor tiles to the battered gray walls and metal folding chairs, none of whose legs all touched the floor at the same time, and Jim's metal desk that was too wretched to laugh at and too ridiculous to regard with sympathy, the office looked like a film set in a Graham Greene adaptation.

"Do you ever get out of here long enough to see how other people live?" Harry asked Jim, who was sitting at his desk, bent over an open file and surrounded by stacks of similar files awaiting his attention.

Jim looked up. Seeing Harry, he unfolded his considerable length from his chair and reached across the desk, his large hand extended.

"Don't you know you can get yourself shot in here, coming up on someone like that?" he asked with an accent that planted his roots deep in Appalachia.

"You don't carry a gun, despite all my efforts," Harry replied. "Can I break you away from those case files long enough to ask a question?"

The two men held their handshake a moment or two longer than necessary, reflecting their years of having worked together and their mutual respect and liking.

"Lord, yes," Jim said, coming out from behind the desk. "There's coffee somewhere around here. Where's my sergeant gotten to? Frank!" he bellowed, having thrust his head out the door.

Harry had chosen the least wrecked metal chair available and eased himself into it, knowing that sitting down heedlessly and then finding yourself on the floor was a serious risk.

Jim had reached his chair by the time Frank arrived, a broad, heavy man filling his tan uniform like a sausage in its skin and a round, perpetually red face, framed to wear a smile.

"Harry," he said, his smile widening. "What brings you here, arrested for overly zealous search and seizure of one of them society women you're always chasing?"

The old Florida in Frank Hodges's voice never failed to make Harry laugh, which was all right because Hodges got just as much pleasure from listening to Harry's Yankee twang.

"I'm looking for information," Harry said. "I suppose I could have Googled it, but thought it might give you two something to do other than sponge off the taxpayers."

"Speaking of sponging," Hodges said, lowering his weight onto a chair that squealed miserably as it absorbed the load, "that brother-in-law of mine has showed up again. I was all for sending him on his way with a load of birdshot in his ass, but the wife threatened to set the dog on me if I didn't put the gun down. So he's living large at our table, and the grocery bill is climbing like an air show biplane."

"Frank," Jim said, "do you think you could scrounge us some coffee from the commissariat and leave your brother-in-law to a higher power to deal with?"

"I could do that and maybe, if she's not looking, rustle a donut or two from Evelyn's hoard," Hodges said, brightening at the prospect.

"There," Jim said when Hodges had left. "What is it you want to know?"

"Does the name Meredith Winters mean anything to you?"

"Hodges is better at this than I am," Jim replied, rubbing his hand briskly over the last of the very short, pale hair on the top of his head, something he frequently did when he was thinking. "He probably knows who she is and the names of her second cousins as well. Why are you asking?"

"I had a bad night," Harry said, "and to clear my head, I drove in to take a walk on the pier. I was watching a female dolphin and her new calf fishing near the pier when a woman dressed all in black asked me if I was a PI and gave me her card with her name and address, then asked me to call on her tomorrow afternoon."

"Holly Pike cause you the bad night?" Jim asked, a frown of concern darkening his long face.

"Yes."

"How many months has she been gone?"

"She left for Montana in September."

"I thought you two had found common ground."

"No, whatever it is continues, and it's wearing me out."

"She won't stay here, and you won't go there. Is staying on the Hammock that important to you?"

"Apparently."

"But you're still . . . negotiating?"

"I don't really know what we're doing, but it's damned painful," Harry said, trying to keep the bitterness out of his voice and failing.

Hodges strode in, looking very pleased with himself, carrying three mugs of coffee on a bent aluminum tray and a half-filled box of powdered sugar donuts. "She'd gone somewhere, and I struck," he said, beaming.

"She'll track you down," Jim said, clearing a space on his desk for the tray, "and when she finds you, you're on your own."

"We'll eat the evidence and hide the mugs in your desk," Hodges said, passing Harry a mug, then the donut box.

"Frank," Harry said, taking half a donut, "do you know a Meredith Winters?"

"Anyone planning to eat this other half?" Hodges asked, showing the box around.

Jim, whose mouth was full, shook his head, and Harry waved the suggestion away.

"Then I will," Hodges said, finishing it in two bites. "Not personally," he said, then drank a little coffee and reached for another donut. "From all reports, she's about the third richest woman in Avola."

"Did she marry money?" Jim asked.

He was always telling Hodges not to gossip, but the truth was that Jim liked nothing better than a serious and lengthy gossip-fest, especially if he could quiet his conscience by finding a way to tie it to a case under investigation.

"No," Hodges said. "She inherited it."

"Is she married?" Harry asked.

Hampered by a large bite of donut, Hodges shook his head, then added, "Widow," a moment later.

"Recently made?" Jim inquired, trying not to sound interested.

"A month or so ago," Hodges said. "You should remember that, Captain. He was the guy lost drift fishing. The Coast Guard searched for a week and then stopped, saying there was no chance of his being found alive. *The Banner* gave it a lot of coverage then dropped the story when the Coast Guard quit looking."

"Lord, it's all going," Jim protested, vigorously rubbing his head. "Now I remember. Harry, you must have read about it. Sheriff Fisher was afraid we were going to be brought in on it."

Hodges gave a powdery whoop of laughter and said around a mouthful of donut, "Fisher thinks the department ought to be run like the Salvation Army, on faith and donations."

"Frank," Jim said, "you know better than to talk that way about Sheriff Fisher."

Hodges put up his free hand in acknowledgment of Jim's angry outburst but went on eating.

"The man who was lost, Harry, was Amos Lansbury," Jim said. "Does the name jog your memory?"

"She must have kept her own name after she married," Harry said. "I wonder if it's the same Lansbury who ran Prentice Foster's state senate campaign?"

"Yes, now you mention it," Jim said. "He stepped on a lot of toes getting Foster elected. If memory serves, when it was over, some of the payback landed him in jail."

"Plus this," Hodges said, dusting the powdered sugar off his hands. "Lansbury appealed to Foster for help with the charges, since what he'd done, he'd done to help Foster get elected, but the new senator scraped him off his boot and left him to dry on the road."

"I don't remember," Jim said, "but he was in Eglin Federal Prison up on the Panhandle for a while."

"Vote tampering, as I recall," Hodges said. "There was talk that it was a set-up. Apparently the judge thought so too and gaveled the Assistant Attorney General's call for 'a sentence that would send a message.' Instead, he gave him a six-month slap on the wrist at Elgin."

"Ah!" Harry said, thinking about motive. "Didn't he run against Rycroft Tillman?"

"Right," Hodges said cheerfully, "and there was smoke on the water before old Rycroft hit the canvas and stayed there. He thought to the very end that he was winning."

"So did a lot of his supporters," Jim said. "The whole developer crowd was with him. A lot of their oxen were gored in that defeat."

"And they've got long memories, not the oxen," Hodges said, followed by a roar of laughter.

"Sergeant, remember where you are," Jim told him with a frown.

A short, square officer with a shock of gray hair and steel-rimmed glasses appeared in the office doorway.

"Oh, oh," Hodges muttered, making a grab for the empty donut box.

"Lieutenant Orwell," Jim said, already on his feet and making a pathetic effort to look and sound pleased.

"Leave that box where it is, Sergeant," she said in a hard voice, "and tell me how it got here. No, on second thought, don't bother."

While she was speaking, she came further into the room and picked up the box, looking at each of the men as she left as if memorizing their faces. At the door she paused and said, "You might have had the decency to ask me."

"I don't know what it is about Evelyn," Hodges said in a pained voice as the three men remained standing and avoided looking at one another, "but every time she looks at me, even when I haven't done anything, I feel guilty."

Harry could no longer contain his laughter.

"It's not funny," Hodges said, "the Captain and me will pay and pay."

"It's your fault, Frank," Jim said. "Why didn't you get rid of that box? I would have but I couldn't see it from behind the desk, and when I stood up it was too late."

"Anyone have any idea why Meredith Winters wants to see me?" Harry asked, remaining on his feet when Jim and Hodges sat down, still wrangling.

"Not a clue," Jim said, obviously still preoccupied with the donut caper.

"Me neither," Hodges added, "but watch yourself. She runs with a nasty crowd. They've got too much money and no respect for anybody."

"I'll keep that in mind," Harry said, amused by the thought that Hodges had probably struck that sour note because he'd been caught pinching Lieutenant Orwell's donuts.

Chapter 2

Meredith Winters lived in Sandy Point, a section of Avola Harry seldom visited. Neither did anyone else except the people who lived there and a small army of service and delivery people who maintained the huge houses and acres of lawns, gardens, trees, and shrubberies that shielded the houses from the silent, nearly empty streets.

But the Point couldn't escape the Florida plague, the roar of lawn mowers and leaf blowers, that greeted Harry when he stepped out of the Rover onto the raked chipped stone drive under Winters's porte cochere. Once out of the SUV, he was confronted by the pale veined marble stairs leading to the white-pillared entrance to the house.

A large, heavy door swung open at his approach, and a solidly built man in a black suit, polished black shoes, and a white shirt and black tie stepped onto the landing to greet him. A slender woman stepped out from behind the man.

"Ah, Mr. Brock, good." She came forward to shake Harry's hand. She wore a black jacket and skirt and a cream-colored blouse with a ruffled front. Her long black hair shone like the marble floor behind her. "I am Raquel Morena," she said, adding a smile. "Mrs. Meredith's secretary and general factotum."

"I'm pleased to meet you," Harry said and meant it, returning her firm grip.

Through sometimes painful experience, Harry had learned how to cope with the very rich, which was best done as with any other large predator, holding meat in one hand and a gun in the other. Nonetheless, he felt slightly uneasy as he walked through the door and into a foyer the size of a tennis court, with a soaring ceiling and a black marble floor that glistened like a moonlit pond.

Raquel Morena was a very attractive woman and her large dark eyes were bright with intelligence. She was, he thought with pleasure, unmistakably one of those people who make you feel better just meeting her.

"Don't be surprised to find Mrs. Winters out of mourning," she said, leading him toward the sweeping stairs that curved up to the second-floor balcony. "Yesterday was the final day. If she seems remote or unresponsive, it will not be in reaction to you. The loss of Mr. Lansbury has been difficult for her."

"I suppose the fact his body was not recovered makes acceptance that much harder," he said.

"Con certeza," she responded, but Harry didn't think she sounded altogether certain.

Meredith Winters was standing in front of one of the tall windows on the side of the room overlooking the mouth of the Seminole River, the white-flecked Gulf beyond. Beneath the windows a manicured lawn ran down to the water and was dotted with palms and clusters of white, salmon, and red oleander bushes in full bloom.

"Mrs. Winters," Morena said quietly, "Mr. Brock is here. Would you like me to stay?"

"No, Raquel," Winters said in the same lifeless voice Harry recalled from their meeting on the pier, "you may leave."

Morena glanced at Harry, gave him an encouraging nod, and left. Not until then did Winters turn away from the window.

"Thank you for coming, Mr. Brock," she said, waving him

toward one of the large chairs nearest him as she sat down facing him.

Once seated, she said, "Just off the shore, a flock of terns and gulls are diving into a school of bait fish, being driven up to the surface by something. Nature is beautiful but cruel. Do I exaggerate?"

"No, I don't think so," Harry said, "but *cruel* isn't adequate to describe what's happening out there. But I'm being pedantic. I'm sorry."

"Of course, you're right."

In the silence that followed, Harry looked more closely at Winters and saw that her long, wavy hair had been brushed, she had made up her face very lightly, and the perfect fit of her pale orange, sleeveless dress set off her brown eyes. She possessed, he thought, a quiet elegance.

"Would you like something to drink, Mr. Brock?" she asked, leaning forward slightly as if tardily remembering he was there.

"No thank you," he said. "Is there anything I can say that would make it easier for you to tell me why I'm here? I know these things can be difficult."

"I find it difficult to focus," she said with a tremulous smile, "and I feel that even attempting to do something is ridiculous."

"I understand," he said. "I felt that way for a while after my first wife died, even though we had been separated for years."

"Amos and I were married for fifteen years," she said as though the information was something Harry needed to know.

Harry waited, sensing that she had more to say and needed to say it.

"He made some mistakes and was sent to jail, not for long, but long enough and for something that made it impossible for him to continue in politics when he was released. I remained with him, but I didn't forgive him, and he knew it. Now it's too late to say to him, 'I forgive you, Amos.' "

Harry did not ask himself why she was telling him this. Instead, he was listening hard, and by the time she finished speaking, he thought he knew what to ask.

"Is that why I'm here?" he said. "Do you want me to help you do something to say you're sorry?"

She had been leaning forward, arms crossed, staring at the floor. Her head snapped up as she straightened, unfolding her arms, her eyes fixed on his. "His death was no accident," she said. "Amos was murdered."

The accusation, delivered with force and harshness, left Harry momentarily without a response. Recovering himself, he paused long enough to sort through his options and asked quietly, "How long have you known this?"

"Since the moment Lieutenant Grover of the Coast Guard told me he was missing."

"Then the news that the search was terminated did not come as a further shock?"

"Not really."

"Did you think he was in danger before you heard that he was missing?"

It occurred to Harry that this lovely woman about whom he knew almost nothing might be unbalanced or intending to use him to help her take revenge on someone for real or imagined wrongs. On the other hand, he thought, perhaps not and asked, "Why haven't you gone to the police?"

"I let Sheriff Fisher know. He was courteous, called someone, came back on the line, and told me he was making some inquiries and would get back to me."

"Did he?"

"Oh, yes," she said. "He told me the Coast Guard had concluded that Amos died while drift diving, probably by drowning, and that there was no indication of foul play. He then told me there was nothing more to be done, expressed sorrow for my loss, and hung up."

"You waited some time before contacting me."

"Yes, I thought I would think about my situation for a while, to be sure it wasn't a fantasy brought on by grief. Having decided to go ahead, I began looking for someone to help me, and I found you."

"And you're sure I can help you?"

"Absolutely certain."

She'd said virtually the opposite to him on the pier the other day. He chose not to address it and said instead, "What do you want me to do?"

"Find the person who killed my husband."

Harry sat for a while before answering. While they talked, her voice had grown stronger and her face more animated. *Whatever else is true about her,* he thought, feeling his heart begin to beat a little faster, *she is a beautiful woman.*

"Mrs. Winters," he said finally, with reluctance, "initiating a search for whoever murdered your husband, if such a person exists, is not something a woman in your position should undertake lightly. By that, I don't mean you take your husband's death lightly," he added quickly, anticipating her objection.

"No, I certainly don't," she said sharply, her cheeks coloring slightly from what he assumed was anger. "What do you mean by, 'my position'? What does it, whatever *it* is, have to do with searching for Amos's killer?"

Harry had anticipated some resistance from her once he began speaking but not the flaring anger he was encountering, fully evident in her voice and her flushed face. *The lady,* he thought, summoning his patience, *has a temper and is not accustomed to being crossed.*

"You're a prominent person in the county," he continued. "You are also wealthy, which adds to your visibility. And, you are the widow of a man who once wielded a lot of political clout in Southwest Florida and who played a key role in getting Prentice Foster elected to the state senate."

Harry paused to let his words register with her and watched the results. Some people get up from sitting down as if rising from a throne, the rest as if sitting down had been a crippling experience. Meredith Winters rose like one of the royals. She walked back to the window with a straight back and the unself-conscious grace of a woman who, Harry observed approvingly, knew herself and her place in the world.

"You will now tell me," she said, raising her chin as she turned back to face Harry, "that my husband's notoriety is alive and well in the community."

"He also has or had enemies, a lot of them."

"Beginning with the man who owes his present position to Amos and will never forgive him for it."

"You're referring to Prentice Foster?"

"No."

Harry had risen with her and spoke as she turned away from the window to face him. "I had Rycroft Tillman in mind."

She gave a short, bitter laugh. "That wretched man," she said. "Would you like some tea? I'm parched."

"Yes," Harry said with a twist of sympathy, "I would like that."

She picked up a cell phone from a large cherry desk between the two windows and punched in a number while Harry watched her, reminded that she was in pain however much she tried to hide it.

"One of the girls will bring it up," she said, returning to her chair.

Once sitting down again, she leaned back for a moment, sighed, and said, "We have a houseful of people waiting on us. Ridiculous, really, except that in the winter months, there is constant entertaining, and it's either keep a staff that has grown accustomed to the activities or bring in a temporary staff two or three times a month."

She closed her eyes, and Harry had begun to think she'd forgotten him when a sharp rap on the door was followed by Raquel Morena's entrance.

"Mrs. Winters," she said, "tea is here," and stepped aside to let a young, dark-haired woman wheel in a brushed steel trolley, freighted with a teapot in a dark yellow cozy, surrounded by plates of scones, jam, marmalade, and cucumber sandwiches cut into triangles.

"Thank you, Genevieve," Winters said, suddenly coming to her feet. "I'll deal with things."

When the two women had left, she said, turning to Harry, "I'm sorry. I go away like that. I'm so ashamed of myself."

"Stop, no apologies," Harry said. "Are you sleeping at night?"

"Not a lot, no."

"Then sleep when you can."

She gave him a somewhat sharper look as if she had missed something then poured their tea. "Please help yourself to sugar and milk and whatever you want to eat."

"I'll eat a sandwich if you will," he said.

"I'm not hungry."

"Neither am I, but it would be a sin against the gustatory gods not to eat a sandwich that looks as good as these do."

Winters smiled, picked up the sandwich dish, and offered it to Harry.

"You go first," she said.

He took the dish from her.

"Pick one up," he told her. "Then I will."

She looked slightly grim but took one. So did Harry after putting down the plate.

"Now we bite together, and if they're poisoned, we both die."

"Mr. Brock," she said, having swallowed some of the

sandwich, "you are very strange."

"You should see where I live," he replied, and when she had eaten all of her sandwich, he said, "Now I will go on telling you why you should think twice, then again, before setting out on your crusade."

"What do you mean, *crusade*?" she protested, putting down her bone china cup forcefully enough to make Harry wince.

"I mean that you will be going to war with a large segment of the world, a segment that will not be happy with you because people don't like answering questions that connect them with a murder investigation. Nearly everyone in the world your husband inhabited has something to hide."

"Does that mean you won't help me?" she asked quietly, giving no physical signs of being fazed by what he had told her.

"It means I don't like the idea of your being exposed to unnecessary pain."

"Does that mean you will help me?"

"You haven't asked me."

"Christ!" she exploded. "Are you always like this?"

"I don't answer rhetorical questions."

That made her laugh. It didn't last long, but Harry saw the shadow lift briefly and her face shine for that moment with life.

"All right," she said, "will you help me find my husband's killer?"

"I will help you try to find out," he told her, "whether or not your husband was murdered, but I want you to know up front that the chances of getting an answer one way or the other are slim. I can't interview the very large things that swim where your husband died."

"Granted. Then how?"

"By doing things you're not going to like."

Chapter 3

When Harry and Meredith finished negotiating the terms of their contract, she stood up from her desk and extended her hand, which he took. "I knew before you told me, Mr. Brock, what the odds were of our coming up empty, but I want, no, I'm compelled, to make the effort."

"Call me Harry. I dislike being called Mr. Brock."

"All right. I'm Meredith or Merry, which I'm not."

"Then Meredith it will be. Do you want to tell me what's compelling you to do this?"

"No," she said with a rueful smile, "but I will. I stopped just short of divorcing Amos after I sat through the trial and learned what he'd done. I did not visit him in prison, and his coming home after being released wasn't a reunion of souls or the renewal of our vows. A problem with the IRS had come up and our tax attorneys pressured us into staying together."

"There's no doubt that he was guilty?"

"Only in the judge's mind."

"How can you be so certain?"

"I asked him and he told me."

"Okay, this can't be very comfortable for you," Harry said. "You don't have to go on."

Meredith's face sagged, and he saw he'd miscalculated.

"But," he said quickly and with feeling, "I'm really interested in what you're telling me. If it's not too painful, I would like to hear all of it."

"You're good, Brock," she said, "but be honest. How much of that did you mean?"

"All of it," he said. "The more I know about you and your husband, the more likely I am to make the right decision when I ask myself whether or not you had anything to do with his death."

"That's the nastiest thing anyone has ever said to me."

"Would you rather I, who am on your side, said it to you or a detective from the Criminal Investigation Division?"

"But no one except you has ever suggested I murdered him!" she protested angrily.

"No, but if you and I find something that makes it possible he was killed, the question will be asked. Are you sure you want to risk that?"

"You mean being asked if I arranged my husband's death?"

"Yes."

"Why not? I had nothing to do with killing him."

"The three legs of the law enforcement stool are motive, means, and opportunity."

"Do you mean did I swim out there, stab him, drop the knife, then swim back?"

"Very funny, now try this on: You hired someone else to do it. You've already admitted you had a motive, and your wealth provides means and opportunity."

"But I didn't."

"I believe you, but your denial and my belief still make a two-legged stool."

When Harry reached Bartram's Hammock, the sun was well down the afternoon sky, and the soaring trees were casting long shadows across his house and the narrow white sand road in front of it. Winding along Puc Puggy Creek, the road ran the length of the Hammock, a state nature preserve. He and Tucker

LaBeau, an elderly farmer, were the only people living on the Hammock, which could be accessed dry shod only by way of a humpbacked bridge near Harry's house or less comfortably by miles of slogging through water, cypress swamps, saw grass marshes, and alligator-infested sloughs with moccasins, coral snakes, rattlers, pythons, and the occasional monitor lizard for company, not to mention hosts of biting insects.

Harry was living on the Hammock only because the state had bought his house through a forced sale and as part of the deal made him a state game warden, tasked with keeping track of the wildlife, collectible orchids, and myriad other living things on Bartram's Hammock and the adjoining Stickpen Preserve, a vast stretch of cypress swamp, lying north and east of the Hammock. It had astonished and frustrated Harry to learn how many wild animal dealers would risk arrest and heavy fines to poach baby alligators, snakes, turtles, newts, tadpoles, and a dozen other species of lizards and plants.

After leaving New England, Harry, already a private investigator, drifted south and finally washed up on Bartram's Hammock. He settled, married a woman with two children, had a son with her, but after he had been shot and nearly killed in various other damaging ways related to his work, she'd had enough and left him because he would not find a new occupation.

As a game warden in Maine, he had been charged with murder after fatally shooting a man while making a contested deer-poaching arrest. The jury cleared Harry of all charges, finding he had shot the man in self-defense, but the shooting cost him his job and his wife, who left at the conclusion of the trial, taking their two children with her.

Having parked the Rover under the huge live oak at the front corner of his lawn, mostly the same white sand as the road, and taken a long look around to make sure he didn't have any unexpected company, human or otherwise, he pulled on his hat, walked back to the road, and set off for Tucker's farm.

Like most of the Hammock, the sandy road was deeply shaded with the late but still fiery sun casting only shifting flecks of light on the ground. Although when he began walking his mind was still filled with thoughts of Meredith Winters and their conversation, the Hammock soon drew him out of his mind and into awareness of the throbbing life around him. It began with the whiff of some heavily perfumed flower and the call of a hidden bird in the branches over his head.

The Hammock was never silent, or if it was, then only for a breath-stopping moment when time itself seemed to pause on the brink of some great chasm until the sudden hunting cry of a red-tailed hawk or the slap of a fish falling back into the water after taking a fly signaled the forward rush again of everything that is. Harry never experienced one of those moments without feeling his heart lift at its end, not usually with relief, but with a powerfully recharged sense of being a part of all the teeming life around him.

This time it was neither a hawk's cry nor the slap of a fish but a solid crunching sound that brought him fully into the present. Puc Puggy Creek, stained with tannin, drained the brush-covered swamp to the east of the Hammock and ran another fifteen or twenty miles into the Seminole River that joined the sea in front of Meredith Winters's palatial home. But she was well out of Harry's thoughts when he moved quietly to the side of the road and looked down the tangle of pucker brush, raspberry canes, and wire grass thronging the bank and saw what he expected to see. A sleek and busy female otter was making short work, bones and all, of a small gar she had caught. Her two middle-sized cubs were scrabbling in the mud at the water's edge, ferreting out frogs and crawfish and chewing them up with relish.

An instant later the mother gave a short, sharp chirp. A large alligator's eyes and nostrils appeared above the surface less than ten feet from the otter family, attracted to them either by the sounds they were making or their smell. The young otters raced up the bank without pausing for an instant, and when they were out of reach of the alligator, the mother followed, watching the big reptile over her shoulder as she went.

"Well done," Harry said to her when she loped past him.

The two youngsters had shot by without even a glance. The mother paused, her small, bright eyes fixed on him, until she could say, "Oh, one of those," then loped away in that strange, humped-back run so characteristic of otters. The brief meeting with the otters brightened Harry's spirits, as always when encountering a wild creature that looked, saw nothing to fear, and went on with its life.

Harry found Tucker kneeling in a dark patch of newly turned earth in his kitchen garden, planting tomatoes. A large black mule, wearing a straw hat with holes for his ears and a white ibis feather stuck in its band, and a big blue tick hound, lounging under a blue plumbago bush, were supervising the work. Seeing Harry, the two hurried forward to greet him. The mule dropped his head to press his nose against Harry's chest and blew softly in a show of welcome. The hound pushed his nose into Harry's stomach hard enough to shove him back a step, while Harry was rubbing the mule's shining black neck. Reaching down, he grasped the hound by the loose skin on both sides of his heavy neck and gave his head a good shaking while the dog grinned and growled with pleasure.

Tucker got up, knocked the loose dirt off the knees of his bib overalls, shook out the sleeves on his perfectly ironed long-sleeved white shirt, and walked out of the garden to shake hands with Harry. "Oh, Brother! was just telling me you were coming," he said, taking off his straw hat. With a red-checked bandanna he wiped the sweat off his nearly bald head, fringed with white hair.

"Want some help setting out the rest of the tomato plants?" Harry asked.

"Yes, as a matter of fact. I waited till the sun got behind the trees before setting them out, so as not to stress them too much, and maybe with your help we can finish up before dark. There's a square of canvas in the wheelbarrow you can use to kneel on."

Harry knew Tucker did not like to talk while he was working because, as he put it, "it takes away the concentration and lets error creep in," which was either true or just Tucker's way of extending the silence of his life, which he prized and protected. Tucker's total absorption in whatever he was doing was one among many things Harry admired about the old farmer.

Although Tucker's age was a well-kept secret, Harry knew he was well beyond the threescore and ten allotment, but the old man worked all day, every day attending to the flower and vegetable gardens, his citrus orchard, his hens, and his dozen beehives. When Harry first came to the Hammock, his life wrecked and his interest in living burned to a crisp, Tucker began to recruit him for projects he pretended needed four hands until, a spark at a time, he reignited the flame of Harry's life from its ashes.

"There," Tucker said with obvious satisfaction, sitting back on his heels and giving his face and head another wipe with the bandanna. "We've done it. Now it's in the hands of the Great Spirit."

"And none too soon," Harry said, groaning as he pushed himself to his feet. "My back feels as if it's broken."

"Do you have your dinner in the oven?" Tucker asked, starting to gather the empty tomato seedlings' flats and pile them on the wheelbarrow.

"No," Harry said, shamed into helping.

"Eat with me. I've got a smoked ham that's been baking and ought to be done," Tucker told him. "You wheel the barrow, I'll bring the tools. Oh, I've also got a pitcher of cider chilling in the icebox. Do you think you could help me decide whether or not the barrel's worth keeping?"

"I think I could force myself to drink some of it," Harry said, "and I'll take you up on dinner."

Chapter 4

Half an hour later the two men were seated in bentwood rockers on Tucker's back stoop. A poor-Will's-widow was calling from somewhere in the woods behind the house, and a new moon was hanging in the patch of sky above the stoop. A soft yellow light, falling through the kitchen screen door onto the small table, kept them from being marooned in the dark and winked quietly on the beads of water gathered on their glass mugs and the half-empty pitcher. Tucker had just taken an apple pie out of the oven to cool, and its aroma, mingled with that of the ham, drifted out to them as they talked.

"How old is Meredith Winters?" Tucker asked.

"Mid-forties, but that's only a guess," Harry said, then added, "and a very attractive woman."

"Did you ever meet one who wasn't?" Tucker asked.

"I could probably name a couple," Harry answered, leaning his head back against the chair to watch the moon. "Bats are out," he said, seeing one dart across the bright crescent.

"That would be about right," Tucker said, obviously following another train of thought. "She's Lansbury's second wife."

"She said they'd been married fifteen years."

"I would have guessed longer," Tucker said, going silent for a few moments. "He married up," he added. "His first wife worked in Chandler's Bakery."

"Divorced?"

"Yes. She's still living in Avola, but I doubt she has to work in the bakery."

"I could look all this up in the *Banner*'s archives, but you're closer. Was it an amicable separation?"

"From what I ever heard about him, almost no transaction involving Amos Lansbury was amicable, but by then he'd made a pile of money and she got a comfortable settlement."

"Did she remarry?"

"Not that I ever heard," Tucker answered, pushing to his feet. "After we've dealt with supper, what say we have some plum brandy from the keg I opened last week. You haven't tried it. I think you'll like it."

"Sounds like a plan to me," Harry said, showing considerable courage because when he stood up and followed Tucker into the kitchen, he found the cider had set his world slowly and gently revolving. Fortunately, the meal, in addition to being delicious, ended the circling, and he was able to give his full attention to Tucker as he told Harry about his intention to add a flock of bantam hens to the Plymouth Rocks.

"Are you planning to keep a bantam rooster?" Harry asked.

"Oh, yes, but I haven't settled on a breed yet."

"I've heard they're aggressive," Harry said.

"So is Longstreet," Tucker said, "but he's tame enough with those he knows. Even he and Sanchez get along."

Harry decided not to take his doubts any further. Tucker had apparently made up his mind, and once that happened, Harry knew from experience there was no point in arguing. After washing and drying the dishes, the two men went back to the rockers, each holding a small glass, the kind pimento cheese once came in, of the plum brandy. Having sampled it, Harry agreed it was excellent. He guessed, since his first swallow nearly took his breath away, that Tucker had been very liberal with the grain alcohol when the fermentation was complete.

"After marrying Meredith Winters, Amos Lansbury gradually

became a very influential man in local and state politics," Tucker said, picking up the conversation that washing the dishes had interrupted, "largely because she brought him into a very nearly closed circle of men and women in Tequesta County who provide either directly or indirectly almost all of the money behind the area's successful politicians."

"Off and on over the years," Harry responded, "I've heard such a group existed, but since no one, as far as I know, has ever been named as a member of this shadow cabinet, I assumed the rumors and assertions were largely mythic."

"You've even known intimately one or two of them," Tucker said, needling Harry in a tender spot.

"I suppose you're bringing up Gwyneth Benbow again," Harry said huffily.

"The name sounds familiar," Tucker said innocently.

"I'm going to tell you again, Gwyneth and I never slept together."

"Really? Too bad. She was a lovely woman, that black hair and those sky-blue eyes. Are you sure . . . ?"

"Yes."

"I'm fairly certain she was in the group," Tucker said, "but it never accepted that husband she dumped."

"Wise choice," Harry said, thinking about Gwyneth. "I wonder where she is. Last I heard, she was selling her place."

"My information stops at the water," Tucker said.

"Nonetheless," Harry said, "it always puzzles me how you and your friends know as much as you do about the people in Avola."

"Nothing mysterious," Tucker said, pausing to sip his brandy, "we're all old. Most of us have children and grown grandchildren who, taken collectively, work and live in every corner of the city. Also," Tucker continued, "we inherited from our parents the habit of taking note of what others were doing.

They lived in places, for the most part, where they needed to know their neighbors and took an interest in them. You never knew when you were going to need them, and they responded to the same need. It was what community meant."

"Yes, I can see that," Harry said. "What else can you tell me about Amos Lansbury?"

"He made a lot of enemies."

Just then there was a scrabbling sound under the floor that made Harry jump up. Oh, Brother!, who had been grazing in the grassy area between the stoop and the woods, lifted his head and cocked his ears. Sanchez, stretched out on the grass close to the stoop and looking ready for burial, groaned his way to his feet.

"Florinda and her family are going hunting," Tucker said, continuing to rock.

"The skunk," Harry said and laughed. "I'd forgotten about her."

A moment later, she emerged at the edge of the stoop floor and, followed by three small duplicates, set off in line toward the trees, tails erect and paying no attention to either Sanchez or Oh, Brother!, who watched them out of sight in silence, making no move that Florinda might mistake for aggression.

"Have you kept track of how many babies she's had since she took up residence under the house?"

"Around fifteen. She's fairly small," Tucker added. "Larger females might have had more."

"They've learned to cope with the alligators, and the panthers and coyotes leave them alone," Harry said, "but now they've got the pythons to contend with and, maybe, the monitor lizards. I expect the populations anywhere near water are going to come under pressure."

"Probably," Tucker said, shifting uneasily in his chair.

Harry had noted that in the past year or two Tucker had

begun showing signs of distress at the thought of his world being disrupted by the intrusion of new predators or the possibility that the state might open sections of the Hammock to the public, and guessed it might have to do with his increasing age. If Tucker knew how old he was, he kept it to himself, fending off all attempts by Harry to approach the subject.

"Back to Amos Lansbury and his enemies," Harry said, hoping to get Tucker's mind off whatever it was that had distracted him. "What did he do to acquire them?"

"One way or another, he caused them pain, either by keeping them from acquiring something they wanted or making them do something they didn't want to do to get it. He also cost a lot of powerful people a lot of money by seeing to it that the people they were supporting for office were defeated in elections."

"I assume his methods didn't come out of the Good Book."

"No. He pretty well wrote his own book and broke a lot of laws."

"Meredith Winters thinks he was murdered," Harry said, letting the statement hang.

Tucker responded by drinking some more plum brandy.

"Tucker?" Harry asked after the forest's night chorus of frogs and insect fiddlers had dominated the scene for a while.

"She and most of Avola," Tucker said finally.

Harry was just back from his morning run when Holly called.

"Hi, Harry," she said as if she had just stepped onto his lanai.

"Why are you up at four in the morning?" he asked. "Is anything wrong?"

"No, I'm going trout fishing and the guy taking me insisted on being on the river at sun-up."

"Fishing?" Harry asked, surprised by her news.

"Yes, I'm taking fly fishing lessons in Livingston. This will be my first time on the river with Rolf."

"And Rolf is?"

"My teacher, Rolf Petersen. He's wonderful."

"I'll bet he is," Harry said, the snake of jealousy hissing as it uncoiled in his stomach.

"Are you sure you won't come out here and join me?"

"I was a Maine game warden, remember? I don't need fly fishing lessons."

"Then come and fish with me. It's stupendous out here, and Rolf says you can't throw a rock into any of our rivers without hitting a trout."

"Cutthroats?" he asked.

"Yes, and rainbow, some of them are huge and fight like grizzlies."

"Is that what Rolf says?"

"That's what the man says."

"I'll bet he ties his own flies."

"Oh, yes. He's promised to get me started once I've been fishing a while. But there's a place in town called Dan Bailey's. It's a famous fly shop. Rolf's going in with me soon to explain what's on offer."

Harry thought he knew what was on offer, and it wasn't trout flies.

"Is he catching a hatch at first light?" Harry asked, tormenting himself by stoking the fire of his smoldering anger.

"A hatch? Oh, yes, flies come out of the water in a big swarm, and the trout rise to feed on them, and if you're there, Rolf says, it makes for a spectacular experience."

"And a long breakfast afterward in a quiet, private place?"

"Yes, Rolf cooks, it's part of the package. We'll have trout if we catch any."

Harry suddenly felt something inside give way. He pulled a chair out from the table and sat down.

"You've missed everything I've said, haven't you, Holly?" he said, giving up.

"Harry, are you all right?" she asked in a voice heavy with concern.

"No, yes, yes, I'm okay. You're happy, aren't you?"

"Yes, but I miss you terribly."

"Rolf must fill some of the gap," he said.

"He's wonderful for a man of his age, but no, he doesn't, and it hurts like hell to have you suggest that."

"I'm sorry, Holly," he told her, feeling lower than the sole on his sandals.

"You thought I was starting an affair with a handsome young Danish woodsman, didn't you?" she asked, a triumphant note in her voice.

"Yes."

"Good," she said. "Now I feel compensated for the nasty comment."

"Enjoy yourself," he said contritely. "Fill your creel."

"I intend to, and Harry, I'm not going to give up on getting you out here! I love you. Come out and share this place with me, at least for a little while. Please believe me. It's something that has to be experienced to know it. No pictures do it justice."

"I've just taken on a new client," he said, feeling the need to defend himself, "who wants me to find proof that her husband was murdered and was not the victim of an accident."

"Harry," she said more softly, "why won't you engage with me? What are you afraid of? No! Forget it. Forget I asked. I've got to go. I love you. Oh, yes. I put my brood mares out to pasture yesterday. It scares me to death, but I'm told that's the way it's done around here."

He started to say, "And I love . . . ," but she was gone.

CHAPTER 5

Haley Sloane had not been easy to find. Harry caught up with him in Key West at the Foundered Ship bar, across the street from the Sunrise Marina where he kept his boat. The bar had no door, and when Harry inquired about it, the barman told him no doors were needed, as the bar never closed.

"You're a hard man to find," Harry told Sloane, having introduced himself and shaken hands, raising his voice to be sure he was heard over the Johnny Cash imitator crucifying "Ring of Fire."

"You could have reached me by radio," Sloane said, sounding a little offended as though everyone had a ship-to-shore radio and used it every day.

Harry looked at him a bit more closely and saw a man set up much like himself, a little older, but his body, where it wasn't covered by his shorts and A-shirt, looked as if it had been soaked in brine, dried in the wind, and baked by the sun.

"If I'd had a radio," he said.

"You want to go fishing? My *Sally Ann* is a thirty-seven footer, and she'll take you wherever you want to go."

"Where is she?" Harry asked.

"About thirty yards behind us."

"What would it cost me to rent the two of you for half an hour?"

"You won't do much fishing in half an hour," Sloane said, his blue eyes snapping to Harry's face.

"I don't want to leave the dock. I just want to look at her and talk to you."

"About what?"

"Amos Lansbury."

"Oh, shit. You with the police?"

"No, and that's why I want to talk on your boat and not in here."

"Buy us a couple of Yuengling amber bocks and follow me," he said, spinning off the bar stool, "but I won't guarantee you'll learn anything."

The *Sally Ann* was rocking comfortably in her berth. Harry stepped down into the boat, expecting the reek of fish, but was surprised to encounter a whiff of engine oil and cleaners. He was also impressed by the gleaming white boat's dazzlingly clean turnout.

"This looks like a working boat," Harry said, admiring the gear and the open day boat configuration.

"It is," Sloane said, displaying pride. "Let's get into the shade."

Ducking his head, Harry followed his host into the cabin, which was as polished and clean as the cockpit.

"If you're not a cop," Sloane said, waving Harry into a folding canvas chair and setting the opened bottles on the small table between them, "what the hell are you?"

"Private investigator," Harry answered.

"And why are you asking about Amos Lansbury?"

"My client doesn't think his death was accidental."

Sloane shook his head as if he'd been over the ground until he was sick of it. "How much do you know about drift diving?"

"Enough to make me sure I'm not going to try it."

"Wise decision," Sloane said, taking a swallow of the beer. "Lansbury and friends had been out with me three or four times before. They were all experienced divers, top of the line equipment, sober, serious about their sport."

He paused, pulled off his faded Red Sox cap, ran a hand through his sparse, gray-streaked hair and resettled his cap, all the while looking over Harry's head as if watching something on the cabin wall.

"We were out twenty miles, and in the Stream," Sloane said, as though something had suddenly switched him on. Then he stopped just as suddenly and fixed a cold gaze on Harry. "Who are you working for?"

"I can't tell you."

"Then get the hell off my boat."

"Okay," Harry said, getting up, "but I was looking forward to drinking the beer. I haven't tried that brand for a while."

"Sit down and drink your beer," Sloane said with a grin tacked on. "What can you tell me?"

"A couple of things. First, there's money behind this inquiry as well as very strong personal interest. Second, it was bound to happen. At the moment I don't know squat about the men who were with Lansbury, but I'll give you good odds that they're part of an elite, wealthy, hard-living group of men and women in Avola, who are socially, economically, and politically very powerful."

"What makes you think bringing up Lansbury's death again was 'bound' to happen?"

"From the little I know of him," Harry said, "Amos Lansbury was a nasty piece of work, well suited to twisting and yanking political strings in a way that finally landed him in jail. But in the lead-up to being jailed, he put Prentice Foster in the state senate and trod on a lot of toes doing it."

"I know he thought he had enemies," Sloane said, showing interest. "I heard him say once when he and his friends were kicking back after a dive that he'd been set up on that vote-rigging charge, and two of the three listening agreed with him."

"Interesting," Harry said. "Did anyone suggest how or why?"

"I don't know. A squall hit us, and I had my hands full for a while. They went into the cabin to get out of the rain and stayed there until we was in the mooring. But I still don't see why reopening the investigation was sure to happen. Hell, Brock, it was plain as the sun in the sky, either Lansbury's equipment failed and he drowned, he had a heart attack or stroke or embolism, or he was hit by a shark."

When Sloane stopped talking, Harry set his bottle back on the table and thought Sloane was probably right.

"Did you recover his float?" he asked.

"No, which adds to my conviction that something took him and dragged him down. He was hooked to his float."

"Could a boat have picked up him and his float and gotten out of sight before you came back to check on him?"

"Yes, it could have happened that way. I was gone about twenty-five or thirty minutes."

"How does drift diving work?" Harry asked, switching away when he heard the defensive tone in Sloane's voice returning.

"It's pretty simple. You go out about twenty miles and drop the first man into the water with his gun and his float, move on fifty yards or so and drop the second diver, then repeat the moves until everyone is in the water, all the time watching the compass."

"Is there any current out there?"

"Yes, the Stream is moving them north, northeast in that area about five and a half miles an hour. If your boat is idling, it's going with them. So when the last man's in the water, I move on a ways, to give him room, come about, let the *Sally Ann* idle for a while, then move back along the drop-off line, keeping an eye out for the floats."

"How is it working for very rich people?" Harry asked.

After a moment's pause, Sloane replied, "Somebody said the

rich are different. I don't think that. They're just the same as everybody else, only worse. You know that squall I mentioned? None of them asked if I needed any help."

"You might have taken that as a compliment," Harry offered.

"I might have, but I didn't."

"You've got four bunks in here," Harry said, "but there were five of you."

"Diving day trip," Sloane said. "When I go to the Dry Tortugas or the Marquesas Keys, for an overnight, I will take three but prefer two. With three rods in the cockpit and me handling the boat, the bait, the gaff, and what-not, things get pinched."

"Thanks for your time," Harry said, getting up and taking a card out of his shirt pocket. He passed it across the table to Sloane then shook his hand, deciding not to ask him the names of the other three men. *Let him think I'm convinced Lansbury's death was accidental.*

"Thanks for the beer. If this business with Lansbury turns into a murder investigation," Sloane said, narrowing his eyes at Harry, "I'm going to be suspected of having a hand in his death."

"A piece of advice," Harry said without hesitation, putting in the stick a little. "If you didn't have a hand in Lansbury's death beyond what you've told me, you've got nothing to worry about."

"As I see it, Brock," Sloane told him, "being caught up in a murder investigation is like being at sea in a thirty-seven-foot boat. If you want to stay alive, you had better worry."

Harry drove back to Avola and went straight to Jim's office. He found the lawman at his desk, laboring over case files.

"All I can say is," Jim said to Harry by way of a greeting, his long face drawn even longer in disgust, "I must have done something very wrong in a prior life, to account for my being chained to this desk."

With that, he slammed shut the manila file folder he had been reading and thrust his six-foot-three frame to its feet.

"Sorry, Harry," he said, calming down, "but sometimes I think I'll go back to the home place and take up where my father left off, farming, moonshining, and preaching Sunday mornings. How's the Winters investigation going?"

"I could be the excuse you're looking for that would let you think about something besides the crime wave gripping Tequesta County," Harry said, keeping his face straight despite desperately wanting to laugh at Jim's uncharacteristic outburst.

"All right, let's hear it," Jim said, coming around to sit on the front of his desk, bringing his head down closer to Harry's and making it more comfortable for them to talk to one another.

"I've had a talk with Haley Sloane, the man who owns the boat Amos Lansbury and his friends were on the day Lansbury died."

"Learn anything new?"

"I'm not sure," Harry admitted. "Unless he's a champion liar, he believes Lansbury died out there either from natural causes, mechanical failure of his breathing apparatus, or a shark hit him."

"That's what the Coast Guard people concluded," Jim put in.

"I was ready to close the book when I thought to ask two more questions," Harry added. "The first was, did he find Lansbury's float? And the answer was no."

"That doesn't carry any weight," Jim said. "It could have floated off anywhere."

"No," Harry said firmly. "They were twenty miles out and well into the Gulf Stream. Once you're there, according to Sloane, the current is moving north, northeast at a steady five and a half miles an hour, carrying everything in it at the same rate. If Lansbury had died on his dive, his float would have gone on floating above him—or above where he ought to have been."

"Well, well," Jim said, "live and learn."

"Second," Harry said, getting into his story, "I asked if a boat could have come up on Lansbury, picked him and his float up, and gone off with him, without Sloane seeing the boat. The answer was yes."

"So," Jim suggested, "if someone had shot or clubbed him, cut off his tank, picked up the float, he would have sunk without a trace."

"That's a possibility," Harry agreed.

"But you'd never prove it," Jim said, shaking his head.

"You'd have to prove a negative: that he didn't drown because of a system failure or by misadventure," Harry said with a sigh. "But there's something else."

"And that is?"

"There were three other men out there with him. Were they ever questioned?"

"We didn't question them," Jim said.

"Do you have their names?"

"I'm sure I do. They're bound to be in the Coast Guard report."

Jim picked up the phone and asked the person who answered to bring him the Coast Guard report on Amos Lansbury's death. In less than five minutes Jim was scanning the report.

"Here it is," he said, looking up.

Harry had his BlackBerry in his hand.

"Arthur Hornsby, Kevin O'Malley, and Jonas Amstel," Jim read aloud then snapped the report shut and dropped it on the desk.

"I don't recognize any of the names," Harry said. "What about you?"

"No, we need Frank," Jim said, "and I don't know where he is."

"He's right here," Hodges said, announcing himself as he walked into the office, his face redder than usual and some of his shirt hanging outside his trousers, "but it was a near thing. I thought I was going off the six-mile bridge right into the Luther Faubus Canal."

He dropped himself onto one of the folding chairs that sagged and shrieked under the impact.

"I was on my way to deal with a complaint from the casino," he continued. "Last night somebody from Avola got sore after having bottomed at the roulette table, upended it and went after the croupier, decked him and two of the Indian policemen who had tried to subdue him without the help of their sticks. Big mistake."

"Frank," Jim said, failing to conceal his impatience, "what does that have to do with your nearly being thrown into the canal from the six-mile bridge?"

Frank turned to Jim and said, "I'm getting to that, Captain," then shifted his attention to Harry. "By the way, I don't recommend anyone jumping into the canal right about there. There's a sixteen-foot alligator that's made that stretch of the canal his own."

"I gather you caught up with the man who wrecked the roulette table," Harry said, tickled as always by Hodges's love of storytelling.

"Security at the gate had his plate number," Hodges said, easing back in his chair, settling himself for an extended narration, only to be cut short by Jim who demanded he say right then what happened at the bridge.

"Well," Hodges said, his face registering his disappointment, "on my way back into town, I drove right up on the car, parked just beyond the bridge, and the driver was hanging over the bridge rail, watching that alligator I mentioned."

"What happened when you reached him?" Jim asked, urging Hodges along.

"I asked him for I.D., and he tried to throw me into the river," Hodges said, his eyes widening as if he was still astonished by the experience.

"I gather you didn't go into the river," Harry said, thoroughly enjoying both the story and Jim's impatience with his sergeant.

"I let him know it was something I didn't want to do right then," Hodges said. "So I hung him over the railing for a while by his belt until he cooled off and began answering simple questions as soon as I asked them. I don't ever get over being puzzled by people and what they do."

Hodges shook his head at the mystery of life and stared at the wall until Jim stopped fidgeting with his pen and demanded to know what the outcome was.

"He was sober and as sensible as he was ever going to be, so I sent him back to the casino, to come to an agreement with the management."

"His name?" Jim asked.

"Atherton B. Scrubs. Draw your own conclusions."

Harry and Jim exchanged looks.

"Surprising how fast the prospect of being fed to a sixteen-foot alligator will make a man cooperative," Hodges said as if he'd just stumbled on truth at the Luther Faubus Canal.

Chapter 6

As soon as he left Jim's office, Harry called Meredith. The beginnings of investigations, he had found, have a tiresome resemblance. Nothing seems to be happening, and the clients become restless and disappointed with the lack of progress.

Renata Holland, an old friend and briefly a lover, had once called him the Hermit of Bartram's Hammock, which had caused him extensive ribbing for a while. Although the epithet stung and stuck and irritated him, it finally made him admit that he would rather not see nearly everyone, especially his clients, than see them. The admission led him to make a rule for himself: When he found himself not wanting to see a client, it was time to pick up the phone and make an appointment.

Raquel Morena answered and told him, without enthusiasm, that if he would wait a moment, she would ask Mrs. Winters if she was free.

She was and Harry found to his surprise that his spirits lifted in anticipation of seeing both women. Harry liked and admired women, but had displayed an astonishing incapacity to make long relationships work. Two marriages with children and a long and passionate love affair had all collapsed in heartbreak and loss.

Nonetheless, it had not dimmed his lively interest in women, and his weakness for them, if it was a weakness, had been something of a built-in redemption. Fortunately, he only fell in love with women who loved him. Of course, that made the separations all the more painful. Also, loving him had not kept them with him, a fact that had not escaped his attention.

"How nice to see you again, Mr. Brock," Raquel Morena said with what Harry saw was a forced smile when she came out of her office to greet him.

"Did you think I'd run away?" he asked, trying to assess the problem.

She was pale, and although she was beautifully turned out in an Indian yellow blouse and black skirt, Harry had the sense of something seriously wrong.

"Have you been ill?" he asked.

"No," she said, starting toward the stairs, but turning back to him when she saw that he was not following her. He stood looking up at her, waiting.

"I'm divorcing my husband," she said. "I'm not doing a very good job of hiding it. I'm sorry."

"Don't apologize," Harry said quietly. "You have my sympathy and deserve it."

"Have you ever been through one?" she asked tentatively.

"Two," he said, joining her on the stairs, "and in both, while they were in process, I constantly wanted to curse God and die. I only found the courage to curse God, who seems not to have paid any attention."

A smile flickered at the edges of her mouth and died.

"I am riddled with guilt," she said, looking disgusted with herself, "even though I know it has to be done, and I suppose I do have to share the blame."

They had started slowly up the stairs again, side by side, talking as they went.

"Don't even think of trying to assess blame," Harry said a bit more forcefully than he had intended. "It's like falling into quicksand. Once in, the harder you struggle, the more you sink."

"All right," she said, giving him a surreptitious glance and growing a little pink when he caught it and smiled.

"And don't give up trying when you fail," he said.

They had reached Meredith's office. Raquel knocked on the door, opened it, and said, "Mr. Brock's here, Mrs. Winters." Then, as Harry stepped past her, Raquel asked with some mischief waking in her glance, "Was that Rule Two?"

"Yes," he said, but she had already closed the door.

"Come over here," Meredith said, not bothering with greetings. "I've got tea laid out for us: sandwiches and other things. Do you drink sherry? If not, gin, vodka, scotch, and a bottle of single malt's on offer."

"Yes," he said, and she laughed.

"I'm dry and starved," Harry said, "in any order, but on second thought, a glass of sherry to start and then the rest would work for me."

Then he wondered, as she poured the sherry, if he should say she appeared to have thrown off some of the pain burdening her. She certainly looked better. Her face had lost its lines of suffering that had been so obvious when he last saw her, and the pale blue shorts and white top seemed to mirror her improved mood. Still, he decided to say nothing. Any comment on her appearance might be a mistake, and so he settled for listening while she described some work on the house she had contracted for after being delayed by her husband's death.

When that subject was exhausted and they had finished their sherry and were sitting down to eat, he said, "I've interviewed Haley Sloane, captain of the *Sally Ann.* Do you know who I'm talking about?"

"Yes," she said, "I know the name. I've never met him."

"I gather he's spent most of his adult life on boats. Although you can never be certain, I think he told me the truth. He's a man who takes pride in what he does, and his boat is spotless and beautifully maintained and equipped."

"Does that count for anything?" Meredith asked, watching him closely.

"With me it does. Men like him tend to be reliable, for practical reasons if no others. He told me he had taken your husband and his companions out drift diving three or four times. He said they were skilled divers, sober and serious about what they were doing."

"Do you know who was with Amos?" Meredith asked, a question that surprised Harry.

"Don't you know?"

"Yes, do you?"

"I do now. Kevin O'Malley, Jonas Amsel, Arthur Hornsby. Were they and your husband good friends?"

Meredith put down her teacup and rose.

"Amos did not have friends," she said with a hard smile. "He had contacts, divided between those to whom he owed something and those who owed him."

Harry found her cynicism, or bitterness, unlikeable. Then he thought perhaps it was simply an accurate description of Lansbury's relationships.

"What about you?" he asked, possibly cruelly.

Her responding laugh was free from humor.

"Money and social status. So he owed me, not that my investment ever paid much in the way of dividends."

"I took advantage of you in asking that question," Harry said, "and I'm sorry."

"Thank you but it's not necessary," she said. "If it brings you closer to finding whoever killed Amos, I'll be satisfied."

"I'm afraid you'll find that launching this investigation will result in being hurt in all sorts of ways, but I'll do my best to shield you from as many as I can."

"Thank you," she said.

They finished eating and moved to a pair of leather barrel

chairs close to the center window with an unimpeded view of the lawn and the Gulf beyond. After having let the conversation lapse for a few minutes, a pause that Harry gave over to enjoying the view, enhanced by the pleasant stirring of air in the room caused by the varnished blades of four ceiling fans slowly turning above their heads, Meredith asked, "Would you like to hear my take on what held Amos, Jonas, Arthur, and O'Malley together?"

"Very much," Harry said, relieved that she had taken the initiative.

"All right," she said, leaning forward in her chair, looking as if what she was about to say was difficult for her. "Someone once warned, 'Keep your friends close and your enemies closer.' Who was it?"

"Probably Michael Corleone in *The Godfather, Part II,*" Harry said, "but it's been attributed countless times to Sun-Tzu and Machiavelli."

"So many," she said dryly. "Well, Amos and company needed and feared one another. So they constantly watched one another while at the same time strategizing to get someone elected or someone else defeated. When they weren't doing that, they were trying to increase their own influence at the expense of the other three. Of course, *influence* had a habit of morphing into money."

"Wasn't your husband barred from being involved in politics?" Harry asked.

"Yes, and Canute told the tide to stop coming in, and you know what that got him."

"Wet feet."

"That's it."

"Did you think of your husband as a force of nature?" Harry asked, trying a tease.

"A man obsessed with what he did."

"Managing political campaigns."

"Yes and no," she responded, displaying more animation. "It was figuring out how to manipulate an outcome and thereby defeat an opponent."

"And your husband, Amsel, Hornsby, and O'Malley all worked for the same candidate?"

"Oh, no!" she cried. "That's the beauty of it. Amos and Hornsby worked for Foster. O'Malley and Jonas Amsel worked for Tillman."

Harry let that sink in, then asked, "Was your husband a man of strong political opinions?"

"If he was, he never shared them with me," she said. "I think politics to him were what pots and pans are to a cook."

Harry laughed and got up.

"Thank you for the sherry and the tea, Meredith," he said, "and also for talking about your husband. It's been a help to me, but it must have been very hard for you."

"What I find difficult," she said, walking with him to the door, "is not talking about him but believing that he's dead. There's no real evidence that he is."

"No, you can't, I suppose, find a closing."

"Nothing to bury." She paused a moment then added sourly, "I might have been talking about my marriage."

"Has the court issued you a death certificate?" Harry said, avoiding a response and glad he hadn't mentioned Haley's telling him that Amos could have been picked up by another boat without being seen.

"Finally," she said, "but only, my lawyer told me, because the Coast Guard said the circumstances warranted it."

"Has that been of any help to you?"

"Oddly, no, but shifting focus, aren't you and Holly Pike friends?"

The question took in Harry's belt a notch, and for an instant he stopped breathing.

"How did you know . . . Yes, at least I think we are."

"How did I know? Holly and I have known one another for years. I'm a little surprised she never mentioned it."

More discomfort, this of an even more personal variety.

"I guess there was no occasion to," he said, not believing it for a moment.

She hadn't mentioned it because *my world is not your world.* That was what he thought but not what he told Meredith, who had been watching him closely.

"Have I walked into an Indian burial ground?" she asked, showing some concern.

"She and I have been more than friends for a while."

"Ah," she responded at once. "I'm sorry. We haven't talked much since Amos got into trouble. That's my fault. She's bought a ranch in Montana, hasn't she?"

"That's right."

"And you're still here."

"Yes."

"Do you fly?"

"No."

"Right. You asked me earlier if the Coast Guard's report had helped, and I said no. I've found talking with you does help. Will you stay in touch? Talking with you, I find, does help."

"Of course," Harry said, grateful for her quick response time. "Now, I must begin questioning the men who were on the boat with your husband."

"Good luck," she said. "You'll need it."

Chapter 7

After breakfast the next morning, Harry walked to Tucker's farm. He could have driven, but a norther had ridden in during the night and dropped the temperature into the mid-seventies, causing Tequesta County to shiver in the blast of frigid air. Taking advantage of the bright sun and cooler temperature, Harry walked. The sun was still low enough to find its way through the tangle of branches and lianas in the canopy and reaching the road in patches and shifting patterns of shadow and yellow light.

The sun had brought the Gulf breeze with it, stirring and whispering over Harry's head, the softly sibilant sound punctuated by the last of the dawn chorus that had wakened him as it did most spring mornings. He walked with one hand in his pocket and his hat in the other, stopping frequently to breathe the cool, damp, richly scented air of the Hammock. It was his home, and it was what Holly Pike was imploring him to leave for the east slope of the Montana Rockies. He had no idea how he could begin to weigh his love for Holly against his attachment to the Hammock.

He was jolted out of that disturbing challenge by the sudden arrival of a dozen or so glossy ibis, beautiful dark birds with iridescent backs and wings. They came down suddenly with a rush and whistle of feathers, landing almost simultaneously on a small muddy beach a couple of yards wide, running along the edge of the creek, crowding close to the white sand road where

Harry was walking. The birds ignored him but went to work at once, walking together like a small platoon of soldiers, slightly out of step, thrusting their bills into the muck, testing for worms, snails, grubs, lizards, or any crawling, wriggling, or creeping thing that passed the taste test.

Harry watched the flock working its way efficiently down the beach, admiring their skill and composure, thinking at the same time of his conversation with Meredith and the tangled complexity of the picture she had drawn of Amos Lansbury and his companions. His reflections briefly conjured up the image of barracudas circling a school of bait fish and slowly forcing them to crowd together just before they attacked.

He was trying to rid his mind of the image when without warning a very large, broad-winged bird fell like a stone on the flock, flattening one of the ibis under the force of its strike, driving its body into the mud, the remaining members of the flock rising and scattering around their doomed companion as the hawk drove its talons deep into the fallen ibis, ensuring its death. A moment later, the bird, a heavy brown red-tailed hawk, screamed in triumph and rose on its powerful wings, bearing away its prey.

"I didn't have time to wonder what the flock would do," Harry told Tucker a short time later, concluding his account of the incident, "because they reformed instantly over the spot where the attack occurred and rocketed away, putting as much distance as possible, I suppose, between themselves and the hawk."

The two men were standing in a newly scythed and leveled piece of ground adjoining Tucker's citrus orchard, a short walk from the house. Small piles of neatly stacked lumber of varying widths and thickness lay in a row on the ground. The strong smell of newly milled pine gave Harry a jolt of nostalgia, well salted with emotional pain, that instantly snatched him back into Maine and the pine and black growth forests where he had made his life for ten years.

"As far as I know," Tucker said, surveying the lumber and the piece of ground on which it was laid, "crows are the only birds that make it a practice to mob large hawks and owls. Songbirds will congregate around a tree where something is threatening a nest, but only in the breeding season and not with the concentration of crows."

"The other day I saw a merlin threaten a crow, but both of them were in a small tree and nothing came of it," Harry said, bringing himself back.

"No, it wouldn't," Tucker agreed. "Now then, it's been a while since I laid out a foundation. I know the idea is to start by squaring all four corners. Can you remember how it's done?"

"I helped build the cabin in western Maine that Jennifer and I moved into after I got my first warden posting," Harry said. "But that was a long time ago. I remember something about measuring all the sides as a start."

"Sounds right," Tucker said. "Let's lay out these four eight-by-eights, and see what we've got. I want the ten-foot side facing the orchard. That's where I'll put in the run. The eight-footers will go on the ends."

Once that was done, Harry brought the small sledgehammer and four stakes from the wheelbarrow and drove in a stake at each corner.

"This is a generous-sized house for bantams, isn't it?" Harry asked when the fourth stake was driven.

Tucker was standing in the center of the enclosed space, turning slowly, studying the area.

"If things go as I hope," he said, "I'll have a breeding stock and those I want to sell. So I'll need space for nesting boxes, roosts, feeders, water, and . . ." He paused. "I've just remembered," he said, pulling off his hat and slapping his leg with it.

"We measure from one corner diagonally to the one opposite, then the other two corners. When the numbers are the same, the foundation's square."

When the stakes and the eight-by-eights had been adjusted, Tucker stepped back to view their work and said, "Those hemlock eight-by-eights feel a lot heavier than they once did. Do you suppose that has anything to do with the trees?"

"I suppose it might," Harry said, going along with Tucker's joke, and skirting the fact that he had been breathing heavily when they finished moving the timbers and Tucker hadn't.

After a short rest, they slid flagstones under the corners, leveled the timbers and began laying the first floor. That done, they rolled out black tarpaper over the floor, tacked it down, and put on the second floor, laying the boards at right angles to those they had put down first.

"Let's sit on the bench for a few minutes," Tucker said when that was finished, leading them to a rough-cut garden seat in the shade of some oleander bushes.

The bench faced the citrus orchard, and Harry sat down in time to catch the Gulf breeze pushing through the grove, bringing with it the faint but distinct odors of lemons and oranges.

"I may never get up," Harry said, closing his eyes and breathing deeply.

"What brought you out here this morning?" Tucker asked. "Don't waste our time telling me it was my company."

"All right, I won't. I want to pick your brain."

"That won't take long. What do you want to know?"

"When Amos Lansbury died, he was diving with three other men. They all knew one another and had worked together as campaign organizers for several years. According to Meredith Winters, Prentice Foster's campaign against Rycroft Tillman left Tillman bitterly resenting his defeat and blaming Lansbury's team for the way they had pummeled him. Of course, he also blamed Foster for letting it happen."

"As I remember," Tucker said, "Tillman was accused of having sex with a girl under the age of consent. The source of the accusation was never identified, but it was generally understood that Foster's campaign team was behind it."

"I can see that I've got to spend some time in the *Banner* archives," Harry responded. "But Tillman's wasn't the only ox gored. His sponsors in the developer community had spent their money for nothing as well as having a controlled development man elected. Also, two of the three men Lansbury was diving with took a beating. They had worked in Tillman's campaign and came away with empty pockets."

"Which, had their man won, they would have filled from the spoils of victory," Tucker said sourly.

"Yes," Harry said quickly, "but Meredith either thinks or wants me to think that these men are all close to one another because in the end it pays all of them to stay on good terms. When one of their candidates fails, the second-tier actors are moved onto the winner's team."

"Then all three of the divers left alive are taken off the suspect list?" Tucker asked, not sounding convinced.

"No. Kevin O'Malley, for reasons not yet clear to me, was running Tillman's campaign and somehow managed to lose a lot of money when the candidate was beaten."

"Wait," Tucker said, "I just remembered that O'Malley wasn't the man who kept being interviewed as the head of that campaign team."

"You're right," Harry said. "Lansbury and the other three worked at the next level down. From what Meredith told me, they deliberately kept themselves out of sight by refusing to talk with reporters and avoided being caught on film. The candidate and his campaign manager decided what they wanted done and Lansbury and company made it happen."

"I assume," Tucker said, "how they did it was left to them."

"That's right. It gave the principals deniability when something went wrong."

"I haven't heard a question yet," Tucker said, folding his blue and white bandanna and patting his head dry. "What was it you wanted to ask me?"

"What can you tell me about Rycroft Tillman that I'm not likely to find in the *Banner*'s archives?"

Tucker was quiet for a few moments, then said, "Henry Flagler finished building the Florida East Coast Railroad in 1912. It ran from Jacksonville to Key West. The FEC, as it came to be called, started what you see now on the East Coast by building hotels and towns along the railroad and attracting developers with the prospect of cheap land and the attraction of year 'round sunshine."

"Flagler's Folly," Harry said then chuckled, thinking of the irony in the epithet.

"Our side of the peninsular went begging for a while," Tucker said, "and those living on this coast, wanting to get to Key West or Havana, went by boat. Anyway, by the time the Great Depression had sunk its teeth into the back country, people from eastern Kentucky and Tennessee began drifting down the west coast, looking for places to make a living farming, which was usually all they knew."

"Are we going to get out of the weeds anytime soon?" Harry asked.

"Patience is a virtue you ought to cultivate," Tucker replied. "Now, Rycroft Tillman's people were part of that little-known migration. If you've ever read Marjory Kinnan Rawlings's *The Yearling,* which came out a few years before Tillman's people were setting up new lives here, you'll have a good idea how they lived."

"Then he came up in a 'settler culture,' " Harry said.

Tucker sighed and shook his head. "You've known quite a few of them," he said. "The good ones are salt of the earth, but some of them could never give up moonshining. And while their parents made moonshine as a way to get some money to buy the things they couldn't make or grow themselves, their children found they preferred moonshining to the drudgery of farming."

"Crooked."

"As a corkscrew."

"And was Tillman crooked?"

"He didn't rob banks—at least not from the street, if you take my meaning."

Harry laughed. "How did you come to know so much about him and his family?"

"I knew his uncle and worked with him for a while. I knew his father a little, but shortly after I met him he was killed plowing. One of his mules got a hind leg over a trace, and Thompson, that was his name, had bent down to unhitch it. Something probably stung the mule because it lashed out with that hind foot and Thompson's head was in the way."

"That probably didn't enhance Rycroft's love of farm work."

"Probably not. There's another thing about him," Tucker put in more seriously. "He didn't like losing any more than he liked farming."

"Enough to kill someone?"

"I don't know. He's a big man with a short temper who grew up in an honor culture where men were taught to strike hard when they felt insulted."

"I'd better get back to my own farm," Harry said, putting his hat back on and standing up.

"Do you really think Meredith Winters could have had any part in her husband's death?" Tucker asked, getting up with Harry.

"I don't really know," Harry replied, "but I hope not. I'll help pick up the tools and push the wheelbarrow back to the barn. By the way, where are Sanchez and Oh, Brother!?"

"The coyotes have abandoned their old den, and now those two nosy Parkers want to know where the new one is."

"Why?" asked Harry, knowing he was not going to believe what Tucker would say but unable to resist hearing it.

"They've both got a soft spot for coyote pups and like watching them play," Tucker said.

"What do the parents think of that?" Harry asked before he could stop himself.

"It took them a while to feel easy having Sanchez near the pups, but once they worked through their doubts and found their pups weren't in any danger, they'd go off hunting, glad to have someone trustworthy looking after the young ones."

Harry helped Tucker put away the tools and was asking himself once again how much of what Tucker said the old farmer actually believed when Tucker said, "I'm sorry you and Holly can't work things out."

"I didn't say anything about Holly," Harry protested.

"That's right," Tucker said, walking out of the barn with Harry and into the sunlight. "It's how I knew the trouble was persisting."

"She wants me to come out there to see the place," Harry said. "I told her I had a job, but she said, 'Come out when it's finished.' "

"Why don't you go?"

"I don't see the point."

"What are you afraid of?" Tucker asked.

CHAPTER 8

Harry refused even to consider Tucker's question and strode home running over the questions he was going to ask Kevin O'Malley.

O'Malley's office was located on the east bank of the Seminole River two blocks north of the Route 41 Bridge. It was a low, pale green stucco building wedged between a boatyard and a warehouse, not, Harry thought, the kind of place one would expect someone providing services for major political figures to have chosen for an office. And it wasn't as if the costs were low. The land itself with nothing on it would bring several hundred thousand dollars.

Once through the door with its polished brass plaque that read *Kevin O'Malley, Managerial Services,* Harry found himself in a quietly carpeted, low-ceilinged room with fans turning silently, and no other sounds but the soft clicking of a computer keyboard.

"Can I help you?" the woman at the computer asked without taking her eyes off the screen.

Harry was intrigued by her. She looked like someone from Central Casting, made up for a nineteen-fifties movie. Her brown hair curled up at her shoulders, the gray gabardine suit jacket had broad shoulders and wide lapels, and her gold-rimmed glasses were perfect, as was her sharp, clipped manner of speaking. All she lacked, he thought, was a cigarette.

"That all depends," he said, surrendering to impulse.

"Okay," she said, finally turning to face him, "so you're a wise guy."

She really was quite attractive, Harry admitted, unable to stop himself from smiling. He even took off his hat.

"The name's Brock," he said, having reached her desk.

She had steel-gray eyes, and she did not smile, having taken in the shirt that had been washed too many times and the shorts that hadn't.

"He's on the phone," she said in the same voice that suggested she had seen it all at least twice. "There's chairs over there. Take some weight off."

That said, she returned her gaze to the screen and began typing as if he had ceased to exist. Slightly deflated, Harry wandered over to the chairs and sat down.

"Where are the magazines?" he asked, unable to let it go.

"Who reads?" she asked.

Harry didn't answer. The silence grew for a while. Then she said, "Nobody. Go on in. He's off the phone."

"Where is *in*?" Harry asked.

She rolled her chair back and stood up in one motion.

"Helpless," she said to no one in particular and led him down a short corridor, rapped on a door, opened it, and stepped back.

"Thanks," he said as he passed her on his way through the door. They locked eyes for a moment, and he was delighted to see that she was having trouble holding back laughter.

"Brock." The voice belonged to a large man with a broad red face and bent nose that looked to Harry as if it had been broken, probably more than once. The small, darting blue eyes, however, did not look at all subdued.

"Mr. O'Malley," Harry responded, retrieving his hand before it was crushed.

"Kevin I was christened and Kevin I will die," the big man

said. "Mr. O'Malley was my father, God rest his soul. What can I do for you?"

"Unless legal counsel has warned you not to talk about it," Harry said, watching O'Malley's face closely as he spoke, "I'd like to talk with you about Amos Lansbury's disappearance."

The face bent toward him became a comic mask of tragedy. "Ah, that was a bad thing, Brock, a bad thing. Here, let's sit down."

Taking Harry's arm, O'Malley walked them to a pair of worn leather chairs, arranged on what might once have been a Navajo rug but time had not been kind to it. The chairs were the only place in the office to sit, aside from O'Malley's black desk chair.

"Shall I ask Gloria to bring us tea, or coffee, something stronger?" O'Malley asked before sitting down.

"No thanks," Harry said.

"Then let's get on with it," O'Malley said. "Why are you asking me about Amos's death?"

"I'm a private investigator. I'm working for Meredith Winters."

Harry found a different man looking at him. "Doing what?"

"Finding out as much as I can about what happened to Amos Lansbury."

"He drowned, was struck by a boat, pulled down by a shark, or died of a heart attack or stroke. Take your pick. What else could have happened to him?"

"He might have been picked up by someone as step one in a disappearing act. He might have been killed by someone, not accidently but deliberately."

"Is that what Meredith thinks?"

"I can't comment on what my employer thinks."

O'Malley sat back in his chair and stared at Harry, a brooding expression darkening his weathered face.

"What do you expect to find, Brock?" he asked finally.

"I've learned it's best not to have expectations in this business. I'll find out the truth or I won't. Usually I do."

"I don't think I'm going to be of much help, but ask away."

"Did you and the others drive together to Key West or come separately?"

"We fly from Avola. The drive out there is a bitch and takes forever. Cape Air offers four flights a day from October thru May."

"Together?"

"The limited schedules make it the only practical thing to do."

"Do you fly out and back in one day?"

"No, because we want an early start diving. We usually fly out the evening before and return the next evening."

"Do you stay in the same motel?"

"Two of us usually share a room."

"Who stayed with Lansbury on the trip in question?"

"I did."

"Did he seem worried about anything?"

"Only the thing he's always worried about."

This is like bailing out a boat with a teaspoon, Harry thought but took care not to let his impatience show. "And what was that?"

"They didn't get along, and he was always bitching about it. Pain in the ass."

"He was?" asked Harry, surprised by the comment.

"No, her. Spoiled bitch if you ask me. He wanted to leave her."

"But she had all the money?"

For the first time, O'Malley's broad face broke into a smile. "Something like that," he said.

★ ★ ★ ★ ★

After leaving O'Malley's office, Harry sat in the Rover a few minutes, scribbling some notes in his case book, a tan notebook with a ring binding, the latest of several hundred that Harry had accumulated and that he kept stacked in a back room because throwing them away would be like discarding a significant part of his life.

That done, he looked up Arthur Hornsby's address on the northwest side of the city and drove away, hoping he would get more information from Hornsby than he had from O'Malley. Because Avola was pretty much laid out like a grid, addresses were usually easy to find, and Hornsby's office, in contrast to O'Malley's, was located on a short, quiet one-way street, lined with Canary Island palms and a mix of upscale apartment and office buildings, book-ended with two giant fichus trees.

Hornsby's office building was located near the south end of the street. When Harry got out of the Rover, he paused to listen for a long moment to a ring-necked dove's bubbling call, tumbling down to Harry from somewhere in the upper branches of the dark-leaved fichus that spread above his head and stirred elegantly in the Gulf breeze.

Nesting, Harry thought and then allowed himself the gift of simply experiencing the bird's haunting call.

It was clear to Harry from the moment he pulled open the brass-trimmed door of the building that Arthur Hornsby's approach to his craft was at the opposite end of the stick from O'Malley's. His assessment of the man was confirmed when he walked into Hornsby's deeply carpeted office with watercolors of the islands on the walls and a giant, variegated philodendron dominating the space between the two wide windows on the street side of the room.

He was greeted by a tall, smiling young woman with thick, carefully brushed reddish-blonde hair, who had risen like Venus from the sea at his entrance and come around her gleaming cherry desk to greet him.

"Mr. Brock?" she asked in a pleasant voice almost scrubbed of its Georgia accent.

"Yes," Harry said, wondering how she could endure the near-arctic chill in the room without a sweater. "It's freezing in here," he said, suspecting his bare legs already had goose bumps.

She was dressed in a pale blue skirt, open high heels, and a long-sleeved white blouse with a ruffled front. Her smile widened at his comment. "The air conditioning is a bit freaky," she said. "I'm Sandy. It will moderate."

"The curse of Florida," he added.

"I thought it was mowers and leaf blowers," she said.

"Those too," he agreed.

"Well," she told him, "this is fun, but Mr. Hornsby wants to see you, and he doesn't like being kept waiting."

She made a wry face and laughed quietly. She had dark-lashed violet eyes, not lost on Harry. He had been admiring the entire ensemble and was interrupted by her taking his arm and saying, "Shall we go in?"

"What brings you here, Brock?" Hornsby asked with a trace of challenge in his voice once Sandy had made the introductions and left, leaving a very faint trace of her perfume drifting on the air-conditioned air.

"Hasn't Mr. O'Malley already told you?" Harry asked, softening the question with a smile.

Arthur Hornsby looked, Harry thought, like a crow, a comparison enhanced by the tall, lean man's dark face, long, sharp nose, slightly stooped way of carrying himself, and his thin black hair slicked straight back on his head. His eyes were also black and sharp as a crow's. Leaning back against the front of his desk, he appeared to be assessing Harry as a crow might a kernel of corn, or so Harry surmised with some amusement.

"Yes, Kevin called to alert me that Meredith Winters was on the prowl. What does she expect to find? Sit down. I'll join you," he said, pushing away from the desk and following Harry to a double-carpeted section of the room closer to the glass wall and its view of red-tiled rooftops. In the distance Harry caught a blue glint of the Gulf.

"She thinks her husband's death may not have been an accident. What do you think?" Harry asked, having sat down in one of the half-dozen padded chairs arranged around a low table with what Harry took to be a bristlecone pine about a foot tall in a dark green Japanese bonsai bowl at its center. The tree conferred an authenticity and dignity to the setting that Harry doubted it deserved.

Hornsby folded his long, limber frame into a chair facing Harry with the tree between them and thrust out his legs as though emphasizing his lack of concern over Harry's presence.

"I think Meredith Winters is a woman with too much money and too much time on her hands," he said harshly. "I wish she'd book passage for a round-the-world trip," he added with a dark scowl. "She's becoming a damned nuisance."

"On the night before Amos Lansbury died, you and Jonas Amsel shared a room at the motel. Is that right?" Harry asked, pretending he had not heard the man's comment.

"Yes, the Conch Motel. It's a short cab ride to where Sloane docks his boat and not too flea-bitten."

"Did you and Amsel discuss Lansbury that evening?"

"No, we talked mostly about diving and went to bed early," Hornsby replied, turning his head to look out the window.

"Why did you say Meredith Winters was becoming a nuisance?" Harry asked.

That got Hornsby's attention. "I said, 'a damned nuisance'."

"Was Lansbury also a 'damned nuisance'?" Harry asked.

"Amos Lansbury was a man who would put a knife in you if

you were between him and something he wanted," Hornsby said in an affected drawl. "Aside from that little shortcoming, he was good company and one of the best divers on the island. We've had some good times together, and Amos was an important part of them. So, no, he wasn't any kind of nuisance."

"But he bore watching."

"You might say that," Hornsby replied, his mouth twisting into a thin-lipped grin.

"In what ways has Mrs. Winters been a nuisance?"

"Why would you ask that?"

"Because I don't like driving at night with the headlights off," Harry said, returning Hornsby's bitter grin.

"She was always poking her nose in where it didn't belong, giving Lansbury a hard time over the things he did—had to do—while he was working on a campaign. And if one of us was with him, we'd get the sharp end of her stick as well. Furthermore, she'd pry things out of Amos she had no business knowing and a few times got us all in trouble."

Hornsby stopped talking to stare at the bonsai tree as if he had lost his train of thought or was intensely following another one.

"I'm going to say something off the record. Understood?"

"All right, and unless you tell me you've committed a crime or intend to, you have my word," Harry said.

"It was probably Winters who first gave the Assistant Attorney General the nod about Amos and the vote-tampering scheme that got him canned."

Harry was unable to get Hornsby to elaborate on his accusation beyond saying, "You ought to know going in, Brock, you're not working for Little Goodie Two-Shoes."

"How could she have done that without having to testify at the trial?" Harry asked.

"Wake up, Brock," Hornsby said, getting to his feet and ending the interview. "She and the A.D.A. are Assyrians and run this county."

CHAPTER 9

Having heard that, Harry decided he needed some professional help. He turned off Meredith's clock and set off for Jeff Smolkin's law office.

"Do I know you?" the woman blocking his advance into the office asked.

She was a little shorter than Harry and had a pencil stuck in her upswept brown hair. Dressed in a severely cut black suit and a blazing white blouse that had rejected all gestures toward ornamentation, the severity of her turnout was reinforced by the expression on her narrow but beautifully sculpted face. Only her hazel eyes, liberally flecked with gold, offered any hint of warmth.

"Biblically speaking, yes," Harry said, "but perhaps you'd rather not remember."

"Where the hell have you been, you damned hermit?" she demanded. She threw her arms around his neck, and, pressing her body against his, gave him a long kiss on the mouth, which he returned.

When that was over, they stood, holding one another, both smiling, the smile wiping away all traces of severity from her face.

"I suppose it's too much to expect that you came in here to see me," she said, stepping out of his arms.

"It's the tragedy of my life," he said, "that I always find myself loving someone committed to someone else."

Her shoulders slumped a little, and she made a sour face.

"Spoilsport," she said, her face brightening as swiftly as it had darkened. "I suppose you want to see Number One."

"That's it," Harry said. "Have you been keeping him out of trouble?"

"Between that and whipping his paralegal harem into shape, I have no life of my own."

Harry laughed and then became serious again.

"Are you happy, Renata?" he asked. "Glad you came back?"

"I tried you, flight, marriage, and renunciation," she said wryly, a hand on one hip, "none of which worked. And as the man said, 'I'm singing in my chains like the sea.' Why don't you come in, the water's fine."

"I never for an instant doubted it," Harry said, "but I'd fall back into love with you, and then where would we be?"

"Up that well-known tributary without a means of propulsion," she said and laughed ruefully. "Come on." She took his hand. "I'll lead you to Number One. He'll be mooning over one of his para's racks. Let's put him out of his misery."

Jeff Smolkin was one of Avola's most successful lawyers and a firebrand litigator. Harry remembered when he chased ambulances—not really, but when he had to scratch for a living. Not any longer, and as Harry well knew, a great deal of his success was due to Renata Holland, who had carried a torch for him with a passion that was not reciprocated. Yes, it happens and is funny only to those who find train wrecks amusing.

"Harry!" Smolkin shouted, jumping up from behind a desk that looked as though its builders had started to make an aircraft carrier and changed their minds late in the process. "Great to see you."

A lovely young woman with glistening black hair and blue eyes, and wearing a dark red suit, rose with Smolkin from her chair at his side. A Welsh beauty, Harry thought.

"This is one of my paralegals, Wyndham Davis," he boomed, his round face blooming. "Wyndham, Harry Brock, one of the city's finest private detectives."

"Come on, Davis," Renata said, "let's get out of here and leave these two to themselves. They deserve one another."

She had dropped Harry's hand before knocking and stepping into Smolkin's office, but as she turned back toward the door, with Davis hugging half a dozen files, hurrying to catch up, she caught Harry's eye and gave him a parting wink.

Harry watched the two women out the door, then turned to Smolkin and said, "Do you even have a clue as to how lucky you are?"

Smolkin, following in Davis's wake, was a short, round, bald man, bursting with energy, whose face suddenly lost its smile and settled into what looked like a default position of worry with deep lines between his eyes.

"I have a special prayer of thanks that I repeat every time I take a leak," he said, pumping Harry's hand. "Where the hell have you been? I haven't seen you for months."

"I've got a telephone," Harry said.

"Who's got time to call anybody but clients? Sit down. What's brought you out of the jungle?"

"I'm working for Meredith Winters. Know her?"

"Of her, married to Amos Lansbury, wasn't she?"

"That's right."

"Spooky how he died," Smolkin said, giving a small shudder. "What do you suppose killed him? I know there are some really hair-raising things out there, but having someone actually grabbed by one of them gives me the creeps."

"Brings reality a little too close, do you think?" Harry said, teasing Smolkin, whom, he knew, had a low regard for the natural world and preferred to engage it through glass.

"I don't even want to think about it," he said, pushing his

hands out in front of him as he perched on the edge of his chair, looking ready to flee.

"Meredith thinks he was murdered by one of the people connected to Rycroft Tillman's failed campaign against Prentice Foster."

"She's one of the Assyrians, isn't she?" Smolkin asked.

"I don't know how I could have lived in this town as long as I have without having heard about the Assyrians and it's not as if I've never associated with wealthy people. I've had half a dozen clients who grew money the way a shark grows teeth."

Smolkin laughed and bounced to his feet. "Answer the question. Want some coffee?"

"Hodges thinks she does," Harry replied and added, "No," to the coffee, "and neither do you. Come back here and sit down, and stop trying to get the Welsh goddess back in here."

Scowling and grumbling, Smolkin slouched back to his chair and dropped onto it, giving the impression that he wanted to sulk.

"Here's why I'm keeping you from playing with your toys," Harry said quickly while he had Smolkin's attention. "Can you find out for me who provided Harley Dillard with the information that led to Amos Lansbury's arrest?"

"You and I both know, Harry," Smolkin protested loudly, perching again on the edge of his chair like a bird about to take wing, "getting that kind of information out of the Assistant Attorney General's office is like pulling teeth with your fingers."

"I need it, Jeff."

"Who told you?"

"Can't tell you yet."

"Okay," he said, bobbing up, "let me give it a try. You want anyone to know who's asking?"

"Not yet," Harry said. "How's Renata doing? I thought she looked tired."

"The last time you took an interest in her, she left for the West Coast," Smolkin complained. "And speaking of that, what's going on with Holly?"

"She's still trying to get me to go to Montana."

"Are you going?"

"Not right away."

"Idiot," Smolkin said disgustedly and closed the door on Harry.

That left Jonas Amsel, but the sun was well into the west, and Harry wanted to talk to Meredith. True or not, Arthur Hornsby's assertion that she had ratted on Lansbury had seriously tangled Harry's ideas about the person he was dealing with. He had no intention of confronting her with the accusation—certainly not until he heard from Smolkin—but he wanted to press her a little all the same.

Although he didn't admit it, he very much wanted to hear from Smolkin that someone else had launched the investigation against Lansbury. He did not ask himself why he felt as he did any more than he had confronted the question of why he refused to visit Holly in Montana.

"Hello, Mr. Brock," Raquel said after Luis had met him at the door and passed him on to her. "Mrs. Winters is waiting for you."

"Rule Three is that when I've shared Rules One and Two with a person, they're obliged to call me Harry."

He had deliberately stretched that bit of banter out in order to assess the damage the divorce had done since seeing her last. It was extensive, he concluded, but might have been worse. Her face looked thinner and still pale, her eyes less lively.

"Well, Harry, it might get me sacked, but down here I'll risk it. Different rules apply up there," she said and pointed at the stairs they were approaching.

"Noted. How are you?" Harry asked.

"Mas o menos," she said with a shrug. "I try to follow your advice. I don't always succeed."

"Neither do I," he replied, and managed to elicit a brief laugh.

"The worst thing," she said, "is finding myself going over the same scenes and the same pieces of conversation, the most painful pieces, again and again as if I expected them to be different or less demeaning or less humiliating or less painful."

"I'm with you. How are you sleeping?"

"Not much."

"Are you talking with a therapist?"

"No."

"You must, and you must have sleeping pills. I used whiskey, but I don't recommend it. Someone told me to drink a lot. I tried it but in the end it made me feel worse and I quit."

"How will talking about it with a therapist help? I talk to myself about it all the time, for all the good that does."

"I'll give you the name of a therapist who really knows what she's doing, her name's Rachel Holinshed. She pulled my daughter through a very bad situation when neither her mother nor I could reach her. She also helped me, and I was a very tough sell."

Harry stopped midway up the stairs, tore a page out of his pocket notebook, and fished a pen from a side pocket. He wrote a name and a number on the paper, using the banister for a desk, and passed it to her.

"Thank you, Harry Brock," she said, looking at him with renewed interest.

"Give her one session and you'll understand what I mean. Promise?"

"All right and thank you," she said. "I can't feel any worse."

Yes, you can, Harry thought, but he said, "Let me know what you think of her."

"If you were to think that I live in this room," Meredith said, showing some level of disgust after Raquel left, "you wouldn't be far wrong."

She was wearing flat beige sandals and a pale yellow sundress, her hair caught back in a gold ring, looking, he thought, younger and happier. Harry was pleased with the change.

"Why *do* I always find you home?" he asked.

"Work!" she said, planting her fists on her hips and glaring at him as if it was his fault.

When Harry came into the room, he had found her standing in front of the long windows facing the Gulf, watching a gathering of terns and laughing gulls swirling over a patch of churned water beneath them. He had joined her, but now the frenzied feeding on the bait fish was tapering off, and flocks of sea birds were breaking up and dispersing.

"Explain," Harry said, "before I begin to think you're laughing at me."

"Perhaps I am," she said. "I could use a laugh. Actually, for reasons not fully clear to me, the more money I make, the harder I have to work, not in making it but in looking after it."

"Don't you have accountants and so forth to look after it for you?"

She took his arm and led him back past her desk, which, he had already noticed, was stacked with what looked to him like financial statements in colored binders of various shapes and sizes, piled around her computer. When they reached the easy chairs, she pointed him toward one of them and sat down in the one facing it. He noticed with an inner smile that she had chosen the one with most light falling on it.

"Yes, but then I have to keep track of what they're doing,

which is almost as much a nuisance and time-consuming as having to make the investment decisions myself. By the way," she added, "before I was married, I was head of an equities group in the Swift River Management Company. Ever hear of it?"

Harry said he had and wondered where she was taking this conversation. She had been sitting on the edge of her chair, legs crossed, leaning forward as if anxious she might not have his full attention. Now she bounced herself back in the chair, uncrossed her legs, smoothed her skirt, and propped her elbows on the arms of her chair.

"I suppose," she said with much less vivacity, "I should have been paying much more attention to what Amos was getting up to."

"What was that exactly?" Harry asked.

"Trying to get Prentice Foster elected to the state senate," she said, bitterness creeping into her voice, "and losing sight of everything but the need to win."

"It was a tough race," Harry said, not sure why he was putting in a sympathetic word for Lansbury.

"When I finally lifted my eyes from my computer," Meredith continued, "I saw too late that Amos was wading knee deep in the blood of a vicious, ruthless, utterly personal, slamming attack on Rycroft Tillman."

"Tillman's campaign wasn't exactly playing patty cake with Prentice Foster, if I remember right," Harry said, surprising himself a second time.

"No, both sides had lost all sense of decency. And when I tried to pull Amos out of the fray, it was too late. He had already taken the step that undid him."

"Attempted to buy votes," Harry said.

"Yes," she said, "and there was nothing I could do to save him, not even by buying the best criminal lawyer in Miami to defend him. It didn't help that Amos refused to make the slightest effort to defend himself."

Harry waited for her to go on. When she didn't, he asked quietly, "Remorse?"

"I don't know. By then I had stopped speaking to him."

"What were the circumstances leading to his arrest?" Harry asked.

"Harley told me it was an anonymous phone call from a payphone in the court building," she told him, staring past Harry with what he read as a lost-in-thought expression.

His question had certainly not startled her as far as he could tell.

"Are you and the Assistant Attorney General friends?"

"What makes you think that?" she asked, coming back from wherever she'd been and looking slightly confused.

"You called him Harley."

"We know one another."

"Are you both Assyrians?"

Harry thought that might make her angry, but he wanted her reaction.

"I hate being called that," she said crossly. "It's insulting."

"Sorry, no insult intended. It's only recently that I've learned such a group existed. Was your husband a member?"

"No," she said, frowning at him and straightening her back. "Why are you asking me these questions?"

"Do you remember my saying if you started this investigation, things would happen you didn't like?"

"Yes."

"These questions and more to come are in that gathering of unpleasant things. Why didn't he belong?"

"The people you call Assyrians are mostly wealthy. It's not a club, you know. It's a somewhat fluid group of like-minded people, interested in seeing the city and the county and the state, for that matter, properly administered."

"Interesting," Harry said blandly. "Which candidate did the Assyrians support in the Tillman and Foster election?"

"As far as I know, no canvass was ever taken, but my guess would be Rycroft Tillman. Of the two, he was the more strongly pro-business."

"Were you subjected to any unpleasantness following the election?"

"You mean because of Amos's role in defeating Rycroft?"

"You know Rycroft?"

"Yes. I've known him a long time. Feelings, you know, ran very high during the campaign."

"What form did the unpleasantness take and was it directed at you or through you to Amos?"

"When did you decide to stop being nice to me?" she demanded, her voice rising and ending in a forced laugh.

"Meredith, who made the threats, and what were they?"

"None of my acquaintances said anything threatening," she said after some hesitation, "but a few of them asked if there wasn't something I could do about that 'damned husband' of mine."

"That's all?"

"Yes, I think so."

"All right," Harry said, certain she had been lying, "I'll let you go. You've answered enough questions for one day. Wait, I have one more. Did you make that anonymous call to Harley Dillard?"

She was on her feet, eyes blazing. "That's a terrible thing to suggest, Harry. How could you?"

"Someone thinks you did," Harry said, getting up with her, speaking calmly. "So I'm asking you, not accusing you."

"How dreadful!"

"Maybe and maybe not," he said. "Whoever made the call might have thought it was the only way to save his life."

CHAPTER 10

Midmorning the next day Harry drove east five miles on Immokalee Road. Ahead of him, over the Everglades, enormous white thunderheads were already building their ice crystal mountains that looked like the crowded domes of gigantic cathedrals. Harry never tired of admiring them and thinking that all they lacked were dreaming spires, to conjure an alabaster city.

Immokalee Road was straight as a die, and between morning drowsiness and fantasies of cities in the skies, he almost missed his turn and had to brake hard, yanking the Rover off the tarmac onto a dirt track with a small, rectangular pale blue sign on an iron post. The rectangular sign bore the name *AMSEL* in chipped black paint.

Once on the one-lane road with its grassy center line, Harry drove more slowly. It had not rained for a while, and he did not want to raise a dust funnel behind him. The road, such as it was, ran along the top of a gravel berm. Heavy tangles of green and brown swamp grass and an occasional cabbage palm, curving up from the wet ground and wearing a thin circlet of palm fronds at its top, pressed up on both sides, giving the berm the somewhat sinister impression of a gigantic snake emerging from some god-awful depths beneath the swamp.

The image pleased Harry and he arrived at Jonas Amsel's wooded hammock in a cheerful frame of mind. The brown-stained, lap-strake sided house was less than a foot higher than the surrounding swamp. The open area in front of the house was covered with crushed oyster shells, and Harry parked beside an ancient jeep with no top and a windshield in a crudely welded frame, red with rust. Once out of the Rover, Harry was surrounded by the fiddling, stridulating orchestra of locusts, cicadas, crickets, and mystery bugs, hidden in the dense canopy shading the hammock. The house itself, Harry noted with approval, was a classic Florida structure, surrounded on three sides by a deep, shingled and screened lanai.

He couldn't see the back of the house, but he looked up to confirm that a rectangular, roofed but open and screened wooden frame was raised above the house roof proper for another three feet. Once inside, he thought with satisfaction, he was sure to see that the center of the house was open from the ground floor to the framed gap, creating a perpetual upward draft of air in the rooms, pulled in from the lanai and exhausted through the rooftop, creating no-cost air conditioning.

Satisfied with his examination of the house, Harry crunched his way to the lanai door, to make his presence known. As he walked, he became increasingly aware of birdsong, growing louder as he approached the door. Before he could figure out where it was coming from, the door swung open and revealed a small, lean barefoot man, burned nearly black by the sun, wearing a pair of faded denim shorts and an equally faded Red Sox cap with thick, gray hair curling out from under it.

"Come right in, Brock," he said in a gravelly voice. "Can't keep the door open long. A couple of my parrots think they want to try life in the rough. I've told them times enough that they wouldn't last longer than it takes me to shave, but you know parrots, minds of their own."

He shook Harry's hand as Harry stepped through the door. "What brings you to Paradise Place?" he asked.

Harry realized, just in time to keep himself from laughing,

that the man wasn't joking.

"It might be something you won't be all that interested in revisiting," Harry said as he followed Amsel to a pair of tattered rocking chairs that had once been green.

"Sounds like most of my life until I moved out here," Amsel said, this time grinning at Harry. "How about a beer? It's going to get hot by and by. We might as well prepare for it."

"Sounds right," Harry said, easing himself into the rocker, the cane seat not looking too strong.

A pair of brightly colored birds flew past Harry at eye level and a moment later banked around the corner of the lanai to his left.

"Did I just see . . . ?" Harry began.

"Probably. What color?" Amsel asked, having stuck his head back out the house door.

"Orange, black, some pink, that's my best guess."

"Patch of red on the forehead?"

"I think so."

"Those are my olives. They're heading for the fruit and veggie table. The four chicks in their nest are keeping them busy."

Between then and when Amsel came back with the beer, an African gray parrot, a white macaw, five house sparrows in a tight formation, and several pairs of canaries flew by Harry, indifferent to his presence.

"Hornsby and O'Malley called," Amsel said, passing Harry a bottle and seating himself. "What do you want to ask me?"

"First," Harry said, "what about the birds?"

"Started out with an African gray that somebody left on my doorstep years ago, and I got hooked, but for a long time my life didn't have space in it for more than one parrot. Then I came to my senses and moved out here. I'm a licensed breeder of African grays, but I've cut way back because of overproduction in the country, and focus more now on canaries."

"I saw a gray fly by," Harry said.

"That's Watson," Amsel said with a nod. "He's about twenty-five now. If we sit here a while, he'll stop by to check you out."

"I'm surprised you have time for this in your line of work."

"I don't travel. That's one thing," Amsel said in his most gravelly voice, "and I've cleared all the trash out of my life. That's another."

Harry wondered if that included people and had just decided not to ask, when Amsel said, "It does, male *and* female. Now, to business."

"Who blew the whistle on Amos Lansbury?"

"Well, well, start with a biggie."

"I'm waiting."

"Hornsby thinks his wife did," Amsel said, holding his bottle up to study it.

"What do you think?"

"I think he's lucky to have lived as long as he did," Amsel answered, lowering the bottle and turning his head toward Harry.

Harry tried to judge the thoughts behind that cold, blue-eyed stare but decided he didn't need to get beyond the indifference he saw there—acquired before or after Amsel migrated to his hammock?

"Is he dead?"

"As a door nail."

"What did it?"

Amsel smiled. "I think the question ought to be, 'Who did it?' "

"Harry," Hodges said, loud enough to make Harry pull his cell away from his ear, "the Captain asked me to tell you Arthur Hornsby was found in his garage this morning, shot through the head. So far, we've got no leads. Millard Jones and his people are on it. You interviewed Hornsby the other day, didn't you?"

"That's right," Harry replied. "He worked with Lansbury on Prentice Foster's campaign."

"The Captain and Jones would like you to come in, to see if anything he told you might cast a light on Hornsby's death."

"He was murdered then, not a suicide."

"Nope, no weapon at the scene."

"Robbery?"

"Doesn't appear to be. Door to the house was still locked and his wallet was in his jacket pocket."

"Okay, I'll be down."

"That's the second person who worked for Prentice Foster's campaign that's died a violent death," Harry told Jim and Millard Jones, a small, dark-haired man with a ferociously trimmed mustache. "Do you think we should have a word with Senator Foster?"

"Not yet," Jim said quickly, fiddling with a pen on his desk.

For a big man he was very restless. Jones, on the other hand, had the gift of stillness. He could sit, as he was doing now, comfortably relaxed on his chair, his legs crossed, his hands resting in his lap, for long periods of time, only his black eyes, which Harry knew seldom missed anything, studying the face of whoever was speaking.

"No, not yet," Jim repeated. "Sheriff Fisher would not approve, and I agree with him. The less contact this department has with politicians the better. They're a tetchy lot."

When he was nervous, as he had become after listening to Harry's question, he tended to revert to the way he had spoken back in the hills. He had scarcely finished speaking when Evelyn Orwell knocked and blustered into the room, carrying a manila folder and scowling as if she was ready to take off someone's head.

"Captain," she began darkly. Then her glance fell on Jones and everything changed. "Oh, Lieutenant Jones," she cried in a bright and cheerful voice. Her back straightened and her shoulders went back, and a hand headed toward her hair but was quelled. "How nice to see you."

She glanced quickly at Harry and Hodges and back to Jones. "Hasn't Sergeant Wylie offered you any coffee? No, I see she hasn't. I'll be right back. I'm sure there's been a delivery from the bakery. Just give me a moment."

With that she was gone. The other three men stared at Jones, who had sat through the performance without stirring, smiling quietly at Orwell.

"Do you ever get tired of it?" Harry asked Jones.

"Of what?" Jones responded.

Hodges gave a roar of protest.

"Suppress that!" Jim barked, looking as if he'd like to wring someone's neck.

They went on discussing the shooting until they were interrupted again by Orwell, shepherding a beaming Sergeant Wylie, a short, plump young woman with corn rows and large brown eyes, pushing a trolley into the room, loaded with white cups and saucers, napkins, and dishes piled with donuts, Danish pastries, crullers, a gleaming coffee pot, spoons, and a creamer and sugar bowl.

"Now!" Orwell said. "Shall I serve?"

"No thank you, Lieutenant," Jim said, probably a little louder than was called for. "We'll take it from here. Thank you, Sergeant. We're very grateful for what you've brought us, but we'd better get on with our meeting."

The two women were nearly out the door when Sergeant Wylie, blushing brightly, turned back and said, "Lieutenant

Jones, there's an apple Danish on the dish. I know you especially like them."

Jim closed the door before Jones could respond. After a brief pause for Harry and Hodges to stop laughing, Jim said, "Lieutenant Jones, what can you tell us about the Arthur Hornsby shooting?"

"Not much yet," Jones said quickly. "His wife is a nurse at Avola Community Hospital. She came home about one-thirty this morning, and found him. He had been shot three times in the chest at close range. From the position of the body, I'd guess he was either just getting into or just getting out of the car. He had fallen between the car door and the seat."

"Caliber of the gun?" Harry asked.

"No. We'll have to wait for the autopsy."

"What time?" Hodges asked.

"The M.E. thought between ten and twelve."

"Any indications of who it might have been?" Jim asked.

"So far only this, I think Hornsby knew his assailant," Jones said without hesitation. "He was shot at very close range. There are powder burns on his shirt front and no indications of a struggle or an attempt to escape."

"Anything else?" Harry asked.

"Not much, but he was killed in the garage. The door was still up when his wife arrived, and it's a good forty yards from the garage to the street."

"Meaning," Hodges put in, "had it been a stranger coming up on him that way, he would likely have bolted."

"Or at least gotten back into the car," Jim said without much conviction. "Thank you, Lieutenant. Keep me posted."

"Of course, Captain," Jones answered. "Enjoy the pastries," he added, turning first to Hodges and then to Harry on his way out.

"Coming back to Hornsby's murder," Harry said quickly, "I

think it's a stretch to decide his murder isn't connected to Lansbury's death and not at least notify the other people in Foster's campaign they might be in some danger."

"You going to warn Winters?" Hodges asked.

"I am," Harry said.

"Harry," Jim put in, speaking quietly as if hoping to spare his feelings, "there's no proof Lansbury was murdered and no evidence to suggest Hornsby's death had anything to do with the Foster and Rycroft Tillman senate race."

"Meredith Winters and both Hornsby and Amsel told me they thought Lansbury was murdered," Harry replied. "Beyond that, I have no evidence or proof their deaths have anything to do with the campaign. You're right."

"But you're not persuaded," Jim said.

"No, Jim, there's something about this whole situation that's made me very uneasy. I have the feeling that I'm poking my stick into a volcano looking for an excuse to erupt."

"Maybe you're just worrying too much," Hodges offered, obviously not being sarcastic.

"Frank," Harry said, his feathers ruffled, "I'll tell you what Haley Sloane told me about worrying too much. 'If I didn't, I wouldn't be alive.' "

"Now who's being dramatic?" Jim said with an indulgent smile. "You know as well as I do, there's a time to worry and a time not to. I'm saying this is a time not to. By the way, what are you hearing from Holly Pike? I think of her now and then, and when I do, it always comes to me that a ranch in Montana with your own trout stream might be the answer."

"To what?" Hodges asked.

Jim leaned back in his chair and sat staring into something a long way away for a few moments and then said, "Everything, Frank."

Harry, who had been ready to be further irritated, suddenly

remembered the problems Jim had with his wife Kathleen, the County Medical Examiner, which was the reason no one mentioned that the medical examiner's comment on Hornsby's time of death was made by Kathleen Towers, Jim's estranged wife.

"I'm off," Harry said, getting to his feet and pulling on his cap, "and thanks, Jim, for including me in Jones's report. I've promised Tucker I'd help him build a coop for the bantam hens he's buying and had better get to it."

"The man's going to have a zoo out there," Hodges said, followed by a loud laugh. "Next come the giraffes, and in a week they'll all be talking to him."

"Don't mention them to him," Jim said, trying to sound cheerful but not quite making it. "And don't forget what I said about worrying."

Harry noticed that Jim had dropped the subject of Holly, which made him feel worse than if he had gone ahead and said she had taken up fly fishing and older men.

Chapter 11

Tucker was laying the building paper on the coop's under-floor when Harry found him and swearing because as fast as he unrolled a length of the black paper and laid it on the floor, it rolled itself up again.

"I know I should tack one set of corners down, unroll the rest of the paper, tack those two corners down, and then tack in the middle," Tucker said, pulling one of his red and white bandannas out of his pocket and mopping the sweat off his face and neck, "but I said, 'No damned piece of black tarpaper is going to defeat me.' Turns out I should have worked with it instead of against it. You ever find yourself doing something stupid like that?"

"Yes. You could have taken one of those short pieces of dimension we sawed off and put that on one end of the roll, then nailed back to it," Harry said, stepping onto the coop floor, having just been escorted up the farm road by Sanchez and Oh, Brother!.

"That's right, I could have, but I didn't, and that made all the difference. Let's get at it."

They worked for an hour and laid the paper then laid the second floor over it, nailing the boards at a right angle to those in the first floor.

"Not bad for beginners," Tucker said as he stood in the middle of the floor looking around him. "Are you ready for the framing?"

"Yes. What kind of roof do you have in mind?" Harry asked.

"A single pitch, high in the front," Tucker said, "but we'll do well to finish with the framing. I've got a plan with measurements in that yellow bucket. While I get it, you can set up the sawhorses. Then we'll see where we are. I've kept things simple: one door at the orchard end, four windows, and a fifteen-by-twelve-inch door between the windows for the birds to go and come through with a slide-down door to close the coop at night. How does that sound?"

"Fine," Harry said. "Have you settled on a breed?"

"Not yet. I'm making up my mind."

"Time is running out."

Tucker made no response to Harry but gave him an odd look that Harry decided to ignore. For the next half hour, the two men worked in silence, allowing Harry to think about Arthur Hornsby's death, a development that worried him because if someone connected with the senate race had killed Amos Lansbury and then decided to add others to his list, there was the distinct possibility that Meredith's name would be near the top.

"Let's take a break," Tucker said an hour later, laying down his hammer. "If you would fetch it, there's a thermos of lemonade in the wheelbarrow along with two glasses. I'll be sitting on the orchard seat, if I make it."

Tucker set off without further comment, and Harry, studying his walk, decided he had just been making one of his self-deprecating comments for his own amusement.

"Once we frame the door," Harry said, arriving with the lemonade and the glasses and sitting down beside Tucker on the split-logs seat, "the front will be finished."

"I might say the same to you," Tucker said, opening the thermos and pouring the lemonade.

"What are you talking about?" Harry said.

He had been thinking how excellent it was to be sitting in the shade of the orange trees and being cooled and dried by the breeze humming softly in their branches. Tucker's question startled him.

"You asked me," Tucker said, handing him a cold glass of lemonade, "if I had chosen a breed of bantams to put in the coop. I said I hadn't, and you said, 'Time's running out.' "

The lemonade was delicious and thirst-quenching, and for a moment Harry reveled in the pleasure of drinking it before responding.

"You might cast your mind over the current attractions in your life and ask yourself if what I said applies."

"Nope," Harry said, hoping Tucker would abandon the subject.

"Holly Pike," Tucker said, undeterred.

"And what about her?"

"That's what I asked you."

One of the few things about his old friend that gave him whatever was the equivalent of hives of the mind, was Tucker's capacity for boring in on what Harry least wanted to think about and certainly not talk about.

"Can we change the subject?" Harry said.

"Sorry, Harry, it's got to be talked about. She's not going to wait forever."

"I'm not moving to Montana," Harry said.

"The last I knew the planes fly there and back," Tucker said comfortably.

"Very funny. She just wants to get me out there and try to persuade me to stay."

"Are you afraid you'll find you like it?"

"I'm not afraid of anything involving Holly and Montana, and I wish you'd stop accusing me of being afraid," Harry protested, scowling at the orange trees with no effect.

"I can't find any other reason for explaining why you're acting the way you are. I know that you are or were in love with Holly, and she gave a good imitation of loving you or else she actually did. Then she sold her stud and began looking for another one. Stop me whenever I veer too far from the truth."

Tucker's words were making Harry feel increasingly worse, first, because they were accurately describing what had happened, second, because he did not want to think about what was being described, and third, because he did not want anyone, not even Tucker, to know how bad he felt about Holly's going.

"If we're going to get this framing done in our lifetimes," Harry said firmly, emptying his glass, "we had better get at it."

"I suppose so," Tucker said with a sigh, following Harry to his feet, "and cutting the uprights to give the roof an even slant is our first challenge."

"Let's saw them two at a time," Harry said, relieved to have been taken out from under Tucker's microscope, a relief that was short-lived. "That way we'll ensure both sides will be the same height."

"Good place to start," Tucker said. "It's always a good idea to plan carefully. It reduces the number of times the future arrives with a nasty surprise."

"I thought it was random," Harry said.

"You should know, Harry, if anyone does," Tucker said sharply, stepping onto the coop floor and picking up his saw, "that except for those catastrophes in which we are simply victims, we are busy creating our futures every minute."

Later in the day, walking back to his house on the white sand road with only the Hammock and its denizens for company, all of which appeared to be taking afternoon naps, except for the cicadas that were fiddling in rising and falling waves of sound, Harry found Tucker's remark about making our own futures unwelcome company.

He knew it had been true in his case. His broken marriages and his loss of Soñadora had all resulted from decisions he had made long before the separations occurred. And he knew all too well that his mistakes, if they were mistakes, were of a kind he would make again if he found himself in the same places.

That thought gave him no satisfaction. Reluctantly, he allowed himself to think about Holly and to ask himself if he was making the same kind of mistake with her that he had made with all the others—insisting on remaining on the Hammock, continuing to live as he had lived since first finding his way here.

"What are you afraid of?" she had asked him.

Harry stepped onto his lanai, heard the screen door slam behind him and echo in the empty house. What, he asked himself, was he afraid of?

"To hell with that," he said aloud and stamped into the kitchen, making as much noise as possible, dispelling the silence and the ghosts that occupied it.

The next morning Harry called Rycroft Tillman's office. The previous night, he had spent some time lying with the moonlight sharing his bed and turning over in his mind whether or not it was likely to be productive to have a talk with Rycroft Tillman. He concluded finally there was only one way to find out. That settled, he did not at once fall asleep but treated himself to another half hour, thinking about Holly and her fly fisherman and the probability that she was one of those women who found older men attractive.

"Tillman," a deep rough voice answered when he called.

"My name's Harry Brock," Harry answered, caught off guard, expecting a secretary. "I'm a private investigator, working for Meredith Winters. Would you be willing to talk with me for a few minutes in your office?"

"I'm free at eleven," Tillman said.

"I'll be there," Harry said, prepared to say something about why he wanted to talk, but Tillman had already hung up.

Not big on small talk, Harry thought, losing some enthusiasm for the upcoming interview. Shaking off that gloomy assessment, Harry called Meredith.

"The Winters residence, Raquel speaking."

"Is Meredith in?" Harry asked.

"Who's calling, please?"

"Harry Brock, your secret admirer," he said, going for a laugh.

"Sorry, Harry," she said, her voice going dead. "I'll call her."

Damn, Harry thought, *another crude mistake.*

"Hey, Harry," Meredith said brightly, "where have you been?"

"Building hen coops. Can you see me in half an hour?"

"Very funny," she said. "Yes, come along."

Raquel met him at the door, looking ill, and before she could muster the mandatory smile, Harry said, "I'm sorry for the thoughtless and feeble joke when I called. It really was not funny."

"I suppose it would be a joke, wouldn't it?" she asked him in a somber voice.

She had turned to lead him to the stairs, but he called her back.

"Raquel," he said, "I've been your admirer since the day we met. You're a beautiful, desirable woman. Please believe me."

"Thank you, Harry," she said, her eyes filling.

"A bad day?"

"Have you heard the Irish ballad with the refrain, 'It's the worst day I've had since yesterday'?"

"I have," Harry said, catching her hand. "Hang on. It's going to get better."

She gripped his hand and held it to the top of the stairs then released it and managed something like a smile.

"Please come back here often, Harry," she said and fled back down the stairs.

"Her divorce is really wracking Raquel," Harry told Meredith after greeting her. "Have you talked with her about it?"

Meredith had abandoned her computer and piles of folders and sat down with him in front of the window she usually chose with a view of the Gulf. This morning she was wearing a pale yellow roll-neck sweater with the sleeves pushed up and olive green slacks and white sandals, a combination that Harry thought very becoming. He also approved of her avoidance of jewelry, other than the blue diamond on her left hand that, he had judged the first time he saw it, would take two crows to carry off.

"No, Harry," she said coolly. "I employ her," as though that explained everything. "And don't look at me that way. It's not fair to people in your employ to pry into their private affairs. Working long hours for someone, being asked to do things you really don't want to do, being polite when you don't feel like being polite, being paid what you know is a pittance compared to your employer's income, and then being fired for a mistake or for nothing, all of that is enough to endure without having to lay out your private life to someone who, despite assurances to the contrary, doesn't really care all that much."

"One of these days you must tell me how you view your employees," Harry said.

"Go to hell," she said. "Why are you here?"

"Seeking guidance, O Glorious One."

"What have you been smoking?" she said, struggling to subdue a grin.

"Don't pry into your employees' private lives."

"Someone has to stop this. I go first. Pax."

"Pax. I've been avoiding an unpleasant subject. Arthur Hornsby's dead. He was shot dead about one o'clock this morning in his garage, while either getting out of or into his car."

"Oh, my God, Harry, how awful," she said.

"How well did you know him?"

"Only to speak to," she said. "I may have met him. I don't remember. Amos said he was an eccentric—something about birds."

Harry saw that she was more upset by the news than her words indicated.

"It's Jonas Amsel who has the birds. What's troubling you?" he asked.

"I don't like it, Harry," she said in a tight voice. "I've been afraid of this. First Amos and now Hornsby. Somebody's got a list, and I might be on it."

"Meredith, it's far too soon for you to think someone's put you on a list," Harry said as confidently as he could. "We don't even know that your husband was murdered. There's not a shred of evidence that he was."

Meredith sprang to her feet and strode to her desk, pulled open a drawer, took out an envelope, marched back, and thrust it at Harry.

"Read this," she said.

Harry saw that it was a mass-marketed, unaddressed business envelope. Meredith had torn open the seal. Harry took out the folded, printed sheet inside and read it. " 'If you think your money protects you, you're wrong.' "

It was an unsigned, printed line.

"How long have you had this?" Harry asked, certain he wasn't going to like her answer.

"Raquel found it in my mail two days after the election."

"Did she open it?"

"No. I've told her never to open mail for me that lacks a return address."

"Why didn't you show this to me when you hired me?"

"I wanted you to prove that I was wrong, and I thought this

note, threat, or whatever it is, would prove I was right. Until you told me Arthur was dead, I had almost convinced myself that I was wrong and the letter was written by a crank."

"Because I haven't found evidence to prove you were right?" Harry asked, not sure whether he should be angry or sympathetic.

"That probably contributed," she said and sighed.

"I'm very sorry you've been carrying the weight of this note all this time," he said gently. "I suppose you haven't told anyone."

She shook her head.

"No, well, there's no use scolding you, but you should have told me or Jim Snyder."

"What difference would it have made?" she demanded, obviously distressed.

"Maybe none, but sharing it with me might have spared you some pain. If nothing else, I could have tried to convince you that this wretched message might have nothing to do with Amos's death or the election."

"Do you believe that?"

"I don't *believe* anything about this investigation," he said sharply. "My task is to find out if Amos Lansbury was murdered or not. This note I'm holding is information that may in time become evidence. I should have had it from the get-go."

"Yes, I see that. I'm sorry I withheld it."

"Never mind. You did the right thing in showing it to me. Now it goes to Jim."

"I don't see what good it's going to do," she said, showing some edge of her own, which pleased Harry, not wanting her spirits broken, the road ahead being, he suspected, long and crowded with trouble.

He got up, the note in hand, and said, "As soon as I've given this to Jim, I'm going to interview Rycroft Tillman. Do you have any last words you want me to hear?"

"Why on earth are you going to see him?" Meredith asked, her eyes wide with either wonder or astonishment at his folly.

"Nothing odd about it," Harry insisted. "Aside from you, he's the person with the most to gain from getting rid of the man who was your husband."

"What, exactly, did I have to gain?" Meredith demanded, obviously not amused.

"Did you have a pre-nup?"

"That's none of your business, Harry."

"Yes it is, and if the police take an interest in you, it will be the first question Millard Jones will ask you."

Meredith's cheeks brightened at the mention of Jones's name.

"I see you've met him."

"Well, I . . . that is . . . yes, right after Amos disappeared."

"Did anything come of it?" Harry asked, delighted.

"I don't know what you're talking about," she protested, the blush deepening.

"Yes, you do," he said, "and if he could bottle it and sell it, he would be the richest man on earth."

"I'm sure I don't know . . ."

"Meredith, don't make it any worse. You're busted. Try to stop thinking about all the ways . . . but I won't go on. Tell me about the pre-nup."

"Right," she said, lifting her chin and bracing herself, her blush fading. "To make it simple," she said in a strong voice, "if I divorced him, he was to take away half a million dollars. If he divorced me, he would have gotten half that and no more. The document carries both our signatures and was legally binding on both of us."

"And in the case of your death?"

"Half a million, the rest going elsewhere."

"The prosecutor would say something like this: 'Deeply

humiliated by Lansbury's criminal behavior, the accused had no intention of either remaining married to him or paying a cent to get rid of him. Not only would a divorce have cost her half a million dollars, it would have insured her exposure to media attention, etc, etc.' "

"You're cruel, do you know that? Do you really see me as being that selfish and ruthless?"

"Certainly not," Harry said quickly. "I don't know whether or not you're capable of killing someone. My guess is you're not, and I played the role of prosecutor to make you understand where the very real dangers lie."

"I hate you."

"I hope not. I like you very much."

She was sitting with her back straight and her knees together, her hands clasped, staring at him, her face drawn.

"It is all so awful," she said a bit unsteadily, "and the idea that people I care about might think I'm a murderer hurts like hell."

"I'm sorry this is causing you pain. Are you sure you want to go on with it?"

"Absolutely, what do you expect to learn from Tillman?"

"How badly he feels about having lost the election and how he felt about Amos are two things. What am I walking into?"

"Rycroft Tillman is a very hard man," Meredith said. "He's clawed and fought his way to where he is and never for an instant considered being anything but one of the people he came from."

"Tucker calls it the honor culture," Harry observed. "If you're insulted, you strike back."

"I don't know what it's called," she replied, "but whatever it is, it's unpleasant and primitive. If you see him frown, and you will, you'll know what I'm talking about."

Chapter 12

Rycroft Tillman lived as far to the east in Tequesta County as possible without having saw grass for a lawn and alligators basking on it. His home, apparently, was his office, and Harry wondered, when he saw the low rambling white structure, if Tillman was strapped for money or lived out here from a desire to be as far away as he could from the people he had sought to represent.

The woman who answered his knock on the screen door struck Harry as being entirely out of place. Her steel-gray hair was stylishly cut, the pale green dress she wore was about as far from a house dress as he could imagine, and her greeting matched her appearance.

"You must be Mr. Brock," she said in a voice with a slight French accent.

"Quebec?" he asked.

"Yes," she said, flashing him a stunning smile. "Maine or New Hampshire?"

"Maine," he said.

"Of course! Are you surprised to find me here?"

"To be truthful, yes."

"Not as surprised as I am," she told him, then said, "The place she is too remove," giving them both a good laugh.

"Please come in," she said as soon as they stopped, "before the mosquitoes find us. Rycroft is expecting you. My name is Céline. Did you have any trouble finding us?"

"None," Harry said, "but the GPS deserves all the credit."

"I'm astonished to hear we are on a map of any kind," she said with an easy laugh, her green eyes glinting with amusement.

The exchange got them into the front hall, which was pleasantly cool and smelled faintly of something familiar, pleasant but slightly astringent. Whatever it was, for the moment it eluded him.

"Have you noticed the odor in the house?" she asked with a fleeting smile.

"Yes, what is it?"

"We're not sure. At night, when the breeze has shifted, we shut off the AC and open the windows and doors. Whatever it is, it comes in from outside. With the windows closed, it stays with us most of the day."

"Of course," Harry said, memory engaging, "it's the night-blooming plants and the swamp exhaling. I don't know why it took me so long to recognize it."

"Oh!" she said. "You're the Harry Brock who lives on Bartram's Hammock. We thought it must be you. You have a reputation."

"It's not true," Harry said quickly. "I'm not a hermit."

"Oh, dear," she said, pausing to laugh. "I had hoped not to have that come up."

"Cee," a man called, "is that Brock down there?"

"Yes, Ry," she answered, "shall I send him up?"

"May as well, unless he's looking to rent a room."

She wrinkled her nose at Harry then led him to a short flight of stairs. "Don't let him irritate you," she said as he started up.

Rycroft Tillman was black-browed, well over six feet, broad and thick as a refrigerator. He had a stomach to match. Dressed in an open-necked, long-sleeved white shirt and black trousers, he might have been an evangelical preacher, but Harry saw nothing in the tanned, heavy face glowering down at him that suggested a close affiliation with the Beatitudes.

"What do you want, Brock?" Tillman demanded as soon as they had sat down in Tillman's office, a large airy room with two silent fans turning slowly over them.

A quick look around the room with its stuffed bookcases and magazine rack had told Harry that whatever else he was, Tillman was a reader.

"I'm working for Meredith Winters," Harry began.

"And she thinks Lansbury was murdered," Tillman said with a sneer in his voice, "and you want to know if I killed him."

"If she didn't kill him," Harry shot back, "you're at the top of my short list."

"You know, Brock, I could snap you in two like a dry stick," he said, giving Harry a wolf grin for good measure.

"Not from where you're sitting, Mr. Tillman," Harry said quietly, "because I would shoot you before you were out of that chair. Shall we go on or do I leave?"

"Finish what you had started to say," Tillman said as though the exchange had not occurred. "I'm listening."

"You're right," Harry said at once. "She thinks her husband was murdered. So far, I can't say. I don't even know that he's dead. I have several questions to ask you. The first is, what's your take on Amos Lansbury's death, assuming for the moment he *is* dead."

"Unless someone did kill him, I don't see how your question can be answered," Tillman said, showing interest. "He had a lot of enemies, but don't we all?"

"Arthur Hornsby also appears to have had at least one," Harry said. "Odd he should have died so soon after Lansbury."

Harry was sitting in a varnished wooden chair with rounded arms. Tillman had pulled its mate out from his desk, turned it around, and was now sprawling in it, his lidded dark eyes regarding Harry closely from under the heavy brows.

"Never met him," Tillman said, "which is unusual. I generally make a point of getting to know my enemies."

"Is that how you saw him and Lansbury?" Harry asked.

"Did you follow the election at all?" Tillman asked.

"I recall it got nasty. Somebody accused you of sleeping with a girl under the age of consent."

"Why do you say, '*somebody*'?" Tillman's voice had darkened.

"Because I never learned who made the accusation. Do you know?"

"Of course I do. Foster would never have done it. It came from that now-dead skunk Lansbury and his team. Foster denied having any hand in the charge, but he didn't fire Lansbury and Hornsby. So, draw your own conclusions."

"Then Hornsby was involved in the charge," Harry said, hoping to keep Tillman talking.

"Had to be. He and Lansbury cleared all the negative advertising their teams could think up. You know, Brock, Foster's sex life isn't likely to be memorialized as one of restraint, but I didn't let my people go near it."

"Maybe that was a mistake."

"Nope, I had to get up with myself every morning."

"Jonas Amsel and Kevin O'Malley worked for you."

"You've done your homework."

"Did you know that Lansbury, O'Malley, Amsel, and Hornsby have been diving together for some time? The four were together the day Lansbury disappeared."

"Sure. They've been doing that for years."

"There are reports around that O'Malley lost a bunch of money on the election," Harry said, wondering if he had stretched his luck too far.

"Unless the people working for me break the law and get

caught," Tillman said gruffly, "I don't know what they're doing."

Harry did not like being lied to, especially by someone who thought so little of him that he didn't try to make the lie believable.

"Want to try again?" he asked.

"Nope. You stuck your nose in where it didn't belong and got it poked."

"You may think you're smart making a comment like that, but I think you're just being stupid. There's the possibility that someone's killing people who worked for Foster in his run for the state senate. If I'm right, it won't be long before suspicion, rightly or wrongly, will fall on you. I think your real advantage lies in finding out as fast as possible whether or not I'm right."

Harry said all of that in a quiet voice, but he didn't take his eyes off Tillman, who was glaring at him as if he was deciding which way to twist his head off. The room had gone very quiet. Even the cicadas had fallen silent.

"Brock," the big man said, relaxing back in his chair, "I'm not sure whether you've got more guts than brains, but I'll give you this: you caught my attention."

"Well, I have to go from day to day thinking I've got a preponderance of brains. Otherwise, I wouldn't get out of bed in the morning. Do you follow my thinking about why you and I should be cooperating?"

"Yes, I see your point," Tillman told him, "but what I don't see is why I should think the deaths of Amos Lansbury and Hornsby are connected."

"That," Harry said ruefully, "goes to the heart of this investigation. I can't even prove that Lansbury is dead. Everyone I've talked to about Lansbury, and that includes Hornsby, thinks he was murdered, including, of course, his wife."

"Has a death certificate been issued?"

"Yes. After the Coast Guard called off the search, a Circuit Court judge in Avola issued a Presumptive Death Certificate that allowed the dispersal of Lansbury's estate."

"And Meredith Winters to become a single woman again," Tillman observed dryly.

"That too," Harry agreed.

"You said she was first on your list, but you're working for her. Any possibility she killed him?"

"Yes, and she's aware of that because I told her, but I don't think that's what happened. So far, I've found nothing that suggests strongly that his was anything but a death by misadventure."

Tillman grunted, nodded, thought a minute, and said, "Anything to suggest weakly that he was murdered?"

"Yes, the four men were drift diving. Do you know what that is?"

"I've heard of it. A good way to shorten your life, if you ask me."

"I agree. They were spread out, and Haley Sloane—he was their captain—circled back every thirty minutes to check on them. There was a period of time between Haley's checking times when they were on their own, diving beneath their floats."

"And someone in another boat who had been watching with a pair of binoculars could have run in and killed Lansbury when he surfaced or hauled him into the boat and run off," Tillman suggested. "I know that area, lot of chop, lot of current."

"That's what Haley said. Want to tell me what you know about O'Malley's losing a bunch of money on the election?"

"O'Malley doesn't let you know when he's mad, and I was telling you the truth when I said I didn't meddle in the business of people working for me." Tillman stopped, scratched his chin as he thought, then said, "But the day after the election, the last day the team was all together, he told me he had lost a bag of money. Then he let go with a string of oaths, and said, 'The son-of-a-bitch who did this to me is going to pay.' "

"Who was he talking about?" Harry asked.

"I don't know. He turned away and hiked off, and I haven't seen him since."

"Do you think he lost it betting on the outcome of the election?"

"As you know, it was too close to call almost from the start," Tillman said. "I can't figure how a smart guy like O'Malley would have bet the farm on the outcome."

"No," Harry agreed, "unless he thought he had an edge, and then learned he'd been led up the garden path."

Chapter 13

On his way back to the Hammock, Harry found his thoughts going back to Tillman's doubts that O'Malley would have bet a large sum of money on the outcome of the election because the outcome had been uncertain almost from the start of the campaign.

"But he lost a lot of money," Harry said as he passed a great blue heron, perched on the railing of the humpbacked bridge. The bird looked at the man addressing him from the open car window with the same aristocratic disdain with which it viewed the world in general.

Once in the house, Harry checked his kitchen wall phone and found a message from Meredith: "If you come back by noon, Harry, call me."

"Why noon?" he asked as soon as he made the call.

"Because I want you to take me out to lunch at a place I wouldn't go on my own," she said. "I need a change of scene."

"Do you like Mexican food?" he asked.

"Some of it."

"Then I know just the place. Dress down and don't wear anything that shouts of money."

"Oh, good, Harry!" Meredith said, gripping the handhold over her door as the Rover rocked and bumped along a dirt road crowded between low, windowless, unpainted buildings of no obvious function, other than holding one another up. "You're going to confine me in one of these shacks and use me to gratify your lust. Am I right?"

"Unfortunately for you, no. We'll soon get to the restaurant. Do you like cats?"

"Do you want to get back to me on that? I'm getting a little seasick. Why are you asking me ridiculous questions?"

"The restaurant has a cat, a large, yellow, one-eyed tom that likes watching people eat."

The conversation lapsed when Harry turned sharply into a space between the shacks, turned again, and parked in an empty space among half a dozen pick-ups in varying degrees of disintegration.

"You're not serious?" Meredith asked in a whisper.

"The cognoscenti always eat where the natives eat," he said, straight-faced.

"And die," Meredith said when she was standing beside him, staring at the restaurant, another lapstrake building that looked as if it had been painted in the distant past. There was an illegible sign over its open door and two windows on each side of the door, also open. A moment later the smell of the SUV was instantly overwhelmed by the mouth-watering odors of roasting chicken, onions and peppers frying, laced with scents Harry couldn't identify.

Meredith actually closed her eyes for a long moment, opened them, and said, "Is it possible what I'm smelling is coming from that shack?"

"The Mezquino Café," Harry said. "Shall we go in?"

A young woman wearing a white blouse and a brilliantly colored skirt welcomed Harry with a flood of Spanish and a wide smile, ignoring Meredith. Harry smiled back and managed a greeting.

"I see you've been here before," Meredith said a bit stiffly.

They were seated at a small wooden table placed in front of

one of the open windows. For a moment conversations going forward among the working men at the other tables ceased while they watched the Anglos being seated. Before Harry could respond to Meredith's observation, a very large yellow tiger cat leaped onto the window ledge, then stretched himself out, giving the arrivals a single dismissive glance before dropping his head onto one of his outstretched front legs.

"Meet Zapata," Harry said to Meredith, "he rules the night. I've been told it's best not to touch him. His temperament is mercurial."

"The thought hadn't occurred to me," Meredith said, eyeing his personal equipment, very much on display, "but I see his appeal. He's very . . . masculine."

The waitress returned. Meredith greeted her with several questions in Spanish, and the two women were off. Harry had understood the first *sì,* and that was all.

"You ordered our lunches?" he asked.

"I did, and she's delightful. She also thinks you are *muy simpatico.*"

"Is that good?"

"Her blush told me it was. You have an interesting life, Harry, filled with things you haven't shared with me."

"I think you know the most exciting parts," he said. "Can we talk some business?"

"Until the food comes."

He quickly told her about his session with Rycroft Tillman.

"I would be very surprised to learn that he had anything to do with your husband's disappearance," he said by way of closure.

"I wish you wouldn't say *disappearance*," she complained. "I'm having trouble enough dealing with him dead. If he's not dead, it's a whole new life unfolding before me."

The waitress brought the food and carried a stick slung over her shoulder from a leather strap. Once the food was on the table, she slipped the strap off her shoulder, grasped the stick, and flourished it at Zapata. The suddenly snarling animal snapped to his feet as if in challenge, but at the next thrust of the stick, he dropped out of the window with a parting growl and vanished.

Meredith asked the waitress something Harry couldn't understand, which brought a mischievous smile to her face and a rapid-fire response.

"I asked her if she ever hit him with the stick," Meredith said, rubbing her hands as she viewed the dishes in front of her. "She said no but others had and paid a price. What the price was, she didn't say. This food looks as good as it smells. No more talking."

When she had cleaned her plate and raided Harry's remaining chilies and been warned off, she leaned back in her chair and said, "That is the best Mexican food I have ever eaten. Whoever the cook is, she is a treasure."

"He," Harry said, polishing his plate with the last bit of tortilla left on the table before popping it into his mouth.

"What?"

"It's a man, the waitress' father. There is no mother. She has a brother but he's married and living in Mexico."

"If you can't speak Spanish," Meredith demanded, "and she can't speak English, how did you learn all this?"

"Gradually," Harry replied, enjoying himself.

"I see," Meredith said, and if she was trying to sound satisfied with his answer, she failed.

"How much do you know about your husband's first marriage?" he asked her, pushing his plate away to make room for his forearms.

"I thought we were talking about Clara?"

"You know her name," Harry said, not wanting to pursue the subject.

"Obviously," she said. "Come on, own up. You've been more than *simpatico* to this girl."

"You have a very suspicious mind," he protested, "along with an inflamed imagination."

"You and *El Tigre* have a lot in common," she snapped. "She's young enough to be your daughter."

"But she's not my daughter, is she? Stop procrastinating. Answer my question."

"All right, I'll stop, but shame on you. I've never met her, and I know very little about Amos's first marriage."

There seemed little point in staying to talk if Meredith wasn't going to say much, and Harry preferred to leave the subject of Clara behind. He took out his wallet and left money on the table, then rose and ushered Meredith out to the Rover.

"You should have let me pay," Meredith said when they were driving away. "I asked you to take me to lunch."

"Not at the Mezquino," Harry said firmly. "It's just not done. Tell me what you do know about Amos and his first wife."

"What were the onions fried in?" she asked dreamily, apparently lost in lunch again.

"I have no idea, but they were brilliant, I agree. Now refocus on the question."

"Okay, this much I do know. It wasn't a happy marriage. Beatrice was not interested in his work or much of anything else in his life. She remained very much absorbed in her family. From what he told me, which wasn't much, there are no children. They finally drifted too far apart to care and divorced with no recriminations on either side."

"Did she remarry?"

"I don't know. Harry, I don't mean anything nasty by saying this, but I don't occupy her world. I've said and thought more about her in the last ten minutes than I have in all the years Amos and I were married."

"I don't think that's anything to apologize for," Harry told her. "The only reason I've been asking you about her is that I've got to talk with her."

As they were saying goodbye, she asked him if he had resented her asking if he and Clara were or had been lovers.

"No," he said, "but I am curious about why you asked me."

"Goodbye, Harry," she said, giving him a bright smile, "and don't let me forget. The next lunch is mine."

Harry intended to interview Beatrice, but his immediate goal was to find Arthur Hornsby's wife and risk irritating Jim Snyder by questioning her about her husband's death. His secret method of finding people was to consult the telephone directory, guessing that there wouldn't be a long list of Hornsbys to wade through.

"Stephanie Hornsby," a woman with a tired voice said.

"This is Harry Brock, Mrs. Hornsby," he responded. "I'm working for Amos Lansbury's wife Meredith Winters, and I would like very much to talk with you."

"Why?"

"Because there's a possibility that Amos Lansbury's death may not have been accidental, and his death may be linked to your husband's."

"Did you know Arthur?"

"Slightly. I interviewed him recently."

"About what?"

"Amos Lansbury's death."

"On Mrs. Winters' behalf?"

Anticipating the next question, Harry replied, "Yes, Mrs. Winters does not believe her husband's death was the result of an accident."

"All right, I'll talk with you," she told him. "Come now if you like."

The Hornsby house was less grand than Arthur's office, and with the statuesque redhead Sandy as his template for Hornsby's taste in women, Stephanie Hornsby surprised him. She was a woman of subdued beauty, and an altogether more restful presence. The ravages of grief were obvious in her paleness and slightly red-rimmed blue eyes, but she was carefully dressed in gray slacks and a short-sleeved lavender sweater with a round neck, and her graying blonde hair was carefully brushed.

"Thank you for agreeing to this," he said as he shook hands with her, "and I'm very sorry for what's happened. If you begin to feel you would like me to leave, don't hesitate to say so."

"Well," she said, followed by a watery glimpse of a smile, "come in. Let's see how it goes. I'm somewhat glad you came. I'm already sick of my own company. I'd be back at work if my returning so soon wouldn't shock my people."

"Where do you work?" he asked.

"I own an alterations business. It's called Alterations because of a total failure of imagination on my part when I was setting up the business, and it soon became too late to do anything about it. It's located on Oyster Street."

"I thought you looked familiar," Harry said, pleased to remember. "You let out some shorts for me last year. Your women are all Latinas."

"And very skilled seamstresses," she said quickly, "far better than I."

"Your shop seemed a happy place, based on the brief time I was there."

Stephanie Hornsby had led them into the sitting room area of the open-plan house. The area Harry saw was furnished and decorated with the quiet good taste that he thought best described her.

"Alterations is practically a landmark," he continued. "You're far too modest."

"Thank you," she said. "What would you like to ask me?"

"Have the police talked with you yet?"

"Yes, a Lieutenant Jones was here. Unfortunately, there was almost nothing I could tell him."

"Had your husband given you any cause to think he was experiencing any difficulties in the days or weeks before his death?"

"No, he was enjoying the rest that comes with the conclusion of the election. We had been discussing a holiday. I have family in Oregon and we were thinking of going there and then to the redwood forests in California."

By the time she finished, she was squeezing her clasped hands so hard that her knuckles were white, and Harry thought she might hurt herself.

"This may be asking you for more than you should be giving."

"No, it's all right," she insisted. "I want to do this. I want to do everything I possibly can to help to find Arthur's killer." She made a visible effort to drop her shoulders and loosen her grip on her hands, took a deep breath, let it go, and said, "Please go on, Mr. Brock."

"Do you know anyone who would want to hurt your husband?"

"That's a very difficult question to answer," she said without hesitation. "Arthur's work was advancing the political interests of those he worked for. That inevitably pitted him against his employer's opponents. Most recently, he and Amos Lansbury were working for Senator Foster in his race against Rycroft Tillman. It was a particularly draining and at times savage contest, as I'm sure you know. Several times, Arthur was on the verge of resigning, the work was so filled with stress."

"Was he ever threatened?"

"He and Kevin O'Malley had words from time to time," she said with a dismissive shrug, "but Arthur thought nothing of that. It was so hard not have words with Kevin if you were around him any length of time. So, I guess the answer is no."

"Try not to be discouraged," Harry told her, getting up. "It's early days. Most inquiries of this kind seem to have no solution when they're first begun. You've been a help, even if you don't think so. If anything, anything at all, occurs to you about this terrible event, please call me, anytime and however unimportant it may seem. You never know when some piece of information is going to lead to solving the puzzle."

She had remained seated and looked up as he spoke, and seemed to be listening. Now she dropped her head as if losing hope or strength.

"Does finding out who killed Arthur really matter?" she asked softly.

Harry wasn't sure whether the question was addressed to him or to herself, but before he could respond, she said, "Arthur is dead. Our lives together are over. Perhaps I should turn my thoughts to my next life, empty as it seems, but where will I find the strength?"

At that point, she buried her face in her hands and began to weep. Brushing away his reluctance, Harry sat on the edge of her chair and, putting an arm around her, drew her against him. Several encouraging words and phrases passed through his mind, but quite sensibly he let them go and just held her. Rather abruptly, the spasm of grief wore itself out or was too exhausting to maintain, and she eased herself out of his embrace, stood up as he made way for her, and walked away. Harry heard her blow her nose, then water running.

A minute later she came back to take him to the door. "Thank you for being so kind," she said.

"I'm glad I was here," he said and was surprised to find he meant it. "Are you on your own?"

"Only because I choose to be," she said. "I seem to need to be by myself for now. Please dismiss my remarks about being without strength. I'm not. I have enough to see me through this. And I am grateful you're looking into Arthur's death. Meredith Winters is, in many ways, an admirable person, who sees her wealth as a responsibility and not a means for self-indulgence."

"I'm glad you think so," Harry said. "And thank you for talking with me, Mrs. Hornsby. I assure you there are people trying very hard to find the person who killed your husband."

"Call me Stephanie," she said somewhat briskly. "After having me cry all over your shirt, it seems the least I can do."

"Then call me Harry. You can cry on my shirt anytime you want to."

CHAPTER 14

The pick-up was blown apart and the driver with it. What was left had burned down to the frame. There were only half a dozen pieces of what was likely Joe Purcell found, large enough to be identified as human and gathered, to give to his family for burial. The windows in Purcell's house and in seven neighboring homes on Snook Street were blown out. Purcell's house and the one across the street lost half their roofs from the blast, and the two coconut palms closest to the explosion were reduced to splinters and had fallen back to earth blazing like a Perseid meteor shower.

"Whoever did it wanted to make sure Joe was dead," Hodges said, taking off his hat to wipe the perspiration off his face and head.

He had been helping the crime scene crew, picking through the charred remains of the explosion. The medical examiner had already left with Purcell's remains.

"Do you know anything about him?" Harry asked.

The dispatcher at the sheriff's office had called Harry and told him Hodges had asked him to come to an address on Snook Street in North Avola. "Somebody detonated a truck is all I know, Brock," she'd said before hanging up with prejudice. "Keep 'em in the dark and feed 'em shit."

"Penny wise and pound foolish," Harry said to the dead connection, thinking that was what his grandmother, who had been English, would have said about the department's cutting staff to balance the budget. No doubt the dispatcher was working double shifts.

"A guy in one of those houses," Hodges said, waving his hat to the right before putting it back on his head. "Millard's got his name, told the CS people that Purcell worked for Prentice Foster. He didn't know doing what. I've got a call in at Foster's office but no response yet."

"Where's Jim?" Harry asked.

"Sheriff Fisher's got him on escort service, riding herd on a delegation from Tallahassee. I imagine he's not having the best time he could imagine," Hodges answered. "I called you when I heard about Purcell's connection with Foster."

"Thank you. Do you mind if I have a talk with Millard?"

"Go ahead."

"We've got traces of the explosive and maybe some pieces of the trigger mechanism, and that's about it," Jones told Harry. He had been wading around the blackened wreckage for the past half hour, and aside from his gloves, he looked as if he might have been on his way to lunch with someone important. His light gray trousers were immaculate and newly pressed. His shoes were polished to an improbable shine, and his white shirt and pale blue silk tie looked as if he had just taken them out of a refrigerator. Not a spot of sweat stained his calm and unblemished brow.

"Too soon to know what was used for the explosive?" Harry asked.

"Maybe. Despite the lack of an identifying smell, I'd still guess Semtex, but we'll run vapor tests on some of this debris just to be sure."

At that moment Harry heard raised voices, with a woman's predominating. A moment later the woman forced her way through the crime scene perimeter and ran full tilt toward Harry and Jones.

"Where is Joe?" she cried. "Where is he?"

"Jesus," Harry said to Jones, "another widow."

She ran straight into Jones and would have flattened him if Harry hadn't caught both of them in a quick embrace. After some staggering and further awkwardness, they sorted themselves out.

"You're Mrs. Purcell?" Jones asked sourly, brushing and straightening his clothes.

She was tall, silver-haired, and more than filled her red-and-white flowered dress. She seemed to be having trouble understanding what Jones had asked. If she saw the rubble and wreckage around her, she gave no indication.

"Where is he?" she demanded loudly.

Harry glanced at Jones but let the question drift.

"My name is Jones, Mrs. Purcell," Jones finally said. "Lieutenant Millard Jones. I have bad news."

Jones had taken the woman's arm and was gently leading her away from the smoking remains of the truck. Both men appeared to realize at the same moment that there was no place to take her.

"Could we move onto the lawn?" Jones asked her. "I have something to tell you. It might be better if we did."

Frowning slightly as if she was puzzled or trying to think something through, she allowed Jones to lead her onto the grass, keeping her back to the blackened wreck. Harry went with them.

Before Jones could speak, she shook off his hand, turned back to the street, and said in a steady voice, "Is that what's left of Betsy?"

"Betsy?" Harry asked.

"Joe's pick-up," she said, glaring at Harry as if he was being deliberately stupid.

"Yes," Jones said in an attempt to regain control of the situation.

"Was Joe in it?" she demanded, shifting her attention to Jones.

"As far as we know . . ." he began, but she cut him off.

"Cut the bullshit! Yes or no?"

"Mrs. Purcell," Jones said, "someone died in the explosion. We can't locate your husband, and a neighbor saw him coming out of the house shortly before the truck was destroyed, but no one so far has said they saw him getting into the truck. The medical examiner will have to examine the remains. They're not recognizable by the usual means."

She nodded as if losing interest and looked up at the house.

"Sweet, loving Jesus," she said, "the roof is gone."

"Mrs. Purcell," Harry said, "if you will let me, I'll get a contractor out here to lay some sheeting over that hole." He glanced up at the sky. "There's rain in the afternoon forecast."

"I suppose so," she said without interest. "Fucking rain. Fucking everything."

With that she collapsed onto the grass like a wet rag, her hands over her face, weeping violently. Both men bent over her, reluctant to touch her. Harry was the first to look up, thinking they were badly in need of another woman.

At that moment, a very large woman in a rainbow caftan, with a red face and a yellow wig a size too small for her head, burst out of the house next to them and came barreling across the lawn in their direction.

"Glass everywhere," she shouted, "it's taken me more than an hour to get all of it off the floor and out of the furniture. Pick her up. Clarissa, can you hear me? It's Doris."

"Doris," Jones said, as soon as they had Clarissa Purcell on her feet, "I'm sorry, I don't know your last name."

"It's Burton, Doris Burton. Let me get an arm around you, Clarissa. We're going to my place."

Mrs. Purcell seemed not to recognize Doris Burton.

"Wait, Mrs. Burton," Jones said, "and please step back. Mrs.

Purcell has had a very serious shock and may even require medical attention. Thank you. Now, I'm Lieutenant Millard Jones. This is a crime scene, and you shouldn't be here, but since you didn't have any choice, we'll move right past that."

"Is Joe dead?" his wife asked, shaking off the men's hands.

"Let me deal with this," Harry said to Jones. "You can get on with your questioning."

He risked taking her by the arm and walking with her toward her house until she stopped and said, "I'm not going in there."

"No," Harry said, "it's too soon for that."

"Is Joe dead?" she asked again.

"I don't know."

"He was supposed to pick me up. When he didn't come and didn't come, I decided to take a cab home."

"Do you have any family in Avola?" Harry asked.

"My daughter's here, she and her husband. They have two children, a boy and a girl. They're nine and eleven. I think I'll sit down."

"Good," Harry said and took some of her weight as she more or less collapsed into a sitting position on the grass. "Do you know her phone number?"

Mrs. Purcell gave it to him in a semi-detached voice that matched her expression.

Harry dialed the number. A woman answered. Without taking his eyes off Mrs. Purcell, he told her there had been an accident, her mother was all right, then asked if she could come to her parents' house as quickly as possible, adding that the police were on the street and not to be frightened. Ten minutes later, she was there, a younger version of her mother.

"My God," she said, coming to a stop beside the blackened truck frame, "what happened?"

Harry told her and recommended that she get her mother away from here as quickly as she could, asking first for her address. He then helped her to get her mother up and started toward the car.

"Here's the daughter's address and phone number," Harry said, passing Jones a slip of paper. "I thought Mrs. Purcell ought to be somewhere other than here."

"Right," Jones said, looking back in time to see Doris Burton go into her house. "A lucky woman, she was in the bathroom when the bomb went off. She said her living room looks like downtown Baghdad."

"A sense of humor?" Harry said.

"I think she was serious," Jones said. "She was no help at all, not even about why she didn't answer the door the first time I tried to talk with her. No one, except for the man I spoke with, appears to have seen anything. Oh, a cat might have seen something, but it was killed in the blast. A sliver from one of the palms went right through its head."

"Sounds right," Harry said, suspecting Jones of having made a very black joke. "All right if I call Tim Petersen and get these roofs covered? I'll give him the Purcell daughter's phone number and tell him to knock on the door of the other place."

"Yes," Jones said, then frowned and added, "Do you really think these deaths are the work of someone connected to Rycroft Tillman's failed campaign for the state senate?"

"There's no evidence to support it," Harry said.

"No," Jones said, "but as of right now, there's no solid evidence that Joe Purcell was in that truck either."

"Semtex," Hodges said. "What do I connect that to?"

"Probably the Irish civil war in the 1990s," Jim answered. "That was when the Irish Republican Army was using it to spread terror in Northern Ireland and drive out the British Army by blowing up civilian targets as well as British Army installations."

"That's it," Hodges said. "It's a long jump from Ireland to here."

"You can go online and find out how to make it," Harry said, "if you ever want to."

"I think it's supposed to smell like almonds?" Jim said.

"I didn't smell anything like that," Harry replied. "Millard mentioned the absence of the smell but said he still thought the bomber used Semtex. It struck me then that if he was right, whoever did it had experience with explosives."

"Sounds right," Hodges agreed. "I'd like to know how the charge was detonated."

"The lab people are working on it," Jim said, sounding but not looking confident.

"Which is the same thing," Hodges put in, "as saying, 'don't hold your breath.' "

Harry saw that Hodges and Jim were going to get into a wrangle over criticisms of another branch of the department and spoke first. "Who besides me is ready to be serious about the possibility that Lansbury's disappearance, Hornsby's death, and Purcell's demise are connected?"

"When you show me a single shred of evidence that they are," Jim said, rising to the bait.

"All of them worked for Prentice Foster during one of the most contentious elections in Tequesta County history," Harry responded.

"That dog won't trail," Hodges said, shaking his head. "And it's too bad because I'm finding it hard to think coincidence."

"Anyone know what Purcell's role was in Foster's team?"

"I don't," Harry responded, "but I intend to find out, probably not from his wife. What she saw when she got to her house didn't penetrate for a bit. Then it did, and she had something like a mental breakdown. I think she asked me three or four times if Joe was dead."

"Her husband," Hodges said, looking pained.

"Yes," Harry replied. "Even Millard couldn't penetrate the fog. As soon as her daughter arrived, I urged her to take her mother away from there. Millard saw there was no use trying to ask her questions and went back to canvassing the neighborhood. Odd thing, only two people came out of their houses, unless they left by their back doors."

Chapter 15

What Harry did not tell Jim was that he had made an appointment to talk with Foster's campaign manager Harkin Smith.

Colin, Smith's private secretary, asked Harry for identification, telephone number—which Harry reminded him he already had—home address, and most recent employer.

"You're looking at him," Harry said in exasperation. "How about my shoe size?"

"Yes," Colin said, looking at Harry with a semi-patient expression, "it's a pain in what we sit on, Mr. Brock, but we live in times when you frequently find the toilet not flushed when it's your turn to use it, and Mr. Foster pays my salary."

Smith banged into the reception area, red hair standing on end as if he'd just been struck by lightning. He greeted Harry, gripped his arm, and led him into his office.

"From start to finish, it was the campaign from hell," Smith said, in answer to Harry's question.

"What did Colin mean by saying we live in parlous times?" Harry demanded. "And why the cross-examination?"

"Purcell's death is one too many," Smith replied gamely. "Sit down. Colin's bringing us some coffee. It's the third death in my crew, two of them clearly murders, and I'm done taking chances. There's a loaded Colt XSE in my desk drawer, and it will go with me when I leave the office today."

"Too heavy," Harry said. "Get something smaller and lighter and wear it in a back holster. I'm glad someone else besides me sees a connection."

"Connection!" Smith shouted. "It's a laser weld. I thought that was why you were here."

Colin arrived with the coffee, set up a folding table, covered it with a linen cloth, laid out cups and saucers, poured the coffee, and left them to deal with the sugar and cream as they saw fit.

"I've been in a lot of offices in this city and others, and this is the first male secretary I've seen," Harry said.

"Colin is a treasure," Smith said. "No p.m. problems, just hard work and a level head. Oh, and a wicked sense of humor."

"Was he inherited?"

"No. My choice. I was tired of distractions. I ended up bonging my last secretary, mostly in hotel rooms. We got careless. It was a bollocks. Her husband put a P.I. on us, and I had to go out a window on a rope made of the bed sheets. We escaped the P.I., but I fell the last ten feet and sprained an ankle, then found myself explaining to a cop, who kept breaking out laughing, what I was doing in the hotel parking lot in my undershorts. The real miracle was that I had anything on."

He sat back, sighed, and said with obvious nostalgia, "That woman rang every last, single one of my bells."

"I take it Colin doesn't."

"No," Smith said. "There aren't many things I'm sure of and fewer every year, but I can say with certainty that I will not be bonging Colin Thompson. Now, to business."

"Was Amos Lansbury murdered?" Harry asked.

"That will lead to who did it? And if I've guessed right, you know the answer to question one is yes. No, I don't know who killed him or even if it's the same person who killed Hornsby and Purcell. I just know I don't want to be next."

"And you have no idea who it might be," Harry said.

"Tillman is a rough son-of-a-bitch, but I can't get to where I think he's the doer."

"I've come at least partway to agreeing with you. But if not him, who?"

"You see, Brock," Smith said, leaning back in his chair and making a tent with his fingers, "Amos Lansbury had a lot of enemies. Of course, I suppose I do too, but it was personal with Lansbury. He said what he thought and laughed if he wanted to. He was also ruthless. We all are in the business but most of us don't go around bragging about it."

"Your point?"

"All right, we may have three killers at work here, and the murders following one another and all involving people who work or have worked for Foster could be coincidental."

"Do you believe that?"

"No, but the dead were all killed in very different ways. It makes one think."

"What does Foster say about it?"

"Haven't you talked with him?"

"The sheriff's department is under orders to stay away from him," Harry said. "And I don't want to ruin my relationship with the department by ignoring the order, at least not for now."

"Wise move. You may not believe this, Brock," Smith told him, rubbing his nose and squinting his eyes, then swearing. "Allergies," he said, fishing for his handkerchief and blowing his nose. "Where was I? Oh, Prentice was far more distracted and disturbed by the viciousness that crept into the race than he ever let on. Once in a while he'd vent to me, but toward the end, he just hunkered down and kept campaigning."

"Couldn't he have ended the attacks by his team if he'd wanted to?" Harry asked, fairly sure he knew the answer.

"No," Smith said, leaning forward in his chair, fully engaged in the exchange, "absolutely not if he expected to win, and he wanted to win. Every campaign has its own life, especially long and close races like ours and Tillman's. Once the tone has been set, it's almost impossible to change it—unless both sides hollow out their campaigns together, and that just doesn't happen."

"They finally just go on slugging one another until the bell rings."

"That's about it, but the wounded don't forget who's responsible for their pain."

"Did Arthur Hornsby wound anyone?"

"As one of a team, of course he did. So did I, but so far as I know he was never involved personally in damaging anyone."

"But Amos did."

"Maybe. You know he went to jail. It was said he was framed, but I don't doubt for a minute that he put out money for some of the votes in that election. He wasn't stupid, but he liked taking stupid chances."

"Like drift diving?"

"I'd say so, but O'Malley and Hornsby were also doing it. Go figure."

"Thanks for your time," Harry said, starting to get up.

"Hang on a minute," Smith said, putting out a hand to stop Harry. "There's a story I want to tell you. I can't verify all of it, but Lansbury's dead and out of harm's way."

"Are you sure?" Harry asked.

"That he's dead? Of course he is. The Coast Guard said he is. That's good enough for me."

Not for me, Harry thought. "Go on with what you were saying. I'm listening."

"Somewhere about halfway through the race, Amos came up to me and said, 'I'm going to have some fun with Kevin.' That's Kevin O'Malley. You've talked with him so you know who he is and what he's like. Well, I've already said Amos liked taking risks, and one of them was needling Kevin.

" 'What now?' I asked him. He said, 'I'm going to tell him I know who's going to win this race. It's a sure thing.' He started laughing, then said, 'I'm going to keep this going right to the end. It'll make him nuts wondering if what I'm telling him is the truth or malarkey.' Then he went off laughing. After Foster won, I heard O'Malley had lost a lot of money, probably on a bet, and I could never learn anything more. Suddenly nobody knew anything, especially on the Tillman side. Apparently, I was the only one on our team Amos had told about the trick he was playing on O'Malley."

"Do you think O'Malley believed what Lansbury was telling him?" Harry asked.

"I don't know."

"O'Malley went on diving with Lansbury after the election. He couldn't have been very angry with Amos for leading him on."

"Possibly so, but on several levels, it's an interesting story. And I wondered if O'Malley had told anyone else what Amos had been telling him."

"I don't know," Harry said, "but I'm finding that everyone has his own story."

Once in the Rover, Harry checked his phone and found a text message from Holly: *Pls cll, Hry.* Harry or hurry, he asked himself as he dialed. She picked up on the first ring.

"I've been rustled," she said, sounding on the edge of tears.

At first he didn't understand what she was telling him. Then the light shone in. "What have you lost?"

"Ten of my best brood mares, all about to foal."

"That's awful," Harry said. "How did it happen?"

"How do you think?" she shouted. "They rounded them up, herded them into a big horse van, and drove away. They're probably scattered over three states by now."

"I'm sorry," Harry said, chastened by her anger and unsure what he could say without further offending her.

"So am I. There's a year's work gone right there."

"Terrible. How many of your mares are left?"

"Eight or nine, and don't try to make me feel better."

"No, of course not. How serious is this financially?"

"Beef prices are up. I'll be all right, but I'm mad as hell."

Harry felt the knot in his stomach begin to loosen as the volume of her responses lessened.

"Was yours the only ranch hit?"

"No," she said, anger still sharpening her voice. "The B&R and the Double S lost steers or horses. White Horse lost its whole remuda, although how that could have happened is a mystery. There may have been others."

"That can't be coincidence," he said.

"Of course it's not a coincidence, you idiot," she exploded. "By now they'll be on feed lots and in horse dealers' corrals from here to South Dakota. Get a grip, Harry. They're organized up to the hilt with horse and cattle vans, horses and ATVs to round up the animals they've scouted days or weeks before, locations off 94 East where the lots are broken up and shifted to smaller vans, rebranding stations ready and waiting, and the crooked dealers are buying low and reselling high."

A welcome silence descended, broken only by Holly's heavy breathing. He thought of asking her how she felt about Montana this afternoon—at least it was still afternoon in Livingston.

"When did you find out?" he asked, having wisely decided to save the question for another time.

"About two hours ago. My foreman brought the news. He checks on them once a day, which is more than the other ranchers do. I've been on the phone with the sheriff's people and alerting the other ranchers ever since. I called you as soon as I could."

"What happens now?" he asked, thinking it might help, at least briefly, to have her looking ahead.

"What do you mean?" she asked, aggression bubbling up in the question.

"Something happened, you learned of it, it upset you, you're dealing with that, and I meant are you going fishing? Are you going to buy more horses? Are you going to shift away from horses to cattle? What are you going to do?"

"I don't know."

She suddenly sounded defeated. The shift away from anger startled and worried Harry. When she was angry, she sounded in control despite the loss. He experienced a sudden stab of guilt. Why wasn't he there to help her?

"You're going to get past this," he said hurriedly. "It's bad what's happened. I know that. It really is, but you're going to get on top of this and move on. I know you. This is not going to defeat you."

"Feeling guilty, aren't you?" she asked with a touch of wickedness showing through. "You want me feeling better and telling you I'm okay, that I've picked myself up, dusted myself off, put on my hat, and climbed back on the horse, all so that you can stop feeling guilty."

"You've nailed it," Harry said, forced to smile at being outed. "What about sheep?"

"Sheep!" she said, sounding insulted. "Are you asking me if I'd thought of raising sheep?"

"Are they rustling sheep?"

There was a long pause.

"You know, I don't know. But they'd rustle juniper bushes if there was money in it."

"I've read that very large breeds of dogs are trained to protect sheep and live with them. Could that be done with horses?"

"Maybe, but we don't lose enough foals to cougars or coyotes to make it worth the trouble. Rustlers would just shoot them. Why am I talking about this? I'm not about to start herding sheep. I came out here to raise cattle and horses."

"And that's what you're going to keep on doing," Harry said.

"The sheriff's here, Harry. I've got to go. Come out here and see how this place works."

Before he could answer, Holly had hung up, leaving him feeling empty and very much alone.

Chapter 16

Harry's responses to Holly's call were numerous, debilitating, and rich in pain, ascending from regret at her loss to extreme guilt that he wasn't there to help her cope with the robbery. Her horses were not merely an investment. They were objects of caring and love, especially the brood mares. She knew all their names as well as their idiosyncrasies, and while they were in their stalls, he knew that she had her hands on their glossy hides every day, currying, brushing, and stroking, all the while talking to them.

He found there was no use telling himself that there was little he could do if he were there. The sense of having failed her just when she needed him could not be dismissed or rationalized away. He knew the reaction was excessive. He also recognized his own hypocrisy in wringing his hands over her situation. He was not with her because he had told her he didn't want to move to Montana. She wasn't with him here because she had made up her mind that a move was necessary to separate herself from the place where every road, fence, pasture, and room in her house were reminders of her husband and his gruesome death.

Morning came as it always does, and he greeted it with a sigh, Holly's difficulties still being with him. Nevertheless, he ran three miles, paused on the plank bridge to watch the sun rise fiery red over Puc Puggy Creek, ate his breakfast with a reasonably good appetite, and swept the kitchen floor, before leaving the Hammock to talk with Beatrice Lansbury.

Just before getting into the Rover, he paused, and in an unusually reflective moment, linked probably to Holly's still being with him, thought that in the world as it had become, there were an increasing number of things about which he could do nothing but stand by and watch the new wretchedness unfold like a flooding river.

Every surface aside from the floor and the ceiling in Beatrice Lansbury's living room was burdened with photographs in Dollar Store frames. The walls also carried their share, spaced out with furniture store art. The clutter, if that's what it was, gave the room the effect of life suspended and time turned off.

"What a peaceful and interesting room," Harry said, surprised by his own response.

"Very kind of you, Mr. Brock," Lansbury said with a pleased laugh. "That's not the response I usually get."

She was gray-haired with a pleasantly attractive face that looked younger than her years and not at all the dowdy, middle-aged person he was expecting. In fact, Harry decided, except for the short gray hair, which made her more interesting in his eyes, she might have been a woman in her late thirties instead of the age she had to be.

"It's very good of you to talk with me," he said, sitting down with her on the low sofa decorated in Florida pastels.

She was wearing beige slacks and a yellow cotton cardigan over a white blouse. She had a figure and had kept her slender waist. Harry found her relaxed but alert with a lovely smile and clear eyes, bright with intelligence, which pleased him very much. He did not like having to talk with unengaged people, and he especially did not like talking to women who didn't want to be talking with him.

"I'm glad you asked," she told him. "I have been very curious to hear what you think I could tell you about Amos that would be of any value after all these years."

"There's always something," he said. "Did I say I was working for Meredith Winters?"

"Yes, and frankly, I've always wondered what she and Amos saw in one another."

She crossed her legs and rested her folded hands on her knee, coloring slightly as she resumed speaking. "I hope you won't be shocked or offended when I say this, but if Amos and I were ever in love, we certainly weren't by the time our marriage was over. I don't think I have ever been as relieved in my life as I was the day the divorce decree came through. If no one else offers, I take myself out for a celebratory dinner every year on the anniversary of it."

Harry couldn't help laughing.

"I wish I could say the same," he replied. "You do seem to have recovered very well from yours."

"Yes, that's true," she said eagerly, pressing her hands against her chest. "I owe my happiness to the failure of my marriage. Marriage taught me two of the most important things I have ever learned: the value of one's freedom, and the gift of one's own company. All the West's wild horses couldn't drag me down that aisle again. Hallelujah!"

With that outburst, she threw up her hands as though she had seen the Light, then burst out laughing. Her laugh was so infectious, Harry joined in, delighted. She was, he decided, one of those rare people who made you feel better just being around them.

"What was Amos Lansbury like when you knew him?" he asked her when they had settled down a bit.

"Driven. He was the most driven man I've ever known, not that I've spent much time around driven men. When I encounter one, I go the other way. Once bitten, etc. And secretive. I never knew more than a fraction of what he was doing. He lived with me on a need-to-know basis, with him deciding what I did and didn't need to know. At first it was creepy, then it became annoying, and finally, unendurable."

"Do you have any idea why anyone would want to kill him?" Harry asked.

"Didn't he drown in a diving accident?" she asked in surprise.

"Mrs. Winters doesn't think so, based on the fact that there were several people angry enough with him to want him dead and that he was a very experienced diver who was unlikely to have died from carelessness."

Lansbury sat back in her chair and looked into some middle distance over Harry's right shoulder.

"Time didn't deal kindly with Amos," she said finally in a quiet, serious voice. "I have followed his career with mild interest. All the bad traits he displayed when we were living together seem to have intensified with the passing of the years. I understand why Meredith thinks he was murdered. There were days when I gladly would have killed him, and I might have done so had I cared enough about him to make the effort."

"What drove him?" Harry asked, liking this woman more every minute he was with her.

"As I said, he never discussed what he was doing or why, so I can only speculate. I think it was some overpowering need to control people in order to bring about outcomes from which he benefitted."

"How benefitted? To make money?"

"A lot of money passed through his hands. He frequently came home with a shopping bag full of twenty-dollar bills that he left on the sideboard in the kitchen or wherever he happened to stop on coming into the house."

"Was he working on political campaigns when you were with him?"

"That's right. I did know that much."

She paused, frowning slightly. "It was an odd thing. He never made a lot of money. The money always went out of the house as casually as it came in. One thing is certain," Beatrice said, her face lighting up. "It never stuck to him. Within a year of our marriage, I went to work to keep us from qualifying for food stamps. I've been working ever since. It's the best thing after divorcing Amos I ever did." That comment was followed by a happy smile.

"What do you do?" Harry asked, not wanting to have to leave.

"Get ready to laugh. I'm in a management position in the Tequesta County Supervisor of Elections Office, been with the office for twenty-five years. I love it."

"I'm impressed," Harry said. "I think I detect some irony in your account. Has the office ever run afoul of your ex-husband?"

"Oh, yes. I'm sure you know about his conviction for voter fraud. We were involved in that. At least the original complaint came to us. I took a little teasing over that."

"I can imagine. Did you find it upsetting?"

"You know," she said on a rising inflection as though she still found it surprising, "I did. For a time I felt as though Amos and I were still together and I was still trying to share a life with him."

She paused, assumed a bland expression, and added, "Of course I got over it rather quickly."

Harry suppressed a grin and asked, "Was he justly punished?"

"Oh, no!" she said. "He got off far too easily, but truth to tell, he was a victim as much as he was a perpetrator."

"How do you mean?"

"His urge to control simply trampled his instinct to protect himself from harm. I think he became more and more his compulsion until it did him in."

"You may well be right," Harry said, standing up. "Thank you again for talking with me. It's been a great help, and I've enjoyed it very much."

"So have I," she said as they shook hands.

Harry went on holding her hand a moment or two longer than was necessary, but Beatrice didn't seem to mind.

After they had said goodbye at the door, Beatrice added, growing a little pink, "If you find you want to talk with me again, you know where to reach me."

"Thank you, I do," Harry said, for some reason feeling obliged to shake hands with her again.

"Every day I become more certain that somebody's systematically killing off Prentice Foster's campaign team."

Harry was talking while holding the door to the bantams' house, allowing Tucker to screw the hinges in place. It was a solid wooden door that opened inward, and there would be a screen door added that would open out. If that seemed excessive in a climate where there might be a frost once in seven years, Tucker was right to be more concerned about the coyotes than the frost. "And add the monitor lizards to the coyotes, and maybe the boa constrictors as well, and it's clear a solid door to close at night makes sense," he had said when the coop was in the planning stages.

"Someone connected to Tillman?" Tucker asked now, stepping back from the door. "Let it swing to."

"I have no way of knowing," Harry said, giving the door a light push, "but with a gun pointed at me, I'd say yes."

"Perfect," Tucker said, eyeing the door with satisfaction. "If it is one of Tillman's people, it would seem to narrow the field substantially."

Harry had known Tucker long enough to recognize the criticism lurking in the apparently anodyne observation.

"Odd," he said, "I had thought of that. Great minds and so forth."

"Don't get huffy. You did a good job of holding the door while I did the skilled work. Don't think I'm not appreciative."

Harry saw this could go on for a long time and wisely sheathed his sword.

"Four men went fishing and three came back," he said. "Then one of them was shot and soon after that a third man died when his pick-up exploded. All of them worked for Foster."

"Two of the divers are still among us. Let's put on the screen door."

When it was successfully hung and approved, Tucker called for a cider break and suddenly remembered he had baked donuts that morning, and added them to the menu.

"Let's sit in the orchard," Tucker suggested.

"I don't think I've ever eaten a donut while drinking cider," Harry remarked awhile later, leaning back on the split-log seat, his feet thrust out.

"How do you like it as far as you've been?" Tucker asked, recharging their mugs from the large thermos he was using to keep the cider cold.

"I'm going to try not to think about that while I'm still eating."

"A good idea," Tucker said. "Donuts and cider are not a match made in heaven. I assume you and Jim Snyder's people have been talking with those left standing."

"Yes, and others. Most recently I talked with Beatrice Lansbury, Amos's first wife. She kept her married name. She's a delightful person, a little older than I am, but she doesn't look it. She and I must have talked for half an hour. She works for the county. From what I've been able to gather, Amos Lansbury was making enemies long before he went to work for Prentice Foster."

"Then it doesn't have to be someone in Tillman's campaign who did him in—if he was murdered," Tucker said, making a sour face and pouring the last of his cider into the grass. "Worst idea I've had this month. I hope it's the last."

Just then Sanchez and Oh, Brother! emerged from the orchard and hurried forward to greet Harry.

"Sanchez," Tucker said, "do you want to finish this donut? I've lost interest in it."

The dog postponed saying hello to Harry long enough to dispose of the donut.

"Oh, Brother!," Tucker said, "remind me when we get back to the house that I've got an apple for you."

The mule paused to listen to what Tucker was saying, then gave his attention back to Harry, who was stroking his shining black neck and complimenting him on the new ibis feather in his hatband.

"I suppose you want me to believe that he understood what you said to him."

"Stick around and see," Tucker said in the voice of one long accustomed to Harry's doubts.

Harry finished the mandatory wrestle with the big hound, who was growling and showing his very large white teeth in delight all the time Harry grasped the loose skin on his neck and tried to throw the big animal off his feet, an attempt that resulted in Harry's landing with a thump in the grass.

"You'd think I'd learn," Harry said, scrambling up while Sanchez stood by grinning.

"It gives Sanchez a lot of pleasure, so it's not all loss," Tucker remarked as he and Harry went back to work on the bantam coop. By the time they finished work for the day and returned to the house, Harry had forgotten about the promised apple. Oh, Brother! had not, or so it appeared. Sanchez had gone off to find a place to lie in the shade, but the mule followed the two men to the back stoop and stood waiting expectantly as Tucker went into the house and returned with an apple in his hand. The mule ate with obvious pleasure.

"What do you think now?" Tucker asked Harry.

"It's a setup," Harry said. "You have him trained to expect an apple about this time of day and all that talk about it in the orchard was to fool me. But I'm not fooled."

Harry was standing on the front edge of the stoop while he talked and was suddenly propelled forward by a soft but powerful push from behind. When he caught his balance, he turned to find Oh, Brother! looking down at him.

"What was that for?" Harry demanded, walking back to look up at the mule.

After a moment, the animal lowered his head, pressed his nose against Harry's chest, and blew softly. Harry stroked and patted him, talking quietly to him. "Okay," he said finally, "I was wrong. You did remember."

At that point Oh, Brother! stepped back with a final snort of satisfaction, and Sanchez gave one of his happy barks.

"Tucker," Harry said, shaking his head, "this is one seriously weird farm."

Chapter 17

"There's some progress on this end," Jim said when Harry had finished describing his interview with Beatrice Lansbury, an account frequently interrupted by Hodges, who wanted further details about all the points in the account where feelings and explanations were or might be involved.

"I knew Beatrice a little over twenty years ago," Hodges said. "That was before she married Lansbury. She was Beatrice Olsen then. If I remember right, her mother was a Seavey. The Seaveys moved down here from Jacksonville, let's see, ten years after Donna struck . . ."

"What year did Donna hit?" Harry asked. "I should know that date, but I don't."

"Nineteen-sixty," Hodges said. "Everybody got to using that date to remember others by. I might have been three years old. I remember my father taking me down to the beach to see that all the water had vanished. Of course we weren't there when it came back, and the surge ran up all the way to Route 41."

Harry had another question, but Jim, rising up like a rower from behind his desk, said in a loud voice, "Enough. We are not here to explore genealogies or review the history of great storms on the southwest coast. We're here to find out who blew up Joe Purcell."

"Don't forget Arthur Hornsby and, possibly, Amos Lansbury," Hodges put in helpfully, causing Harry to fail to smother a snort of laughter.

"Thank you, Sergeant," Jim said. "I don't know how I'd get along without you."

"Not to worry, Captain," Hodges said with moving sincerity, "I don't plan to fly off to Montana, the way Harry here is likely to do, because it's been my experience in married life that when he and she fall out, it's usually she who comes out on top. I'm not referring there to . . ."

"We all know what you're not referring to, Frank," Jim blared, his face red. "Can we just get back to what I was trying to say?"

"Go right ahead, Captain," Hodges said. "I'm all ears."

That was the breaking point for Harry, who had been struggling to keep from bursting into laughter, a development that made Jim fall back into his chair.

"The new development," Harry said, recovering.

"Lieutenant Jones was right," Jim said. "The explosive that killed Joe Purcell was Semtex, but that's only the beginning. It was homemade."

"Then that's why Millard couldn't smell it," Hodges said. "It didn't have that additive."

"That made it smell like almonds," Harry said, finishing Hodges's thought.

"Probably so," Jim agreed.

"The man who made it must be someone who really knows explosives and be something of a chemist himself," Hodges added.

"Frank's half right," Jim said.

"Right," Harry agreed. "Anyone can learn how to make it from what's on the Internet, but very few would be stupid enough to try once they had read the warnings that go along with mixing the ingredients."

"So, as Frank said, we're probably looking for someone experienced with explosives, but not necessarily a chemist."

"Doesn't advance us all that much, does it?" Harry asked.

"No," Jim said, "and that's why I'm considering bringing in the Feds."

"Oh, Lord, no!" Hodges protested. "Don't do that. Our lives will become a burden and a misery."

"Possibly," Jim conceded, "but if we don't find the perpetrators of these crimes, they surely will."

"Why not take the less drastic step of asking for some background checks?" Harry asked.

"Good idea," Hodges said.

"Not so fast," Jim said, obviously reconsidering. "If we ask for background checks, someone in that outfit is going to ask why, and I'll have to tell them. Once they hear that someone's blown up a car with a person in it, they're going to start trying to prove it was an act of terrorism. Headlines, additional money, a media blitz, interviews, a spotlight shining right in our eyes."

"Jim," Harry said in an attempt to talk him down from where he had taken himself, "have you forgotten it was you who suggested bringing in the Feds in the first place?"

"That's right. I allowed myself to get carried away by the prospect that suddenly opened before me. And now I'm even beginning to sound like you!" Jim complained, glaring at Harry.

Harry made a lot of space for Jim, knowing he hated putting a foot wrong, not out of false pride but because he was so serious about his work. Too serious, probably, but his excesses in that direction had made the department one of the best in the state.

"How about this," Harry suggested. "Take one of the people who might have committed the crimes"—Jim didn't seem to notice that Harry had reduced the perpetrators to one—"and slip his name in without providing any eye-catching details. Then, if that ploy works, ease in the rest, one or two at a time over, say, a week, never mentioning the bombing."

"Sneaky but good," Hodges said with a beaming face.

"Might work," Jim said, still showing some reluctance that stemmed, Harry suspected, from his not having thought of doing that himself. He did want to see himself as more than just a bureaucrat.

"Worth a try," Hodges said.

"I'll ask Lieutenant Jones what he thinks and take it from there."

That ended the discussion and once in the hall, Hodges complained to Harry that it wasn't up to standard for Jim to consult with Jones when the decision was clearly his.

"I think there's an acronym that covers it."

"A what?" Hodges asked.

"CYA," Harry said.

Harry had fallen behind on an insurance surveillance assignment, requiring him to determine whether or not a claimant was limited to walking with crutches.

Weilly Cross, the man in question, had given his insurance company a particularly annoying kind of heartburn because two of the three doctors the company had employed to review the medical reports accompanying the claim found the claims not compelling. One of their doctors, however, agreed with the original findings by Cross's doctor that it was likely that for the foreseeable future Cross would be restricted to using crutches or some other mechanical assistance to walk, making him entitled to compensation.

That Cross's doctor was also his brother-in-law was particularly painful for the company. Almost equally exasperating was the fact that Cross was the C.E.O. of Fairfield Witherspoon, a Bible and religious texts and textbooks publisher.

Having already familiarized himself with Cross's work-week routine and observed him being driven to work by a uniformed chauffeur who deposited him at the large brass and glass entry doors to the company, Harry had concluded that he was dealing with either an honest man or a very careful crook. Harry had watched him for several days being helped out of the car by the driver, who passed Cross his crutches once he was on his feet, then followed him into the building, carrying his briefcase and riding up to his office with him. All that remained was to find a way to the executive suite and observe Cross moving around in it.

Today, a few minutes after the chauffeur turned into the publishing house drive, Harry, dressed in a generic delivery uniform, tan trousers, a tan cap with a shiny black visor, and a tan short-sleeved shirt with pens in the pocket, had also equipped himself with a metal-backed clipboard holding printed delivery forms, and a two-foot-square cardboard box, stamped in several places THIS END UP in three-inch-high red inks.

Adopting the fast gait affected by most parcel delivery people, Harry strode into the lobby, holding the box in both arms. "Private and expedited delivery for Weilly Cross," he said abruptly to the dark-haired young woman at the reception desk.

"You can leave it with me," she said crisply, regarding him with complete indifference. "I'll sign for it."

"Nope," Harry said firmly. "I put this into Weilly Cross's hands or I don't deliver it today. My experience is that when whatever is in a box like this doesn't get to the people whose names are on the delivery tag, somebody gets really reamed, usually whoever held it up."

"Top floor," she said, not having changed her expression, and went back to flicking through the magazine she had been looking at.

"Smart girl," Harry said in that same pushy voice and left for the elevator.

He stepped out of the elevator when the doors opened, with an almost indecent sigh, into a crystalline space of tinted glass and gleaming marble floors. To his right he saw a slim, handsome woman wearing horn-rimmed glasses and dressed in a black business suit and black heels hurrying toward him, her shoes clicking rhythmically on the marble as she advanced.

"There's been a mistake," she said crisply.

"Is this Weilly Cross's office?" he asked in a loud voice, interrupting her.

"Yes, but . . ." she began. She had reached him by this time and was frowning darkly at him.

"Personal delivery for him," he said, still speaking loudly.

"Is anything the matter, Ms. Piper?"

"You Weilly Cross?" Harry asked, having stepped to the side to gain a clear field between himself and the speaker.

The tall, tanned man who had spoken to Piper had emerged from a glass office beyond Piper's desk and was striding toward them. "I am," he said in a commanding voice, "and what are you doing up here?"

"Taking pictures of you walking toward us from your office, Mr. Cross."

"Call security," Cross said to Piper, who hurried toward her desk.

"Don't bother," Harry said. "I'm leaving. My name is Harry Brock. I'm a licensed private detective employed by the company insuring you, Mr. Cross."

While he was speaking, Harry had taken a small camera out of the box and slipped it into his pocket. Piper's hand was hovering over her desk phone as she stared at them, uncertain what to do.

"For Mr. Cross's sake," Harry said, "it would be better not to involve any more people than are here now."

"Mr. Cross?" she asked.

"Let it go, Ms. Piper," he said.

Harry reentered the elevator. As the doors slowly closed, he turned and saw Cross and Piper standing frozen in place like figures in a *tableau vivant*.

After checking his watch and adding three hours, Harry called Holly.

"The signal's not very strong out here," she said in place of hello.

"Where are you?"

"In the ranch pick-up, running my fence lines. I'm about a mile from the house."

"And?"

"So far, so good. I've accounted for all but the missing mares, which is a relief."

"How about the cattle?"

"God knows, they're scattered over a wide area."

"Is it open range?" Harry asked in surprise.

"No, when I bought this spread, I became part of a district grazing cooperative that allows me to graze a fixed number of cattle on the land allotted to our district," Holly said. "The group of ranchers in our district has a legal responsibility for the area with each of us caring for our section of the perimeter fencing and a percentage of the taxes."

"Is there much cheating?"

"No, that's watched very carefully, and it's a good thing. A few decades ago the open range was so badly over-grazed the best grasses died out. It took a lot of time and care to restore the range to health and productivity."

"Have you had any word about your lost mares?" Harry asked, thinking he'd better not wait any longer to ask.

"I had a call from the sheriff's office saying they'd tracked the thieves out of the state and then lost the trail. They're still trying, but I have the feeling I'd just better write them off."

"I'm sorry you lost them, but you sound better than you did

the last time we talked."

"I am, and I'd feel even better if I was doing what I'm doing now on a horse instead of bouncing around inside the cab of this truck."

"Why did the sheriff's people lose track of your mares so quickly?" Harry asked, his mind turning again to what really interested him about her account of the failure.

"Damn!" she said suddenly. "Another prairie dog mound. My head went into the roof on that one. It's great to have them here, but this stretch of ground is really thick with them."

"Are they dangerous to the animals?" Harry asked.

"Not really, it's more the damage they do with their digging. Their mound gives unwanted plants, weeds and such, a space to spread from, but they make a place for the black-footed ferrets to live. And since the ferrets eat prairie dogs, they keep the population under control. You know, Harry, if you were out here, you could be doing this with me, and we could do it on horseback."

"You just want someone to laugh at. I remember what you thought of my horsemanship. Back to my question."

"I don't know, but I'm sure the department is stretched pretty thin, and the distances out here are so much greater than anything you have to contend with in Florida. I'm still getting used to it. Several of the ranch families in my district do most of their commuting by airplane. Their kids are on horses at three and flying by fifteen, girls and boys alike. I think they're born knowing how to drive cars and operate tractors, combines, and baling machines."

"Do the sheriff's departments use planes?" he asked, thinking it would be the most effective way to cover a lot of highway and radio the location of horse and cattle vans.

"I asked about that but was told the rustlers do their driving at night, rebrand the first day, and by night send the animals off in small lots and in different directions. Apparently, it's all done with computers and global positioning systems."

"Then if they survive the first night on the road," Harry said, "they're pretty much home free."

"I think that's it," Holly said, swearing again as the truck gave another leap. Then she added in a surprisingly wistful voice, "I wish you could see what I'm looking at."

"Which is?"

"Miles of grassland slowly rising to evergreen forests and beyond them blue mountains with snow-covered tops, and the air is clear as spring water."

"Sounds great," Harry said and, curbing his tongue, left it there.

"Think hard, Harry," she said and then a moment later added, "Oh, oh, lost calf, got to go. Bye."

Harry came away from that conversation with a complex of reactions. It galled him that she was going to have to just give up on the theft of her horses. He felt sure in his own mind that computers or not, you couldn't just make something the size of a horse disappear and keep it in one piece. Also, he didn't think it was possible to alter an existing brand without the change being obvious. The fact that he knew nothing about horse rustling or brands and branding didn't seem a hindrance to his believing firmly in his conclusions.

As for snow-capped peaks and wide-open spaces, he told himself, he had lived all his life so far without living among them and thought he could bear up a few years longer. He turned his mind away from those reflections without being ashamed of the summary dismissal. On the subject of Holly and her appeals and attractions, he had become hyper-vigilant in guarding himself against them.

It has been said, perhaps with some accuracy, that the stories we tell ourselves about ourselves go a long way toward shaping our lives. Harry's personal narrative—and nearly everything he said to himself about Holly fell into that category—had increasingly distanced him from gaining an insight into why he was refusing her invitations to visit the ranch.

If he had asked himself, as Tucker had most recently asked him, why he was so afraid of going to Montana, he might have made some progress toward understanding what he was really doing in refusing to consider her offers. That, however, lay in the Bureau of What-Ifs and had been collecting dust for some time. Unfortunately, only he could enter there, blow the dust off it, and carry it into the sunshine.

Meredith called, freeing him temporarily from his self-justifications. "Is there anywhere I can spend a couple of hours with you looking at something other than these four walls?"

"When was the last time you walked through the Audubon Corkscrew Swamp Sanctuary?" he asked.

"Never. How bad are the mosquitoes?"

"There aren't any."

"Where is it?"

"About a forty-minute drive from where you are."

"Is it off the Immokalee Road, going east?"

"That's right."

"Then I've caught you in a howler," she said in an exultant tone of voice. "That's in the Everglades."

"No and yes. I didn't lie, but I was teasing you. Most of the sanctuary boardwalk is in a cypress swamp, and the gambusia, tiny fish, eat the mosquito larvae so ravenously, there are almost no mosquitoes in the sanctuary. Quite wonderful, really. There's also a carnivorous bladderwort plant that feeds on them."

"Okay, I'll risk it. Shorts and halter?"

"Perfect."

She was standing on the front steps, her face turned up to

the sun, when Harry arrived.

"Someone ought to paint you, standing as you were with the sun on your face," he told her as she climbed into the SUV. He did not say that he found her stunning in her apple-green outfit and matching sandals, her thick, honey-blonde hair gathered in a gold ring.

"Have you been drinking?" she asked, settling into the seat and regarding him with a mischievous look in her eyes.

"Not in the immediate past, and you're no better at taking a compliment than I am."

"Do you want to say anything more?"

"Yes, but because of my menial position as your employee, I've restrained myself."

"Then unrestrain yourself."

"You look ravishing."

"Oh, good!" she said in a much happier voice, blushing and breaking into a wide smile that, Harry thought, made her look about fifteen years younger.

Once they were underway, Meredith released her seat belt and pulled on a white cotton cardigan."

"AC," she said. "My legs seem to be impervious to the cold, but my top and arms are not. What are we going to see?"

"You'll have to wait to find out. The place is never quite the same twice, but I'm never disappointed."

"I have mixed feelings about that display of the process by which they purify and recycle the water from the toilets," she said with a slight frown as they stepped out of the reception area and onto the white sand path leading deeper into the sanctuary. "If their aim was to reduce the use of the drinking fountains, it worked with me."

Harry laughed. "You are a genuinely quirky person," he said, "and I mean it as a compliment. Also, your sense of humor fits mine exactly."

"I was feeling really good listening to you until you reached the personal comparison. That part was a downer."

"Why so?" Harry demanded, prepared to be offended.

"Because your sense of humor is way too mordant for me. I sometimes think you might go to funerals for laughs."

"Not so. I go to interments in order to read the epitaphs, some of which are bracing, such as the one I saw a while ago that read, 'I knew this would happen but not so soon.' Then there was the one on the grave of a man who had outlived three wives that read, 'The rose fades and its petals fall.' "

She tried not to laugh and failed then said, "You made them up."

"No, someone else did."

Quite suddenly, a piercing cry like a soul in torment broke out and Meredith jumped.

"What . . . ?" she said, looking around wide-eyed.

They were walking through a grove of widely spaced, rough-barked slash pines with their branches clustered at the tops of their reddish trunks. The ground under and between them was densely overgrown by saw palmetto shrubs, their deep green fronds creating a carpet three to four feet deep.

"Over there," Harry said, taking her arm and pointing at a very large, garishly colored woodpecker with a crest, hammering away at the tree, making chips of bark fly and pausing occasionally to give a high, loud call.

"What is it?" she asked.

"A pileated woodpecker," Harry said. "Noisy critters."

"These trees look like giant feather dusters," she said when the bird flew off.

"For a reason," Harry said. "Don't laugh, but we're in a terrain that's called an upland forest, which means that it's very dry and burns over every so often during the winter. The fire burns down here at ground level and the pines' foliage is up there out of harm's way."

"What about these palmettos?"

"Most of their trunks are underground, so what's showing burns, then new growth quickly replaces whatever was lost in the fire."

"Cool," she said.

Harry laughed. "You sound like the kids."

"Good. What's ahead?" she asked, pointing at the start of the boardwalk further along the path.

"Shade, for one thing," Harry said, pulling off his hat and wiping his face with it before putting it back on.

"Am I paying you so badly you can't afford a new hat?" she asked, frowning at the remains of the Tilley hat he was wearing.

"This hat has a proud history," he said. "An alligator once tried to eat it, having mistaken it for an ibis. And it's been shot a couple of times."

By now she was laughing. She lifted the hat off his head and appeared to be studying his scalp.

"What are you doing?" he demanded.

"Looking for the holes in your head, but I don't see any. Have you been lying again?"

"I was lifting it up on the end of a stick at the time."

Having reached the boardwalk, they entered the edges of the cypress forest, and there was water under them.

"There's a raccoon down there," she said in astonishment, pausing to look over the railing.

"They've learned that people here won't harm them. So, they go about living as if we don't exist. Some people don't like that."

"Why ever not?"

"They feel diminished."

"That can't be true," she protested.

"Having animals fear them makes them feel superior."

They had reached a turn-off from the walkway, terminating in a roofed seating area that led out into a heavily grassed and shrubbed stretch of land.

"What's that?" she asked.

"A good place to see some of the small Florida deer that live in here. They're nearly as tame as the raccoons but not quite. Quick movements frighten them."

"Are there any panthers in here?" she asked as they made their way to the seating area.

"Sadly, no. They prefer to be where people aren't," Harry told her as they sat down on the bench facing out into the grass and scrub growth. "Also, there aren't very many of them."

"Haven't I read that many are killed each year crossing roads?"

"Yes, they seem to be slow learners when it comes to cars. The best place to see one is on the raised walk in the Fakahatchee Strand State Park off Route 41E."

They had been speaking quietly, and Harry pointed toward a sunny opening in the grass thirty or forty yards in front of them. Two does and three fawns had stepped out of the grass, taller than they were, and stood looking around, their tails twitching.

"The last time I saw a deer in the wild was in Bandelier National Monument," Meredith said in a whisper. "They were more than twice the size of these."

"Mule deer," Harry answered. "Big as cows."

There was disturbance in the grass to the deer's left, and they were gone, silent and swift as smoke in the wind.

Chapter 18

Their walk continued deeper into the cypress swamp and its welcome shade. Gradually, they grew quiet until long minutes passed without either of them speaking. Harry saw that Meredith was relaxing, her tension easing, and the change pleased him.

"Harry," she said quietly after several minutes of silence as they leaned side by side on the railing, watching a very large alligator that had hauled itself out of the water and lay sprawled on the remains of the moss and fern-covered trunk of an ancient, fallen cypress, doing absolutely nothing, "there's something magical about this place. Do you feel it?"

"Every time I come here," he told her. "But it's getting late. I suppose we should be going."

She moved a little closer to him so that their shoulders were touching and her gaze shifted from the alligator to him. He turned his head and found his face close to hers as their eyes met.

"Do you have to be somewhere?" she asked. "Could we stay a while longer?"

He was so close to her that he could see the fine sheen of moisture on her face and her brown eyes that drew him deeper and deeper into them.

This is how she would look if we were making love, he thought. And his next thought was that he must end this, now.

"It's always difficult to say no to a beautiful woman," he

replied, trying to free himself from his speculations, "and if she's your employer, it's foolish."

"What you gave with one hand you took away with the other," she said, her eyes never leaving his.

"How's that?" Harry asked. The boat of his concentration, losing its mooring again, began to drift deeper into her eyes.

"First you said I was beautiful, which was good. Then you said I was your employer, which wasn't."

"Suppress the *employer* part," he said. "I was being sincere only in the *beautiful* segment."

"You don't know how good it makes me feel to have rocked your cradle," she said, finishing with a smile.

"Is that how you see me?" he asked, stung. "As a child?"

"Not entirely, but you are in some strange way, Harry, an innocent," she said, giving him a slight push with her shoulder. "And that's the best compliment I could give you. It makes you very attractive."

"Now you've embarrassed me," he told her, feigning offense.

"Good," she said with an earthier smile, "it's a beginning."

A few minutes later as they were moving on, she took his arm and said in a quiet but serious voice, "I'm not sure I should have come here."

"Why not?" Harry asked, troubled by both what she had said and how it was said.

"Everything involving Amos's death seems far away here and the pursuit of his killer, if there is such a person, meaningless."

Harry caught her hand in his and said, "It's the Eden effect. If you will let it, the place washes you clean and puts things into a clearer perspective."

"Will it last?"

"It never has for me, but remember, you're free to stop any time you want."

Just then, one of the sanctuary's female guides passed them

and said with a weary smile, "Closing time, folks. Please don't linger."

Clarissa Purcell had a long slog ahead on her path to recovery, but she told Harry she was determined to do whatever she could to find whoever killed her husband. She had talked with the police and now she was talking with him.

"Are you sure you want to put yourself through this?" Harry asked, watching the silver-haired woman in front of him with some trepidation.

She was tall, and her perfectly proportioned figure made her look shorter than she was, as Harry found when shaking her hand. Despite the grief visible in her face, her body went on moving with ease and grace.

"Of course I don't want to do it," she snapped, "but I'm damned well going to. Go ahead, begin, and if I start bawling, stay in your seat. I'll recover in a minute or two. Actually, it's a relief for me. Where do we begin?"

Harry looked at her with admiration and increasing respect. He had expected her to turn him down and thought she should. Now, here he was, sitting in her living room, which was still partially wrecked, but the roof had been restored.

"Has Tim Petersen worked out for you?" he asked.

"He's been a life-saver," she answered, brightening a little. "The roof doesn't leak and these temporary plastic windows are keeping out the bugs and the wind and letting in the light. Beyond clearing away the broken glass, I haven't found whatever it takes to deal with the mess you're sitting in."

"Breaking glass is worse than spilling sugar," he said in sympathy. "You can never get it all swept up."

"Right. Moving on."

"Who would want to harm your husband?" he asked.

"I don't know," she said. "He knew a lot of people over the

years, hundreds. So far as I know, he didn't have gambling debts, for example. He was a quiet, pleasant man. I think, perhaps, it was a mistake. That level of violence . . . whoever did this must have been either crazy or so angry he had lost all sense and reason."

"Possibly it was a mistake, and at this point, I have no idea why Mr. Purcell was killed the way he was. I'm not sure shooting someone is more violent than blowing him up. Perhaps we've become hardened to people being shot."

He began enlarging on that theme then stopped himself. This grieving woman didn't need to hear him on the subject of guns.

"I may not have been fully forthcoming in answering your question," she said as if she had been rethinking something while he was speaking.

Harry waited as she turned away from him for the first time since the beginning of their conversation. He had learned that in moments like this one, it was best to sit still and let the other person say or do what needs doing.

"As I've said," she told him finally, turning back to face him, "Joe met a lot of people, some of them ruthless and with very few internal constraints on what they were willing to do to get what they wanted—mostly power and money."

She stopped again, still looking at him, but her mind clearly busy with its own thoughts. When she came back, she continued as if she had not paused.

"At first, I seldom met the people he worked with, but over the years and more often in recent years because he wanted me with him, I got to meet a fairly large number of them. There were some I wish I hadn't."

"Remember any names?" he asked.

"A few. You know," she said after a brief pause, "I think the years were catching up with Joe. He was less resilient. Things got to him that earlier he had easily thrown off. I think now he was probably growing tired of his job. He called it a no-fly zone. I never pressed him for an explanation."

She sighed and gave Harry a watery smile. "I'm sorry. I'm rambling."

"Ramble all you want," he said, and meant it. "I'll go with you. I've learned a lot on rambles."

At that, she actually managed to laugh. Harry smiled. It was a good laugh, and he thought that mattered. There was a lot to learn from listening to a person's laugh.

"Was he upset about anything just before his death?"

"I'd have to think about that."

"Can you give me the names belonging to the people you found obnoxious?"

"Kevin O'Malley," she said without hesitation. "Amos Lansbury," and then added several names that meant nothing to Harry. He wrote them down nevertheless, thinking he would run them past Hodges and Jim.

"What did O'Malley do to offend you?" he asked.

"I'd say being born was his first offense and should have resulted in permanent incarceration."

Harry laughed. " '*Incarceration.*' Where did you find that word?"

"I worked in a lawyer's office for fifteen years," she said, "an experience that didn't improve my opinion of people."

"How about the legal profession?"

"Mine was a good one," she said, leaving no doubt in Harry's mind about what she thought of the rest.

"Coming back to O'Malley," he said. "Aside from being born, what other complaints about him do you have? I've met him but can't say I know him."

Harry was very interested in hearing what she had to say about O'Malley.

"A very cold fish and he gave me the creeps," she replied, her voice losing its brief spurt of energy.

"Did he and your husband get along well? I know they must have been thrown together a lot."

"I don't know of any trouble between them before the recent senate election. That really stirred up the bottom mud. I guess you know by now that Joe worked for the Foster campaign and O'Malley was with Rycroft Tillman's outfit."

She waited for Harry's affirmation and then continued. "Toward the end of the race, which was a nightmare from start to finish, I was afraid that Joe would work himself into the hospital before it was over. Do you want any coffee?"

"No thanks," Harry said, alerted to the fact that her mind had veered away from the subject without her apparently noticing. "Please go ahead."

"What? Oh, Joe would never tell me what it was over, but O'Malley came to see him right after the election, raging mad and accusing Joe of having something to do with his losing a lot of money. It shook Joe, but he refused to tell me more than I've told you."

"This will make at least three times I've heard the story that O'Malley lost a lot of money on the election, but no one I've talked to knows how he lost it or how much he lost. Did you ever hear?" He tried to keep his tone of voice on the level of mild interest.

" 'A lot,' Joe said, but if he knew how much, he didn't tell me."

"Why not?"

She gave him a sharp look, made a sour face, then said, "Some of the things that go on in elections are skating on black legal ice or no ice at all. 'The less you know the better,' was his mantra." She frowned. "I heard it a lot during Foster's senate race, which had Joe sweating bullets before it was over."

Harry got up. He had other things to ask, but knew he had

been holding her under the light long enough.

"Mrs. Purcell, you've been a study in patience," Harry told her. "Thank you very much. Do you think you could talk with me again later on when, hopefully, I've learned things I don't know now?"

"Yes, Mr. Brock, I'd be glad to. There's a question you haven't asked, so I will. Did Joe make any money from the election? The answer is no. Aside from his salary, not a nickel. I'm the family bookkeeper. I would know. Oddly enough," she said, standing a bit taller and smiling a little, "I find talking with you has made me feel better. Thank you."

"That's very good news," he said, cheered by her words. "I just hope you're not trying to keep me from feeling guilty for having kept you so long. And I didn't ask the question because at least so far, I don't think anyone in Foster's team made any crooked money."

Harry paused in his leaving and asked a final question. "Did Mr. Purcell ever say he thought there was any connection between Amos Lansbury's death and that of Arthur Hornsby?"

"Oh, yes," she said at once, "he assumed they were connected. If you're being delicate and not asking me if I think Joe's death is connected to theirs, I will tell you at once that I'm sure it is, and if I'm right, more will die."

Chapter 19

Clarissa Purcell's last comment to Harry stayed with him, especially her certainty that the killing wasn't over.

"How far out on a limb am I in thinking she's right?" Harry asked Tucker.

They had laid the final shingles on the bantam house roof, put away the ladders, and were cooling off in the shade of the barn where the ladders were hung. Sanchez and Oh, Brother! had been supervising the shingling and were now, like the two men, enjoying the shade and the Gulf breeze blowing in its wide door and out the open windows. Above them as they talked was a constant fluttering and twittering of barn swallows, nesting among the rafters.

"Difficult to say," Tucker answered, topping up their mugs of chilled cider and settling back next to Harry in his canvas chair. "If there is no proof, I understand Jim's reluctance to commit himself too deeply. That said," he added quickly, "I don't see how to ignore the fact that all these men worked on the Foster election campaign."

"Exactly," Harry said, "and the only man on Tillman's team who's a likely suspect is Kevin O'Malley."

"Because he lost a bet on the outcome of the race," Tucker added.

"There you are, and O'Malley has a record of being nasty and quarrelsome, but there's no indication in police records or in the tales I've heard about him that he has so much as swatted a fly."

"Frustrating," Tucker agreed. "By the way, and speaking about frustration, has Holly had any luck in recovering her horses?"

"No," Harry said.

"Am I to take it the question has gotten under your collar?"

"A little."

"This is a very boring conversation."

"Change the subject."

"No, what's the matter?"

Harry saw Tucker was not going to let up.

"The thing is," Harry said, surrendering, "their sheriff's department seems to be more inadequately staffed than ours with a lot more country to cover. From what I've gathered, these rustlers, equipped with positioning devices, smart phones, large animal trailers, drop spots, brand-changing locations, and crooked cattle and horse traders to siphon off the stolen animals, have the law enforcement people running in circles."

Once the emotional wall broke, Harry's own frustration and something else came pouring out.

"Seems to me you're a lot more worked up than the inadequacy of the sheriff's department out there justifies. Am I right?"

"I suppose so."

"I know that admitting to any shortcoming is particularly difficult for you, Harry," Tucker said, not bothering to hide his impatience, "but make the effort. We both might learn something."

"All right! I get it!" Harry surprised himself by nearly shouting at Tucker. After taking a deep breath and counting to ten to lower his heart rate, he said, "The thing is, I'm sure that, given some time, I could find where those mares went."

At that point he sank into a black silence.

"And you're feeling guilty because you're not out there with Holly, trying."

"I suppose there could be some of that mixed in," Harry answered.

"With a barn shovel," Tucker said.

"County Elections Office, Jean speaking."

"Hi, it's Harry Brock. May I speak to Beatrice Lansbury?" He waited, and when Beatrice answered, said, "Do you ever take off time for lunch?"

"That's an odd question, Mr. Brock," she said, her voice rising.

"Try number two: Would you like to have lunch with me?"

"Mr. Brock, if you want to ask me more questions, there are less expensive ways of doing it."

There was a distinct chill in her voice, and Harry felt himself being set down hard.

"Try three," he said, trying not to sound desperate. "I'd like very much to have lunch with you, and I promise not to ask a lot of questions about Amos Lansbury's life and death."

"Are you joking?" she asked after a fairly long wait during which Harry forgot to breathe and then had to gasp for air just when she answered.

"No," he said, like a man being waterboarded.

"Are you all right?" Beatrice asked.

"Yes, fine," Harry said, regaining his breath.

"Okay," she said as if responding to a challenge, "what time?"

"How about twenty minutes?"

"All right."

"Oh, do you like grouper sandwiches?"

She burst out laughing.

"I really don't know," she said, regaining control. "I've been eating salads for lunch for so long, I've forgotten."

"I know where they make the best grouper sandwich in Tequesta County. Are you up for it?"

"I guess I'll find out."

The Coral Reef was crowded, but they were seated without a fuss. "Sorry about the noise," Harry said while she pulled a sweater across her shoulders before sitting down.

"I'm used to it," Beatrice said, smiling, then switched to a frown. "What I'm not used to is the temperature public buildings are kept at in Southwest Florida. I take a sweater everywhere I go and would add a scarf if I wasn't a coward, fearing ridicule."

"After losing half a dozen sweaters, I gave up years ago and suffer," Harry said.

Beatrice grinned. The waitress arrived, looking as if she hadn't liked what she'd seen so far.

"Your?" she said, pencil poised over her pad.

"You order," Beatrice said to Harry, "and may it be on your head."

"By the way," Harry said when the waitress departed, "call me Harry, I prefer it to nothing or vulgarisms."

"At work, I'm a five-letter word behind my back, but Beatrice elsewhere."

"I like Beatrice. It has resonance and deep background," Harry said. "Is it a family name?"

"No, my mother thought it was a romantic name, but she misjudged and gave it to an unromantic child—one of her many disappointments," Beatrice said with a jaunty smile that Harry thought was wallpaper. "The last one was my marrying Amos. It proved too much of a disappointment, and she died."

"How badly does that hurt?" he asked quietly.

"What am I doing here, Harry?" she asked by way of an answer.

Harry hadn't expected the question but wasn't surprised by it either, and admired her for asking. "I enjoyed your company the last time we met. I thought you enjoyed talking with me, so I thought we might try for a repeat and see how it went."

"Good answer," she said.

The sandwiches arrived along with their drinks, which went unnoticed and was probably a good sign.

"My God!" Beatrice said upon looking at what was on her plate. "I'll never . . ."

"Yes, you will," Harry said smugly, reaching for his sandwich with both hands, "as soon as you taste it."

"I'm not sure I can lift it," she said, tentatively imitating Harry's approach.

"This not a moment to be faint-hearted," Harry warned before taking his first bite, "nor weakened by doubt. Go forward."

With that he sank his teeth into the sandwich and ignored the spurting juice. Beatrice, holding the sandwich at mouth level, hesitated, closed her eyes, and, opening her mouth wide, attacked.

A moment later, her eyes still closed but chewing, she began making small sounds that resemble those a bee makes before landing on its favorite flower. Harry would have laughed if his mouth hadn't been full and if he hadn't been so preoccupied by thoughts of his next bite.

"Ohmygod," Beatrice said, finally putting down the sandwich, possibly to rest. "This is the best sandwich I have ever eaten, and I don't even like fish."

Without waiting for Harry to respond, she grasped the sandwich again, closed her eyes, and devoted her strength to taking another, entirely unladylike bite and making the "mmmmm" sounds as she chewed.

"Speaking as a chief administrator in the office of elections,"

Harry said finally, leaning back in his chair and wiping his mouth on a paper napkin, "what rating would you give the sandwich?"

Beatrice was staring dreamily at the remaining crumbs on her plate.

"What?" she asked, looking up. "Oh, the rating is off the chart, Harry. Thank you. When I die, if there's a heaven and if I qualify for membership, I want to eat this sandwich for lunch just about every day."

"Good," Harry said. "I would never have guessed you liked it if I hadn't asked."

"Mock away," she told him, "but I notice your platter's clean."

"Yes, and so is yours. Have you seen the lesson in our grouper sandwiches, how quickly we succumb to greed?"

"It's your grim Puritan heritage breaking out of its prison and trying to spoil our lunch," she said. "I'm ignoring it. I advise you to do the same. By the way, I have something to tell you. Though I doubt it will be of any help."

"I'm listening," Harry said, pushing away his plate and leaning his forearms on the table.

"A while ago, after the senate election and before Amos died, one of Meredith Winters's attorneys was in the office, doing something for another client," Beatrice began. "His name doesn't matter, but he and I dated a while and then didn't. Anyway, he stopped by to say hello and mentioned Meredith's name, remembered the connection, and apologized."

"Do people forget you were married to your ex often?" Harry asked.

"Not often, but it happens—worse than that, *I* forget! Anyway," she said, "I guess Amos and somebody from Tillman's campaign got into a tangle and had to be pulled apart. I asked who the 'somebody' was but he didn't know. Then I asked where it happened, and he thought it was in Arthur Hornsby's office.

Of any interest?"

"Yes. Did your friend know what they were fighting about?"

"No."

"Did he say who else was there?"

"No."

"Is there a chance of your telling me your friend's name?"

"I'm sorry, but . . ."

"It's okay. I get it."

"Why not talk with . . ." Beatrice began then stopped herself. "Uh oh," she said, making a face, "you can't, they're dead."

"I could have said that line of questioning reached a dead end," Harry said, signing the credit card slip for the waitress.

Beatrice groaned. "That will get you extra time in purg."

"Not to worry," Harry said. "I know someone who must have been very close to the fracas, someone who's been forgotten."

"Of course," Beatrice said, "the secretary. There, I'm glad we did."

"What?" Harry asked.

"Try a repeat. Want to try for a third?"

CHAPTER 20

On his way to see Sandy Lufkin, Harry asked himself what the hell he was doing taking Beatrice Lansbury to lunch and where the hell did he think it was going. *Of course, idiot, into her bed,* and then where the hell would he be?

These questions were not all geographical or interrogatory. They were also strongly critical of what he was doing. But as he had not asked *why* he was doing what he was doing, none of his answers gave him any satisfaction, nor were they likely to. Enjoying himself, seeking companionship, looking for someone to talk with—he nearly said easing his loneliness, but he shut that one down, probably hoping he hadn't noticed what he had almost acknowledged.

"How did you find me?" Sandy asked, opening the lanai door to him. Although it was afternoon, she was dressed in a pale blue wrapper and wore no makeup.

"Mrs. Hornsby gave me your address," Harry said. "I hope you don't mind. How are you feeling?"

That question came a few moments after stepping into the lanai's shade from the blazing sun. Once his eyes adapted to the shift in light, he saw that Sandy looked pale, unkempt, and emotionally wasted.

"Not good, Mr. Brock," she said, leading him into her modest but carefully decorated living room.

"I'm sorry and it's Harry, please," he said. "Is it losing Mr. Hornsby?"

"The sofa? A chair? Please sit down."

She dropped onto the sofa and Harry sat down beside her. She looked as though she might need propping up. "I'm sorry things aren't as clean as they should be. Time seems to run through my fingers. I can't stop thinking of Mr. Hornsby and how he died."

"A sad thing," Harry said. "Have the police questioned you?"

"Yes," she answered. "There was nothing improper between us," she said in a frail voice, staring at her clasped hands resting on her knees, "but I feel bereft, and I can't sleep. He was a lovely man."

"Are you working?"

She shook her head. "Mrs. Hornsby's lawyer called me the morning after it happened and told me the office was shut permanently. I was given a month's wages and let go."

"Are you looking for work?" he asked.

"No, I can't seem to make myself do anything. I hardly eat. I know it's not good, but . . ." Her voice trailed off.

"No family here?"

"No. I'm pretty much on my own."

"Excuse me a minute," he said and left the house, took out his phone, and punched in a number. He spoke briefly with the person who answered then returned to the house. She was still sitting on the couch and seemed not to have moved.

"Sandy," he said, sitting down beside her and taking her hands in his, "please look at me."

She did, but her focus struck Harry as tenuous at best.

"You need a woman to talk to whom you can like and trust, someone who can help you deal with your loss. Are you listening to what I'm saying?"

"Yes, but I don't . . ."

"I know you don't, but I do, a very gentle, sympathetic woman who's trained to help people in your situation. If I drove you there, would you be willing to talk to her?"

"How would I get home?"

"I'll wait for you and drive you home."

"Will it cost a lot?"

"No, and don't think about that now. If you like her and want to go on seeing her, which I'm sure you will, she will work all that out with you. She already knows a little about you because I told her."

"What's her name?"

"Dr. Gloria Holinshed. She's an excellent therapist. She has helped me and members of my family over some very rough patches. Will you go with me?" he asked.

"Yes," she said after a moment's hesitation.

"Then get yourself ready. She'll see you as soon as we get there."

The question he was going to ask her could wait.

When Sandy stepped out of Holinshed's office, Harry asked her to wait a minute and slipped in.

"Hi, Gloria," he said. "What do I have to know?"

"Hello, Harry," the tall, blonde woman said, coming around her desk to shake his hand. "To do what?" she asked with a wry smile.

"Not what you're suggesting," Harry said, smiling back. "Is it going to be safe for me to leave her alone?"

"Harry!" Holinshed said sharply, her smile vanishing. "Would I have let her out of here if it weren't?"

"There, I feel better," Harry said, squaring his shoulders.

Holinshed laughed and pressed her hand against his cheek. "Why have you been such a stranger?" she asked.

"Well, when I found out I couldn't have you in the biblical sense, I was too badly hurt to go on seeing you and having my heart broken over and over."

"Good," she said. "Have you married yet and made some other woman miserable?"

"I'm trying, but having very little luck. The current object of my affections has gone west."

"Holly Pike?"

"How did you know?"

"I'm not telling. Why aren't you out there with her—no, wait, don't tell me. You don't want to leave Bartram's Hammock."

She sounded disgusted.

"That might be part of it," he admitted.

"Well, remember, Harry, I'm here if you come to your senses and ask for help. Oh, and one other thing. Sandy is too young and too fragile for you to mess with."

"I knew that before you did, for once. Was she really in love with Arthur Hornsby?"

"I'm not going to say, but the ways of the human heart are strange and stranger. Now take her home and don't ask her what we talked about."

CHAPTER 21

"I thought you should see this," Raquel said.

"When did it come?"

"Yesterday around three. I opened it, thinking it looked strange, and I'm not sure why."

"It's strange all right," Harry said, holding the sheet of lined yellow paper, obviously torn from a pad, on which were pasted cut-out letters from a newspaper that read, *HE'S DEAD STOP LOOKING LAST WARNING.*

"I suppose I could have, maybe should have, called the police, but this morning I decided to call you. And I didn't know what to do with it, but I wasn't going to just hand this to Meredith—and not just because she told me not to open any mail without a return address. I'm not sure what it means. How does this person know Mr. Lansbury's dead?"

"The police will have to see this, but I'm glad you called me," Harry said, not surprised by what Raquel had given him. He expected the danger to Meredith to intensify.

"I'll take it and think how best to tell Meredith, and then give it to the police," he said. "How are you doing?"

She was still pale as well as thin, which made her dark eyes look even larger than usual. Although they were beautiful, their sadness wrung Harry's heart.

"Perhaps a little better," she said bravely. "The worst thing is that my family thinks I'm condemning my soul to Hell for divorcing him. And it doesn't help that our two families were friends back in Mexico, which was three generations ago, but who's counting?"

Her sudden flush of anger pleased Harry and was, he thought, an encouraging sign. If she could get angry with somebody, she might get angry with *him,* whose name she had never mentioned, and Harry certainly wasn't going to ask.

"Families," Harry said, "are closed kingdoms, each with its own history, culture, geography, and minefields. Make a personal decision at your own risk."

Raquel managed a shaky smile. "Thank you, Harry. Talking with you always makes me feel better, more a person, and less a cog in the train."

"Cog in the wheel," Harry said, risking a smile.

She grew slightly pink and for an instant she was a woman aware of herself again. She arched her back slightly and shot him a glance from the corners of her eyes.

"Do you think I'm a cog in the wheel, Harry?" she asked, her voice deepening.

"If you are, you're the loveliest cog I've ever seen," he told her.

"Thank you," she said, hesitated, and went on more boldly. "I've had something of a breakthrough in the past week. A lot of my pain has been coming from fear, not grief that we've broken up. I feel it's a big step forward."

"What are you afraid of?" he asked, surprised by her declaration.

"Of being alone, of facing a new life and way of living," she said decisively. "I married right out of business school and living at home. I loved my life at home, and when I married, I moved from one home to another with my husband replacing my mother and father. For the first time, I'm truly alone in the world."

"And good for you," Harry said. "I think you're ready."

"I hope so, but that's enough about me. What do you think about the letter, or threat, or whatever it is? It looks as if some child put it together."

"It was no child," Harry told her. "Someone wanted to frighten Meredith badly enough to make her stop what she's doing."

"Who would want to do such a despicable thing?"

"Someone who has something to lose."

"What should I do?" Meredith asked Harry, dropping the letter onto her desk almost as soon as it was in her hands.

"You don't have a choice. The letter has to go to Jim. I'll take care of that part."

"Am I supposed to take this seriously?" she asked in a rising voice.

"Meredith," Harry said quietly but firmly, "it's very possible that if Amos was murdered, the person who sent you this warning is the killer."

"And I'm supposed to be frightened?"

"You should be," Harry said. "That's what whoever sent this message intended, and I suggest you think very carefully about whether or not you want me to go on with this investigation."

"You mean call off my search?"

"This note is going to galvanize the sheriff's department," Harry said. "Even Sheriff Fisher can't pretend after this that your search is misguided."

"What does that have to do with it?" she demanded, looking angry again.

"If you're asking me what you should do, my answer is fire me and take a month's holiday somewhere, letting Jim and his people do their work. You've flushed out the killer, if there is one. You've made your case."

"Then you think I'm in danger. Whoever sent this note

intends to do more than frighten me," she replied.

"Yes, Meredith, I do. The good news is that he's just burned his best defense. Until now the law has doubted such a person existed. Now there's a strong reason for thinking he does."

"You're sure it's a man, then."

"Do you know of any woman in Avola capable of putting together a Semtex bomb?"

"I don't think that's an appeal to reason, but to prejudice and gender stereotyping," she retorted.

"Let's not get off on that subject. We'll be here all day."

"Or what's left of it. What am I going to do, Harry?"

"I've already told you."

"No, you haven't. You just ladled a load of crap onto my plate."

"Not so! What I said was perfectly reasonable. Why put yourself at risk when you don't need to?"

"Why live?"

"Good question. I've asked it myself a few times. Look, sleep on it. I'll talk with you again tomorrow."

"I thought you were working for me."

"I am."

"Then let me decide what I'm going to do and when."

"Call me when you've decided," Harry said, and left.

On the Hammock bridge, Harry stopped and got out of the SUV to watch the resident female otter and her two cubs fishing beneath it. He had just put one foot comfortably on the bottom rail and leaned his forearms on the top one when his phone rang.

"This is off the record, Harry, agreed?"

"Of course, Gloria," Harry said, astonished that Holinshed had called him.

"Here's the situation. I am aware that you're investigating the death of Amos Lansbury. It travelled on the wind, so don't ask. Shortly after the election, Arthur Hornsby held a meeting in his office, called by Kevin O'Malley, Amos Lansbury, Arthur Hornsby, Joe Purcell, and a man with the improbable name of Harkin Smith. There was a loud and ugly quarrel with O'Malley shouting the loudest, something about money."

"And they're all dead but O'Malley and Smith," Harry told the otters, closing his phone.

As soon as he got home, he called Harkin Smith.

"We had a good talk, Brock," Smith said when Harry managed to get his secretary to put the call through, "but I'm neck deep in fundraising for the senator's next round and don't have time to think about the last one."

"Wonderful. I'm going to be in your office in about twenty-five minutes. You are going to see me the instant I get there. Do you understand me?"

"Brock, are you drunk?"

"Sober, and very serious. Do you understand me?"

"Oh, all right. I can see it will be quicker to see you than argue. Come along."

"Is this office clear of bugs?" Harry asked as soon as the secretary had closed the door.

"What is all this shit?" Smith demanded, sprawled in his desk chair and visibly irritated.

"Is it clean?"

"Of course it is. It's cleared every day. Do you think this is preschool?"

"It's an office that's going to be looking for a new occupant if you don't sharpen up."

Smith sprang to his feet. "Are you threatening me?"

"Why in hell didn't you tell me about that quarrel with Kevin O'Malley in Hornsby's office? And haven't you noticed that you and O'Malley are the only men in the group left standing?"

"So what?" Smith said, paling with anger or some other strong emotion. "What fucking business of yours is it?"

"Three of you in that group are dead and you all worked for Foster. I don't think Lansbury died an accidental death and neither do you. So talk to me. What's kept you away from the police?"

Smith suddenly dropped back into his chair as if his legs had failed him. "It's that asshole Lansbury's fault," he said in a cracked voice, avoiding Harry's eyes. "He's the one that had the bright idea to pull O'Malley's leg by telling him Tillman was going to win by a narrow margin. It was baked in, and Foster's crew were all going to bet on a sure thing."

"Why didn't you stop the joke before any harm was done?"

"Fair question. First, we didn't find out that Lansbury had actually done it until a week before the election. Lansbury was so pleased with himself that he told us, expecting we'd think it was a laugh riot."

"But you didn't."

"No. I got hold of O'Malley and said the whole thing was a send-up and he wasn't to put any money down because there was no poll saying Tillman was going to win and that as far as we knew Foster had a very thin advantage in the numbers."

"But O'Malley had already bet the farm," Harry said with disgust, seeing it all.

"That, I don't know. But I couldn't make O'Malley believe me. Then Arthur called him, then Joe, but by then O'Malley had decided the calls were all part of the scam, and we were going to make a truckload of money and then laugh at him for pulling his bet."

"What about Lansbury? Did he try to dissuade O'Malley?"

"No. He said if O'Malley was stupid enough to believe anything about the election any of us had told him, he deserved to lose his money."

"Get in your car—no, get into someone else's car—and drive straight to Jim Snyder's office. Tell him what you've just told me."

"Nope, I'm not giving O'Malley or whoever it is any further excuse to come after me. He hasn't so far, but if he does, he's going to get a surprise. None of my family is driving. We walk or use a taxi. I took the police training course in handguns, and I'm carrying. There's two AK-47s at home, one on each floor. Every door and window in the house is fitted with an alarm."

"Does your wife know the danger you're in and they're in?" Harry asked.

"No details, but they don't need them. Given my job, they know to be careful. Besides, whoever it is hasn't bothered other people in the family."

"If the Secret Service can't keep the president from being shot, what do you think your chances are?"

"Presidents aren't armed. I am."

Harry decided to make one more try.

"Harkin, listen to me. I know what I'm talking about. Go to the police. Send your wife and kids to a relative and you get some armed protection."

"Nope," Smith said, checking his watch. "I've got an appointment. Thanks for your concern, Harry, but I'll be okay."

He stood, picked up his desk phone, and punched in a number. Harry left.

Chapter 22

Harry's next stop was Jim Snyder's office, and his news did not please the captain.

"Fisher will have a conniption fit if he hears you've been questioning Harkin Smith, and he will land on me with both feet," he complained loudly.

"Jim," Harry said calmly, "forget about the sheriff. He'll howl louder if Smith is killed and he finds out you knew the risk he was in and didn't do anything about it."

"He's right, Captain," Hodges put in, wearing an expression as close to concerned as his congenitally happy face could get.

"I don't need to hear that!" Jim roared.

"You do, Jim," Harry persisted. "It's gone way past the time when your department can rationally insist there's no connection between these killings. Just because the sheriff has an election in his future, you don't have to be governed by his obsessions."

"They're not obsessions, they're existential issues—or so he believes."

"Amos Lansbury, Arthur Hornsby, and Joe Purcell, three men out of the five who were quarreling in Hornsby's office, are dead," Harry insisted. "Only Smith and Kevin O'Malley are still standing. All three of the dead men worked for Foster. How long do you think Smith's going to last?"

"And you've talked with him," Jim said, scowling at the top of his desk, ignoring Harry's question and circling back to his own concern.

"Yes."

"You're not much of a team player."

Jim sounded so downhearted, Harry almost felt sorry for him.

"No, I'm not," he said, pressing his concern, "and in this case, luckily for you."

"How is he taking it?" Jim continued as if Harry hadn't spoken.

"I told him he should send his family away and come to you for armed protection. His response was that he was legally armed and had an AK-47 on every floor of his house."

"Looks like he's planning to turn his place into the OK Corral," Hodges said, following that up with a wide grin.

"Not funny, Sergeant," Jim said, scowling.

"There's something else," Harry said, picking a manila folder off the chair beside him. "I wasn't going to show it to you until tomorrow. Because Meredith was having trouble dealing with it, I suggested she think about it overnight and call me when she'd decided. Now I see you should be told at once." He passed the open folder to Jim. "Her secretary showed it to me before showing it to Meredith. That made it necessary for me to show it to you if I thought it was serious, which I did and now do."

Jim read the note and said, "You're going to tell me that the person who sent this to Mrs. Winters killed her husband, Hornsby, and Purcell."

"I can't prove it," Harry admitted after Jim had passed the folder to Hodges, having warned him not to touch the letter, "but I think it's likely that whoever sent this to Meredith is our killer."

"If he is," Hodges said, returning the file to Harry, "he's made a serious mistake in sending Winters this note."

" 'He's Dead Stop Looking Last Warning,' " Jim recited.

"There's nothing there to hang a criminal charge on. Harassment? Probably not even that."

"Jim," Harry protested, "you're not going to walk away from this?"

"Before I answer, I'd like to ask a question. Why do you suppose Harkin Smith is refusing to ask us for protection? Because," Jim said, providing his own answer, "if his name becomes associated with the death of three of his colleagues, he can say goodbye to his work in the political game, that is to say, his career."

"Aren't you coming at this from the wrong end, Captain?" Hodges asked.

"Meaning?" Jim demanded.

"Isn't the right end the safety of Winters and Smith?" Hodges asked, a bit more forcefully.

"If the department begins questioning Smith, it will have to question Foster," Jim shot back, obviously stung by Hodges's questions. "If you're right, Harry, about the deaths being linked, involving Foster in the investigation—which would happen—will turn into a field day for the media, and his chances for reelection will be seriously reduced."

"Are you suggesting your department shouldn't make an effort to determine whether or not the deaths are connected because it might endanger Foster's reelection?"

"I'm pointing out that other than the Coast Guard's statement you haven't any evidence that Lansbury is dead. We have only begun our investigations into the deaths of Hornsby and Purcell and, so far, we've found no evidence linking the two murders. None! But you want us to expand the investigations to include Senator Foster on the strength of hearsay and speculation. In fact, Harry, there's nothing to support the theory but what people have told you."

"Post hoc, ergo propter hoc," Harry said glumly.

"What?" Hodges asked, looking alarmed.

"After this, therefore because of this," Harry said. "It refers to a kind of flawed reasoning, Frank, which, by the way, is very often true."

"And is just as often wrong," Jim said, throwing his pen onto the desk as if suddenly disgusted with clicking it, which was what he had been doing with increasing vehemence as the argument developed.

"Then there's *cum hoc, ergo propter hoc,*" Harry said, "meaning, happening at the same time and, therefore, caused by the same thing—Lansbury, Hornsby, and Purcell's deaths."

He was angry with Jim's refusing to see the nose in front of his face and couldn't recall the lawman's ever doing it so blatantly before. Furthermore, he thought Jim knew what he was doing, hiding behind the smokescreen of lack of evidence and bogus logic.

"Don't get hot under the collar," Jim said, "just because we're looking at this mess from different perspectives. Everybody in this department knows we've been running on damned near empty, financially speaking, since the last cycle of budget cuts. The people who control our budget are political animals."

"Captain's right," Hodges said. "If we put a nail in Foster's reelection tire and we don't prove our case, the sheriff may be looking for a night watchman's job, and this department may lose even more people, me being one of them."

Harry hated to, but he saw the problem.

"Okay, point made," he said, "but having a number of very bright people on your team, you might find a way to quietly go about doing what you both know should be done without making anything official. Leave no tracks, so to speak."

"We might pretend we're collecting for the department's widows and orphans," Hodges said and was prepared to laugh until he saw Jim's face. "Or not, probably not," he said.

"We'll look into the letter, Harry, but I'm promising nothing more," Jim said grimly.

Harry left in a foul state of mind, thinking he had completely mishandled Jim and now Smith was left hanging there, twisting in the wind, a man who seemed not to understand fully the danger he was in—or had it been bravado and was Jim right that going to the police would endanger his livelihood?

His phone brought Harry out of his sour reflections. He had parked in the shade of the pin oaks lining the parking lot and stood beside the SUV to answer the call.

"Hi, Harry, it's Beatrice."

"A pleasant surprise," Harry said, surprised that she would call from work. "Are you in your office?"

"Actually, I'm in the Starbucks across the street. What's that strange sound I'm hearing?"

"Cicadas. I'm standing in the sheriff's department parking lot, and the oaks here are stuffed with them."

"This is a tough call, Harry," Beatrice said, her voice darkening. "I really enjoyed having lunch with you, but I want whatever we were starting to stop there."

"I'm sorry to hear it," Harry said, lying through his teeth while experiencing a surge of relief.

"I don't want to know why you asked me out in the first place, and I don't want to know because I really had a good time with you. I think you did with me as well, but I'm pretty sure it was the kind of good time that wasn't going to get any better by repeating it or taking it to a different setting."

"I really did enjoy being with you, Beatrice. I hope you don't think I was faking it," he said, suddenly feeling guilty, possibly for being so relieved.

"Oh, no, Harry, I don't think that. I even have the feeling we could have taken this quite a long way," she said, "but in the end it wasn't going to work."

She paused, possibly waiting for Harry to contradict her. When he didn't, she said, "So, Harry, I'm calling it off before we both find ourselves in a situation we can't get out of without losing some skin."

Harry's first impulse was to deny that he thought they couldn't make a relationship work, but he stifled the impulse and said, "I'm sorry because I'm very attracted to you. You're a pleasure to be with, and I would be very lucky to have a relationship with you."

It was his turn to pause and think about what he was going to say next. It came to him that the best thing to do was tell her the truth.

"You're right, you know, and in some ways I'm sorry you are. It would solve a lot of things for me if you weren't right."

"Who is she?"

"Her name is Holly Pike, and about a year ago she moved to Montana. She wants me to go out there with her."

"And you don't want to leave here."

"Something like that."

"Well," she said, signaling departure, "I wish you luck, and it's good knowing you, Harry. Thanks for being honest with me."

With extremely mixed feelings of loss and relief stampeding through his system like wild horses, Harry checked his watch, took a deep breath, blew it out, clambered into the SUV, and drove to his meeting with Meredith.

"I've talked with Jim Snyder," he said, settling down with her near the windows, a cup of tea beside him.

"And?" she asked.

She had been working at her desk when he came into the study and was still wearing her tortoise-shell glasses that made her look, in her black skirt, heels, and long-sleeved white blouse, he thought with considerable pleasure, like an extremely sexy school teacher.

"And it didn't come out the way I wanted it to," he said, speeding up the account. "He feels bound to avoid doing anything that might indicate your husband's death was anything but accidental—if, indeed, he is dead—or that his death is connected to that of Hornsby and Purcell."

"Should I ask why?" she said impatiently.

"If he does and begins an investigation, it will lead to Senator Foster, involving him in a multiple murder investigation connected to his campaign, and that would reduce his chances of being reelected."

"And most of the people who control the sheriff's department's budget are in Foster's party and would punish Fisher for damaging the senator's chance of being reelected," she said in an angry singsong voice. "The system stinks."

"There's an upside," Harry said quickly. "Jim's going to put Jones and his people to work on the letter."

"Praise the cook when you've drunk the broth," she replied with a stiff face.

"Okay, what's wrong?" he asked, abandoning his tea.

"What's going on with you and Raquel?"

"I'm sorry if she's coming to work tired. It's probably because we're spending our nights drinking and . . . well, I won't say more on that subject."

"Very amusing, Harry, ha, ha. I thought we had that settled. You were not to take advantage of her weakened condition and . . ."

"Hold it," Harry said. "What makes you think anything is going on between us?"

"She can't say three sentences without finding an excuse to mention your name. It's 'Mr. Brock' this and 'Mr. Brock' that."

Meredith was flushed and even a little short of breath. Harry decided joking wasn't going to be a safe route to an end of the nonsense.

"Meredith," he said gently, "nothing's going on between Raquel and me beyond our conversations that last from the bottom to the top of the stairs whenever I visit you. She's been having a really bad time with her divorce, but I think she's getting on top of it."

"Well, your therapy sessions certainly have left an impression."

That statement left her face even brighter, a development that puzzled Harry and led to his making a mistake.

"She's a very intelligent and attractive young woman," he said cheerfully. "I hope she comes out of her marriage a stronger and happier person."

"What I don't need," Meredith said, jumping up and striding to the window behind her chair, her back eloquent, "is Orientalism invading my house, especially at this point in my life."

Harry had to scramble to come up with the reference but managed to find it in something he'd learned in a college English class.

"I hadn't thought of her as being an Hispanic exotic," he said in defense of his comment. "And I certainly don't find anything exotic about her."

Meredith spun around and came storming back to her chair, flung herself into it, and said, "Of course you don't. You find that shining black hair and those flashing black eyes wherever you look."

"Whoa!" Harry said, becoming concerned. "What's going on here? I'm not making moves on Raquel. You must know that."

"Your reputation precedes you," she snapped.

"Nonsense, the only woman I have that kind of interest in lives in Montana. I lead a very monkish existence. Besides, why do you care?"

"I don't," she said, yanking off her glasses and tossing her head in a way that sent her hair flying. "Why should I?"

"I don't know. You have beautiful hair, by the way. I never fail to notice it. I hope you don't mind my saying that."

"No. Thank you," she said, crossing her legs and sitting up a little straighter. "I've been thinking about what you said about my leaving town for a while or ending the investigation. I'm not leaving, and I want to go on with the investigation."

"It isn't necessary for you to be here if you want me to go on with what I've been doing. That would be the easy part, but your staying here is gambling with your life."

"Are you trying to get rid of me?"

"Of course not, Meredith, I just don't want anything worse to happen to you than what's already happened."

"That's very kind of you, Harry, but I have to be the one who decides what I want to do. I've made up my mind. I'm staying."

"Okay for now," he said quietly, "but let's keep all your options open."

Chapter 23

"I was told he was run over by a Blue Rock gravel truck," Harry said to Kathleen Towers, the tall, unsmiling medical examiner with a cap of steel-gray hair, bent over the body on the lab table.

He was careful not to say it was Jim who had broken the news. One didn't know from day to day how things were between them or what feelings would be roused by mentioning a name.

"Apparently, he was," she said dryly, probing the small wound in the back of the dead man's head, "if the tire tracks on his back are indicators, but it's not what killed him. This is what killed him."

She stepped back so that Harry could lean in for a closer look.

"A twenty-two-caliber slug?" he asked.

"I think so. It's still in his head. It probably ricocheted around in there for a while, ensuring his death. I gather you know him."

"Harkin Smith," Harry said stiffly, "another of the men who worked for the Foster senate campaign. I told him he was in danger."

"How many does this make?" she asked, plunging her probe into a high-temperature bath attached to the wall behind him and then stripping off her mask and latex gloves.

"Counting Amos Lansbury, Harkin's murder makes four."

Kathleen leaned back against the sink, folded her arms, and

said as though she were making a joke, "Jim and I are observing an armed truce, during which the rules specify limited communication, lest the mutual loathing break out again into open warfare."

Harry winced, then rallied.

"I'm sorry," he said. "Jim is between a rock and a hard place, Fisher has issued a fatwa against the department's taking any action in these murders that would compromise Foster's chances in the next election. His justification for this is that there is no evidence that the deaths are connected to one another and, more especially, to the last state senate race."

Kathleen then unburdened herself on the subject of Sheriff Fisher and her husband's lack of backbone in the matter, concluding with a codicil impugning the character of men in general.

"Present company excepted," she said, pushing away from the sink and dropping a hand on Harry's shoulder. "Why didn't I marry you, Harry?"

"When we first met, you and Jim were just getting it on. Besides, I'm only one of the hewers of wood and bearers of water," Harry said, following up with a hollow laugh.

"That must be why this queue of wealthy women has formed, each waiting her turn in bed with you," she said, smiling for the first time in the past half hour.

"No such thing," Harry protested.

"Let's see," she said, counting on her fingers. "Several names popped up, including Meredith Winters."

"Hold on," Harry said. "My relationship with Meredith is a business relationship, honor bright."

"This is the foreplay stage," Kathleen said, clearly enjoying herself. "Be patient. All right, I'm embarrassing you. I'll stop. Where are you going from here with these killings?"

"Technically," he said, "my only concern with any of the

deaths other than that of Amos Lansbury is finding a connection among the deaths that will prove Lansbury was murdered. But I'm intrigued by Smith's death. Why shoot him in the head and then steal a truck to run back and forth over him?"

"Emphasizing a point?" she asked.

"It could be," he said. "Changing the subject, it's none of my business, Kathleen, beyond you two being among my oldest friends, but aside from the 'agreement' you mentioned, which doesn't sound encouraging, how are you and Jim doing?"

Kathleen had lost her smile.

"I'd say our marriage is like a ball of string, rolling down a hill with one end at the top of the hill and the ball getting smaller and smaller the farther it rolls."

"I'm sorry. How's Clara taking it?"

"We've never discussed it with her, and she's so busy with school and her own life I doubt she's noticed. This hasn't been a loud, dramatic disintegration."

"No," Harry said, "knowing you both, I don't suppose it has been. I wish I had something to say that would be helpful, but I've been through two divorces and a breakup that was as painful as either of the divorces, so I don't think I know squat about mending relationships that are coming unstitched."

She made a face and shrugged as if at the end of her own supply of knowledge.

"There's one thing I can say with some confidence that may or may not help," he added. "It's that no one understands what's going on inside a family in trouble, not even the principals in the drama. So don't be too hard on yourself, Kathleen."

"Hug," she said, holding out her arms.

Harry obliged, and as they were separating, Kathleen kissed him on the cheek.

"Thanks, Harry, she said. "That felt good and was a help, and so was what you said about relationships. It's easy to lose perspective in the fog of war."

Harry left without telling her how good it had felt to him to hold a woman in his arms again. It had been a while, and there was no substitute he was aware of for the feeling of a woman's body pressed against yours.

"Kathleen has probably reported officially on the cause of Smith's death, but I have no idea how it will affect Jim and the department," Harry told Tucker, who had been questioning Harry about Harkin's murder.

"It's an intriguing thing," Tucker said, shaking his head, "running over a dead man with a truck. It makes you ask if the killer's insane or only stressing a point."

"Possibly anger was behind it, but I doubt that's a full accounting."

The two men had backed away from the bantam house to look at the fence they had just finished attaching to the building. It was a chain link fence. Bolted to the house, its top attached to the sides with heavy gauge wire, and the sides buried in a two-foot-deep trench, anchored at the bottom in instant cement and topped up with dirt.

"If that doesn't keep the coyotes out, we'd better let them have the Hammock and head for higher land," Tucker said.

"With those two," Harry said, referring to the pair that had made the Hammock their home, "there is no certainty. So don't tempt fate. Remember, man proposes and the coyote disposes."

"I like that," Tucker said approvingly. "If there's a weakness in what we have before us, those two will find it. I like that too, makes life more interesting. Bonnie and Clyde are good, but this golden pair are masters. We're finished here."

"Are you surprised the coyotes haven't killed those two foxes?" Harry asked.

They had begun picking up their tools and piling them in the wheelbarrow.

"I try not to think about it," Tucker said with a sigh. "So far they seem to be sharing the Hammock on a first come, first served basis. Can I persuade you to stay for lunch? Blue crab cake sandwiches are on the menu."

"That will do it," Harry replied. "We're coming to the end of the crabbing season."

"Let's hope it's only the season and not the blue crabs," Tucker said. "The numbers in the Chesapeake have fallen like a stone."

"We're not that badly off," Harry said hopefully.

Tucker let the statement go unchallenged, which did not mean he agreed. In fact, Harry had learned, the more strongly the old farmer felt about a subject, the less likely he was to argue about it.

"What are you drinking?" Tucker asked when he had the sandwiches on the table.

"Is lemonade on offer?" Harry asked.

"Fresh this morning, and if we're feeling the need of something to aid our digestion when we've finished eating, I opened a new jug of plum brandy yesterday, which ought not to be missed."

Once the lemonade was on the table, they settled down to the serious business of eating.

"This crabmeat is excellent," Harry said.

"Caught and iced and delivered here," Tucker said. "There are advantages knowing people with children and grandchildren who are inclined to put fishing ahead of working."

Most of Tucker's friends were old enough to have grown-up grandchildren, Harry reflected, which increased geometrically the numbers of people likely to drop off fresh game, fish, fowl, and occasionally dressed deer.

"What's going on with your investigation of Lansbury's

death?" Tucker asked when they had retreated from the table to the rockers on the stoop, brimming brandy glasses in hand.

Harry filled in some details about the several deaths that were new to Tucker, and then said, "I'm worried that Meredith isn't taking this thing seriously. Even what happened to Harkin Smith hasn't budged her."

"And you're not expecting help from the sheriff's department," Tucker said.

"Based on past experience, no. But I live in hope."

Tucker laughed.

"You're the least hopeful person I know. Of course, Oh, Brother! is more cynical and doubtful about good outcomes than you are, but I can't fairly compare him with you."

"Am I being insulted here?"

"No, I was speaking of species."

They then decided it was unwise to try to walk on one leg, and Tucker refilled their brandy glasses.

"Did it take a shyster lawyer to make you change your mind?" Harry asked Meredith, deliberately ignoring Jeff Smolkin, sitting on the edge of his chair, as usual, but this time in Meredith's study.

"Harry!" she cried, wide-eyed, and brought half standing by his question.

"Ignore him," Smolkin said. "He's been living in the woods so long he's been dissocialized."

"I take it you know each other," Meredith said, now fully on her feet.

"To both our discredit. Did you know," Harry asked Meredith, "that he maintains a harem?"

"Aha!" Smolkin said, beaming, "the jealousy behind the name-calling reveals itself."

"Do the guy-stuff on your own nickels," Meredith said, reasserting herself. "Harry, please sit down. I've brought you here for a purpose."

"Fine," Harry said, "but before you get to that, I've got something to add to what I said the other day about leaving Avola, at least for a while. Here it is: I've done the job for which you hired me. Assuming that Amos Lansbury is dead, but not dead from natural causes, it's almost a certainty he was murdered. You can declare victory, let me go, and shut down the inquiry."

"I take your point, Harry, but now I want to know whether you've gathered enough information to interest the federal government in becoming involved in this case. I can't persuade Sheriff Fisher to let his people become involved. That's why Mr. Smolkin's here. I want you to tell him what you've learned, and then he'll tell me whether or not I have a case."

"All right," Harry said after a pause and still uncertain what his response should be. Finding no rational alternative aside from refusal, he sat down and told Smolkin everything he knew about Lansbury's death and his involvement with the men who had and had not been subsequently killed, as well as what he'd learned about their deaths, which, he added, wasn't much.

"Have you told Jeff about the threat you've received?" he asked when he finished his recital.

"Yes," she said.

"Why haven't you talked with Foster?" Smolkin asked.

Harry found himself embarrassed by the question but answered despite his reluctance. "Because Sheriff Fisher insisted that no one in the department take any action that might be construed as evidence that the deaths were related to Foster's senate campaign. I have and have had, as you know, a close relationship over the years with Jim Snyder and the rest of the department. I've been trying to avoid interviewing Foster in order to stay on good terms with Jim and Fisher."

Harry did not like the sound of what he'd just said or what it revealed about him, but it had been an honest answer.

"All right," Smolkin said, frowning slightly and disturbing that cherubic look that had charmed so many juries, "that's understandable, but the thing is, Harry, unless you interview Foster you're not going to learn what he knows. Is that an accurate conclusion?"

"It is," Harry said.

"Then we can't do what I'm trying to do unless Harry interviews Prentice Foster?" Meredith demanded, obviously upset by what she'd just heard.

"Well, we don't have the full picture," Smolkin said flatly, "and Harry hasn't found anything that a public prosecutor could take to a grand jury. Just pointing at Kevin O'Malley is miles from being enough to build a case on, and unless Foster has convincing evidence that O'Malley murdered your husband, there's no point in trying to force your case."

Meredith visibly sagged with disappointment.

"Don't be a stranger, Harry," Smolkin said, picking up his briefcase from beside his chair. "Goodbye, Mrs. Winters," he added. "If I can be of any further help, please let me know. I'll find my way out."

"Why didn't you tell me about Prentice?" she asked Harry, as soon as Smolkin was out the door.

"It didn't occur to me that I needed to," he answered.

"You told me earlier that there was enough evidence to satisfy me that Amos had been murdered. Yes, I know, *assuming,* and so on."

"And I was telling you the truth. Meredith, had I thought that Foster had any more information about your husband's death than the men I've talked with, I would have talked with him."

"I don't think that's an honest answer," she said, her eyes blazing.

"How can I prove I didn't lie to you?" he asked, determined not to be angry although he wanted to be very angry—in part because having her not believe him had hurt.

"You were thinking of James Snyder first and me second," she said, her voice breaking a little.

Oh, shit, Harry thought, *she's feeling betrayed.* He closed the distance between them in three long strides and caught her hands in his.

"It's God's honest truth," he said, "you have been first in my thinking from the moment I took this job, and I have never lied to you, not once."

"Okay," she said, "I was wrong to say what I did, but you should have talked to Foster."

Her eyes were searching Harry's as if she was looking for something she desperately wanted to see.

"Yes," he told her. "Perhaps I should have gone to talk with him. You're right, I was influenced by Jim's predicament, but I didn't want to lose the department's cooperation, and I thought that if I could produce enough information that supported your claim, Fisher would come to his senses."

"Would it be way, way out of line, Harry," she said urgently, "if I asked you to hold me for a minute? I'm afraid I'm going to . . ."

By that point Harry had his arms around her and was holding her tightly. He had heard somewhere that holding people tightly reduced their anxiety. That was his excuse but had very little to do with why he had hugged her.

"All my fault," he whispered soothingly. "I'm sorry if I've upset you, really sorry."

She had buried her face in his neck and was clinging to him as if they had just been washed overboard in heavy seas.

Whatever it was she said by way of an answer was known only to his shirt collar, but after another moment or two she leaned away just enough to look at him.

"Harry," she said, blinking away the last of her tears, "that was awesome, but I shouldn't have made you do that. I'm the one who should be apologizing."

"Certainly not," he said, "you were upset, and . . ."

They went on this way for a while, each trying to claim full responsibility for it wasn't clear exactly what. During this time neither made any effort to move away from the other, and they remained glued to one another until Harry found he had not had his mind on the responsibility issue for some time and pressure was rising for him either to fish or cut bait.

"Not your fault," he croaked and released her, moving back against his body's vehement protests.

"Nor yours," she said, sounding as if she'd been running.

"Well." Harry said in a frail simulacrum of normal speech, "I suppose we should discuss how you want to go forward."

"Oh, I don't think it requires discussion," she said in a way that twisted Harry's insides into another knot.

"No," he said, "but you might want to think about it a little."

"Perhaps not right now," she said with some urgency, "because I'm expecting Raquel to tell me I have a business call I must take. But, Harry, let's not put it off very long."

"Certainly not," he said, fairly certain she wasn't talking about his contract.

Raquel knocked on the door, and Harry fled.

Chapter 24

Harry was ushered into the senator's office with the solemnity that might be expected to accompany a papal audience, but the man who came forward to greet him and shake his hand was smiling affably.

"Harry Brock," Prentice Foster said, "I'm pleased to meet you. By the way, call me Pete. Everyone else does—that and other four-letter words. Meredith and I talk now and then—we're both on some committees together. She speaks very highly of you. Have a seat."

That exchange had gotten them across the space in front of the senator's desk and seated on leather barrel chairs under a ceiling fan that had a faint creak. Foster was a large man, long-limbed, broad shoulders with the look, Harry thought, of a baseball player. His hair was a believable brown, his teeth even and a glistening white.

"What can I do for you?" he asked.

"That's what I'm here to find out," Harry said, "and I won't keep you long. You already know I work for Mrs. Winters, Senator. She is not convinced her husband's death was accidental. What's your view on that?"

"I don't have one," Foster answered, frowning slightly as if he'd been moved off the script. "I thought the Coast Guard declared him dead."

"Yes, but he may not be dead, simply gone fishing elsewhere," Harry said in a light tone, not wanting Foster thinking a trap was being laid for him.

"The thought had occurred to me," Foster replied, the frown fading, "but why? The man was on a roll, a successful campaign behind him and the prospect of more to come. I find it difficult to believe he would have walked away from that."

"There's that," Harry agreed, "but I've learned from Captain Haley Sloane, the fishing boat owner whose boat Lansbury was diving from when he disappeared, that it was possible for someone in another boat to have stopped at Lansbury's float and either picked him up or killed him and then moved out of sight without Sloane seeing any of it."

"And one of the other divers may have done it, or a merman or some other alien," Foster said more harshly, displaying impatience.

"I take your point and won't waste your time with any further speculations, rational or not. What isn't speculation is that three men working on your senate campaign have been murdered—four if you count Amos Lansbury, who, I agree, probably is dead."

"Your point?"

Foster was listening with obviously increased intensity and did not look pleased with what he was hearing.

"I think someone is killing off the top people on your campaign team. Have Captain Snyder's people discussed this with you?"

Foster leaned back in his chair, folded his hands across his chest, and studied Harry for a while before answering.

"No," he said quietly. "Do you know why?"

"Maybe, but first I have another question. Were you aware at any point during the campaign of anyone on your staff spreading the story that your people were betting on the outcome of the vote?"

Foster's face became suddenly more craggy, and his eyes narrowed slightly.

"Were they? I suppose you have a reason for asking me that question."

"So far as I know, nobody on either team was actually betting on the outcome of the race until the misinformation was passed along to one man on your team, who did make a wager, and it may be that these deaths are linked to that wager."

"Your evidence for this accusation?"

"First, I'm not accusing you of anything. Yes, I think I could satisfy a judge that the gambling took place and yes, I also know why Sheriff Fisher has refused to allow his department to include you in any of the investigations into the deaths of Hornsby, Purcell, and Smith, or to take the investigation of Lansbury's death beyond where the Coast Guard left it."

"I had absolutely nothing to do with any gambling, wagering, betting, point-shaving by my campaign," Foster said coldly.

"I believe you, but it doesn't change the fact that one of your people almost certainly did."

"Who?"

"You don't want to know that, and I can't prove it in court, in part because the people who could testify to its having happened are all dead. Let me add that if I thought you were part of a conspiracy of silence, I wouldn't be telling you this."

"No, I don't suppose you would," Foster said, seeming to relax a little. "Then why are you telling me this?"

"For a couple of reasons," Harry told him. "Memory is tricky. We see things that seem to be of no importance until later something else happens and we say, 'Oh! That's what I was seeing. It hadn't occurred to me 'til now.' "

"And you think I might have an 'aha!' moment?" he asked, grinning, whether from relief or masked anger Harry couldn't tell.

"Possibly, and to say, although it's not in my job description, that I don't think Sheriff Fisher is doing you a favor by trying to isolate you from this mess because it's going to come out, and when it does it's going to make you look bad. Who's going to believe you then when you say, 'I had nothing to do with it'?"

"Probably the same number as would have believed me had I made the statement a week ago," Foster said in a sour growl.

"Then your position is that you have no knowledge of any betting on the outcome of your senate race by any members of your staff," Harry said.

"Absolutely not," Foster said, looking increasingly at ease, "and, Harry, thanks for your interest, but there are half a dozen people making sure nothing is sneaking up on me. If there had been anything inappropriate going on in my campaign team, I would have known it."

"If you're easy in your mind, I guess I can be," Harry said, mirroring Foster's relaxed manner. "Oh, before I leave, have you received any death threats?"

"Don't be ridiculous."

"I'm trying not to be, and if I were you, I'd wonder why I hadn't."

"Tillman and I have shaken hands and put the race behind us. We're gladiators, Brock. Professionals. We fight for a living."

Harry stood up and shook hands with the senator, and while maintaining his grip asked, "Are you at all concerned that your name might be on this killer's list?"

"No, Brock, I'm not," Foster said decisively. He gave Harry a mocking smile. "The only person who has any reason for wanting me dead is Rycroft Tillman, and he wants me alive, to beat next time."

Harry left Foster's suite of offices in a troubled state of mind because he could not account for Foster's uneasiness and defensiveness at the outset of the meeting and his mood of dismissive mockery at the end. Also, why wasn't he thinking his name might be on the killer's list?

With these questions unsettling his mind, he had driven to the Meriwether Botanical Gardens as he often did when he wanted a quiet place to think and not be distracted by the wildlife, as so often happened when he was walking on the Hammock.

The gardens covered a couple of acres of land bordering the Seminole River. The land and the money for the various structures scattered over the area, to accommodate the needs of special kinds of plants, had been donated by a retired ship captain by the name of Meriwether, which was something of a misnomer because he lost three ships over his career to storms and nearly lost a fourth. At which point the company employing him, fearing the insurance companies would refuse to cover any ship he captained, put him in a golden lifeboat and set him adrift.

He washed up in Avola, where he proved a better stock trader than a ship's captain and became very wealthy, married a skiing instructor he met in Santa Fe, and moved to Grindelwald in the Swiss Alps. All of which accounted for the city's owning two acres of breathtakingly valuable land in south Avola. It also said something about Avola's tax base that the city could reject multiple offers of above a hundred million dollars for the land.

Harry sat on a bench under a trellis, buried beneath a huge jade vine that created a private, shaded space where he could think without being disturbed. And he needed to think because he had missed something while talking with Foster, something that would account for the man's change in mood and attitude.

Gradually, Harry recreated the conversation but found no single thing that provided an answer. With that settled, he found himself shifting increasingly to the conclusion that something that wasn't said explained the change. The watchful waiting, marking the early stages of the interview, had gradually changed to ill-concealed contempt. *At first he feared I knew something potentially damaging to him,* Harry thought, which could only mean that there was something. Otherwise, he wouldn't have been concerned.

What? he wondered as he left the gardens. *Was it something the dead men had known?* So far, Harry admitted, all he could say for sure was that they knew O'Malley had bet on the race and lost a lot of money. *Or,* he thought with a laugh, *maybe Foster's having an affair and was afraid I'd found out about it.*

"Well, Brock, what brings you out here again?" Jonas Amsel asked, inviting Harry onto his lanai with its whistling, cooing, and staccato cries from several members of the parrot families Amsel was housing. Amsel was wearing his beachcomber outfit: ragged sandals, stained denim shorts, and the tattered remains of a Harley T-shirt.

"I guess I wanted to talk with someone who was connected with the Tillman–Foster senate race, but no longer has a dog in the fight," Harry said.

"Our numbers are shrinking," Amsel said. "Beer?"

"Sounds good."

"Grab a seat. I'll be right back. Oh, if a red and green macaw lands on the arm of your chair, don't try to pet him. He bites."

Harry took a porch rocker, looking carefully for bird poop on the seat. Finding none, he sat down to watch the birds whizzing past. One swooped in, sat on the back of the adjoining rocker, and eyed Harry closely.

"Hello, Watson," Harry said to the African gray parrot.

"Cracker, please," the bird said.

"Sorry," Harry replied. "I'm fresh out."

"Pissant," the parrot shrieked and flew away.

"I heard that!" Amsel shouted after the parrot, passing Harry a cold, sweating bottle. "Strange bird," Amsel said. "He'll go for days without swearing, then something will irritate him, and he'll turn the air blue for a while. What's up?"

"Not enough, and that's why I'm here."

"I doubt I can help," Amsel said, studying his bottle.

"What can you recall from the campaign that might shed any light on its aftermath?"

"Very little, I'm afraid," Amsel said, having apparently decided the bottle was designed to be drunk from and tested the theory. "It was a wretched, murderous slog from start to finish. It was one of the worst experiences of my life. Every last one of us came out of it less of a man than he was when he went in."

"And now, four of you are dead, all from Foster's team. What do you make of it?"

"Obvious, isn't it?" Amsel said, showing impatience and disgust all at once. "Somebody's killing them."

"Amazing," Harry said wryly. "I don't suppose you can say who."

Amsel was studying his bottle again. "What do you think I'm doing out here, Brock?" he asked, breaking his concentration to scowl at Harry.

"You told me on my last visit you were getting away from it all."

The sarcasm produced the result Harry wanted. "What the fuck is that supposed to mean?" Amsel demanded.

"Just what you think it means."

"That I'm lying through my teeth?"

"You said it. I didn't."

"Well, I'm not!" Amsel said more loudly. Then he paused and went on glaring at Harry in silence. Harry sat it out, looking as bland as he could.

"Not entirely," Amsel finally said quietly, relaxing as he spoke and settling back in his rocker. He followed the flight of a pair of lovebirds until they vanished around the corner of the lanai, then turned back to look at Harry.

"There are two things," he said. "The first is, I've seen and heard over the years things it would be healthier not to have seen and heard. The second is, I've been on edge ever since Amos disappeared. I don't know more, probably, that you do about what's going down, but I've thought for some time that someone with a screw loose is doing the killing and that it's probably someone on Tillman's campaign team. Who the hell else could it be?"

"I wish I knew," Harry said.

"So do I," Amsel said. "I'd shoot the bastard myself."

"Have you received any threats?" Harry asked.

"No, but this jillpoke doesn't need much of a reason to kill someone. So, why not me if my name happened to come up?"

"How much money do you think Kevin O'Malley lost, betting on that election?" Harry asked.

"There's two things that Irishman keeps his mouth shut about. One is money and the other is information about himself. So, I have no idea, but I think a lot. I asked him once where he grew up, and he told me to mind my own fucking business."

"And yet you and he have been diving together for a long time. You must have learned something about him."

"Why are you prodding me to talk about O'Malley? I don't like it. He's a hard man, good at what he does, but I do not want him hearing I've been telling you everything I know about him. It would be a good way to get my head rearranged."

"So I heard from Harkin Smith when he was talking about the meeting with Arthur Hornsby, Lansbury, Joe Purcell, himself, and O'Malley."

"And where are they all?" Amsel asked.

"Dead," Harry said in a matter-of-fact way, "except for O'Malley."

"Yes, and I've said all I'm saying about that."

"For now," Harry told him.

CHAPTER 25

"Is there something you've forgotten to tell me about you and Prentice Foster?" Harry asked Meredith, standing in front of her desk, having ignored her suggestion that he sit down.

Her face flaming, she came off her chair like a jumping jack.

"What do you mean?" she shouted, a note of either desperation or rage lifting her voice into the high decibels. "How dare you suggest such a thing?"

It was not the reaction he had anticipated, and he actually stepped back from the desk, half expecting her to come over it and attack him with the silver letter opener she held in her right hand.

"Hold it!" Harry said, thrusting both hands at her, palms out. "Foster told me you and he talked fairly often. I figured that meant you had to know I hadn't interviewed him. Why did you pretend you didn't?"

No punctured balloon ever collapsed more quickly. She actually fell back into her chair, turning pale as quickly as she had blushed.

"Are you all right?" he asked.

"Sorry, I will be. Just give me a moment."

She slowly put the letter opener on the desk, and Harry noticed that her hand was trembling.

"The question of your interviewing him never came up," she said, avoiding his eyes. "In fact, I don't recall my ever mentioning you."

"That's not what he said," Harry replied, his curiosity engaged.

"What did he tell you?" she demanded, growing tense again.

"That you said I did everything short of walking on water," Harry said, beginning to enjoy himself and probably showing a failure of perception in not knowing she would not be amused. "I think he was jealous."

"What makes you think he would have any reason to be jealous?" she asked, her anger clinging to her words like a shadow.

"The way I dress comes to mind, and my good looks," he said.

It wasn't that he hadn't seen she was upset, but he had not yet grasped the fact that it was his having associated her with Foster that was causing her pain.

"That's enough," she said, shifting into aggression and half rising from her chair, her hands pressed flat on the desk. "There's nothing going on between Prentice Foster and me, and I deeply resent your implying there is."

Having had it spelled out, Harry got the message. In the same instant he thought of Foster's defensiveness at the beginning of their meeting, and its decline as the interview progressed.

"I'm sorry," Harry said, thinking quickly for a change. "I have no idea what you're talking about, but if I've said anything to make you angry, as you clearly are, I apologize."

His apology left Meredith hanging. She stood all the way up, wearing a puzzled expression. Harry said nothing and tried to look like wallpaper.

"You're sure . . ." she began.

"Positive," Harry said, interrupting her. "Why didn't you tell me you knew Foster?"

It wasn't exactly a defensive attack, but he did regain the status of injured party and turn the focus of attention away from her relationship with Foster, whatever it was.

"I'm sticking with my story," she said and suddenly grinned.

"The 'sunshine of your smile,' " Harry said, responding with a smile of his own. "Welcome back."

She had walked around the desk and was standing in front of him. Harry felt the impact of her presence but it would have been insulting to step back from it. That was his good reason. The real one was he had no desire to.

"Haven't we some unfinished business?" she asked him quietly.

"Yes," he said, "and against the clamor of my hormones and your pheromones, I'm going to suggest we leave it where it is."

"Any compelling reason why we should? What about the consenting adults rule?"

"I can remember voting for it," Harry said, "a long time ago. I'm working for you, Meredith."

"Does that mean we can't be friends with privileges?"

"Now you're laughing at me."

"No I'm not, Harry, I've been without sex even longer than you have, and I'd like you and me to break the drought."

There was a sharp rap on the door. Raquel pushed it open and poked her head into the room. "Sorry," she said. "Somebody's P.A. at Hemlock Pritchett wants you. She's not going to take no."

"Damn!" Meredith said. "Thanks, Raquel. Harry, this is going to be a long call."

"And I've got a lot to do," he said, meaning he had a lot to think about and wanted to get at it.

"I was talking with Senator Foster the other day," Harry said as he and Raquel went down the stairs. "Have you ever met him?"

"No," she said, "but he seems like a nice man."

"He is and took quite a bruising in his last election campaign."

"Do you think Mr. Tillman really slept with an underage

girl?" she asked.

Harry felt bad about what he was doing but not enough to stop.

"Not for a minute," he said, "but if you had asked me if he or Foster were having an affair, I would have said maybe."

"My parents were intending to vote for Tillman, but when he was accused of having sex with an underage girl, that plan died."

"It died for a lot of people—at least enough to get Foster elected. How are you getting along?"

Harry was ashamed of himself for having tried to get Raquel to say that Foster had visited Meredith. Like dirty tricks, he thought, unscrupulous but sometimes they worked.

"Better every day," she said. "Is there really a rumor around linking the boss with Senator Foster?"

"Well done," Harry said. "You nailed me. Not that I've heard. Have you heard anything?"

"No," she said. "They know one another, but she knows a lot of people."

"Are you eating yet?" he asked as they were crossing the foyer.

"I am," she said, coloring. "In fact, I'm going out to dinner tonight."

"That's the best news I've had all day," he told her.

Wondering if it had just been a brainstorm that had linked Foster's uneasiness at the outset of their interview with Meredith's flare-up when he asked if there was something she wanted to tell about her and Foster, he reached out to open the driver's door on the Rover and jump in when something made him hesitate.

At the end of the drive, a car was parked between the gate posts. The car was in deep shadow, but Harry could see the silhouette of a man in a hooded sweatshirt standing beside the driver's door. The figure raised his arm, and Harry leapt away from the Rover and threw himself flat against the crushed rock of the driveway.

"Welcome back," Frank Hodges said.

Harry had opened his eyes and after a moment of confusion saw the large sergeant looking down at him, a welcoming smile creasing his round face.

"What's your name?" a red-haired girl in a white uniform asked from the other side of the bed.

"Harry Brock," Harry said, sounding as if he was surprised by what he had just said.

"You'll do," she said, making a note on his chart and hurrying away.

"Were you in or outside your SUV when she went up?" Hodges asked him.

"Wait!" Harry said, making another sortie into consciousness. "The last I remember, I was hitting the gravel while being shot at by somebody with his hood up. At least I thought I was."

He started to sit up when his back, legs, shoulders, and hips lit up with searing pain. He fell back with a badly stifled groan.

"What the hell . . . ?" he said when he had caught his breath.

"You and about two yards of crushed rock landed on Winters's marble stairs," Hodges said cheerfully. "Lucky for you, you were under the flying pieces of the SUV. The pillars on the portico fared worse. The front doors were splintered, and there isn't a pane of glass in the front of the house. A front wheel with its tire still on rolled halfway up that big flight of stairs."

"That bastard blew up my Rover!" Harry said. "Do you know what that's going to do to my insurance premiums?"

"No," Hodges said, then paused to laugh. "No one in the house was hurt. Who was the guy in the hood?"

"Couldn't see a face, but I thought he was going to shoot me."

"How about the car the guy was driving?"

"I'd guess a light-colored Hyundai, old model."

At that point, a doctor, trailed by nurses, residents, and students, crowded into the room, evicted Hodges, and began explaining to his listeners what had happened to Harry, all the while pressing Harry here, prodding him there, inviting the interns to have a go, and moving him while Harry yelled in protest against being moved at all.

That evening, Meredith came to see him.

"Sue me for damages to your house," Harry said by way of a greeting. "Nothing could jack up my insurance premiums more than being blown up."

"Feeling sorry for ourselves, are we?" she asked with a mock smile.

"Indeed we are," Harry said, making an entirely different face as he tried to hitch into a sitting position.

"I think you'd better lie still," Meredith said, leaning over him and putting her hands on his chest to restrain him.

Her perfume washed over him, and her hair fell and brushed his face, reminding him of how she had felt in his arms. His eyes began to brim over, filling him with shock and shame.

"I can't think what has done that," he began, but she pressed a finger against his lips.

"Enough," she said, took away her finger, and replaced it with her mouth.

As kisses go, there wasn't anything remarkable about it, and it didn't last long, but it dried his tears.

"Magical," Harry said as she sat back.

"Was it really that nice?" she asked, looking expectant.

"Oh, yes," Harry said quickly, "but I meant it stopped me from crying."

"I should certainly hope so," she said. "I talked to the doctor earlier. He said you're bruised pretty much all over, but nothing is broken. Is that what they're telling you?"

"That's about it," Harry said. "I feel as if a barn door hit me. Even my ass hurts."

She laughed and dropped a hand on his arm.

"Why you and not me?" she asked, suddenly serious.

"I don't know, but my guess is that had he killed you, I might keep coming, and by killing me, he gambled on stopping you as well."

"I see," she said quietly.

"Meredith," he said, placing his hand over hers and managing not to wince. "Go away before he comes back for you. This is my job, not yours."

"I don't want to leave," she told him. "We could be together. Wouldn't you like that?"

"Yes," he said, "I would, but I have issues."

"So . . ." she began, leaning toward him again, then stopped. "Aren't we grown-ups?" she asked. "Can't we choose what we want to do?"

"Yes, and that's the problem."

"Holly Pike," she said as if she'd tasted something sour. "Am I mistaken in thinking she's in Montana and you're here and won't go there?"

"That's about it."

"Then I fail to see the problem unless you've embraced a life of celibacy."

"No, I haven't. I'm probably going to see her when this job is finished."

That statement was an outright lie, and he gasped inwardly at his audacity. He had no intention of flying to Montana or going there in any other way.

"We'll see," she said, apparently undaunted, and got up.

"When are you being discharged?"

"I don't know, soon, I think."

"Call me when you know, I'll pick you up."

"Sounds good. Meredith, has anyone from the sheriff's office talked with you?"

"Yes, I have uniformed protection in the house and outside. I guess you weren't blown up in vain."

CHAPTER 26

Meredith parked her silver Porsche coupe under the big oak, hopped out, and ran around to Harry's door, ready to help him to his feet.

"I can do this," Harry protested when she pulled open his door.

He had been wheeled to the curb and all but lifted into the car seat by a brawny volunteer in an ill-fitting hospital uniform and ridiculous cap that made him look like the village idiot, which he wasn't.

"Go, Brock," she said, stepping back.

"There's no need to be sarcastic," he complained between his teeth.

He managed to get one foot onto the ground, and it hurt enough to make him sweat. Getting the rest of him out of the car set new highs in pain, but he persevered, determined not to groan or scream, both of which seemed the sensible thing to do.

"Looking good, Brock," Meredith called as Harry started toward the house.

Her wide grin was not encouraging, and his progress, he found, resembled that of an aged, severely arthritic man beyond the time when he could actually pick up his feet.

"Want to take my arm, Gramps?" Meredith called.

"Don't make me laugh," Harry said. "If I do, I think something would break."

"As long as it isn't anything important," she replied.

"Shut up," he said, failing in his effort to put on some speed.

He did let her help him up onto the granite step and then onto the lanai while she also held open the screen door.

"My God," he gasped, once in the kitchen and settled on the wooden chair Meredith had pulled out from the table, "this may have been a mistake."

"I recall the doctor telling you it wasn't going to be easy. Want to get into bed?"

"The bedroom's upstairs."

"How about the floor with a pillow under your head? Once there, I could take your mind off your troubles, and you wouldn't even have to move."

"Forgive the crudity," Harry said, "but I'm not up for it."

"Believe me, you would be."

"Please don't give me a précis of your plan. I don't think I would survive the consequences."

"Okay, Harry, how about some tea?"

"Excellent, you'll find it in the right-hand cupboard over the sink. The kettle's on the sideboard."

"You have electricity out here? I was expecting lamps and a wood stove."

"I have both of those, but they're rarely needed."

Because it was past noon, Harry asked if Meredith would like some lunch and made a start by getting slowly to his feet. Meredith told him to sit down. He did and made himself of some use by telling her where things were. When they had finished eating and were lingering over the last of the pinot grigio Harry had managed to open and pour, they drifted gradually into a companionable silence, finally broken by Meredith.

"Harry," she asked in a thoughtful voice, "why are you living in this godforsaken place?"

"Because to me it's the best place on this green earth," he replied, suppressing an impulse to get angry.

"You haven't been looking in the right places."

"I've seen this place, and it's enough."

She looked at him as if she was seeing him for the first time.

"But why here?" she asked.

"Because this place and an old farmer who lives half a mile down the road saved my life."

Harry was surprised he had revealed that information. It was something he seldom mentioned. Recalling the tears, he thought the accident might have weakened his resistance.

"Oh! You can't leave me with that answer, which explains nothing but clearly points to a very interesting story."

Harry wasn't sure he liked his life being referred to as a story, but she sounded genuinely interested and not just curious.

"Okay," he said, "but if you're bored half to death, don't blame me."

She planted both elbows on the table, rested her chin on her linked fingers, and said, "I'll be your ideal listener."

"I was a state game warden, married with two children and living in the Richardson Lakes region in western Maine when my life was suddenly turned upside down."

From there he moved quickly through killing a man in self-defense, being charged with murder, tried and acquitted, fired from the warden service, and left with no wife, no children, and no job. After that the long drift downhill and working in Boston as a private investigator, leaving that, and finally coming to rest on Bartram's Hammock where he found Tucker LaBeau.

"And two marriages later?" she asked.

"What do you mean?"

"Is this going to be it?" she asked, unable to suppress her disapproval, if that's what had put the edge in her voice.

"I don't follow you," Harry said.

"It is a very moving story, Harry," she said. "It's wonderful the way in which you put yourself back together, but is that the end of the story?"

"I'm still alive and hoping to see the sun tomorrow," he said.

"Through one of these windows, every day, week, month, year until the man with the scythe finds you?"

"Why are you upset?" he asked, confused by the sudden arrival of anger.

She was on her feet, glaring down at him. "Why are you still here? What are you afraid of?" she demanded.

Had she slapped his face, he would not have been more shaken or angrier.

"You don't know me well enough, Meredith, to ask me those questions. Thank you for driving me home. Now, I'd like to be left alone to catch up on a couple of days' work."

Before he finished speaking, she had run around the table, thrown both arms around him and crushed herself against him. He tried hard, but he couldn't stifle a loud groan.

"Oh, Harry," she said, "I'm sorry. I really, really am."

She said this directly into his ear because she had her face pressed against his.

"Meredith," he gasped, "you're killing me."

"Oh, Harry," she said again, apparently stricken now with guilt for having hurt him, pressed herself against him even harder and cried, "I forgot!"

"Okay," he said weakly, feeling as if he might pass out.

Releasing him, she kissed him on the forehead and said, "You've got to get into bed."

"I don't think I could . . ." he began.

"No, no, of course not. Come on, up, then an arm over my shoulders. Right, here we go."

"Slowly, slowly," he said, squeezing his eyes shut and grimacing.

"Steady as she goes," Meredith responded, having launched them on the stairs.

When she had planted him between the sheets, stripped to his shorts, and showing no interest in his shed clothes, she pulled her own clothes straight and said, "Can I count on you to stay up here until I get back?"

"Just give me my phone, and I'll be here a week from now." Then he added, "Did you say you were coming back?"

"Of course," she said, "did you think I was leaving you alone in this howling wilderness?"

"It doesn't howl," he said defensively. "It hums and buzzes, zings and whines, and the wind can be quite loud."

"If you say so. I have to go back to town, but I'll be back. How about Chinese take-out for dinner?"

Lying down had eased his pain and he got some of his own back by asking, "You're not planning to cook for me?"

"I have *cooked* for you, Harry Brock, for the last time. Believe me on this."

"That's not as much of a disappointment as it would have been had I not eaten the lunch you put together," he said.

"Very quick," she told him. "I'll be back in a couple of hours."

"Watch out for the elephants," he said as she left.

Meredith came back, laden with food and wine. Harry had fallen asleep almost as soon as she left and did not wake until he heard her car go over the loose plank in the humpbacked bridge.

He met her at the kitchen door but let her carry her burdens to the sink counter.

"What are you doing downstairs?" she demanded by way of a greeting.

"We wilderness dwellers have to recover more quickly than city types," he said.

"I had a talk with Bob Fisher while I was in town," she told him, passing him a glass of wine. "Here, drink this. See if it's better than what we had for lunch. He was not happy to see me."

"Predictably," he told her, pausing to taste the wine, then added, "It tastes like about thirty-five dollars. Did he tell you to leave the state?"

"He did, but I had the feeling he was more concerned about the blowback if anything happened to me than he was about me."

"Vintage Fisher. What else did he say?"

"Nothing interesting, aside from blaming you for creating a mess for him. I told him to be realistic, and he didn't like that. Bob isn't accustomed to having his pronouncements questioned."

By the time they finished eating and moved to the lanai with the wine, the sun had set and the long shadows of afternoon merged into the soft darkness that never completely left the depths of the forest behind the house. The last glimmers of day hung in the thunderheads to the east, turning their towers a dusty rose.

"Are you still determined to stay?" Harry asked when they were settled on the lanai, side by side in the wooden lounge chairs.

The lawn, the sand road, the creek and its heavy but low growth of shrubbery provided an open view across the swamp to the sky and the skimpy horizon of scattered palm trees in the distance.

"Yes," she said. "The sky is beautiful, but what is this racket I'm hearing?"

Harry laughed and said, "The night chorus, made up mostly of colony frogs and insects of varying sizes—also the locusts."

"How do you go to sleep?"

"The windows shut out most of it," he said, "but it's wonderful, really. You don't often have the chance to hear life in all its variety and intensity."

"Is that what I'm listening to?" Meredith asked, sounding doubtful.

"The love songs of life. The belling sounds belong to the frogs and the fiddling to the insects. All of these sounds are calling to females who will respond only to the specific call of their kind. Just as those fireflies winking on and off over the creek will mate only with the maker of a particular kind of light."

"Do you ever wish your bottom would light up, Harry?" Meredith asked, followed by something suspiciously like a giggle.

"I think it would look much better on you."

"Oh, good. Something kinky. Have you any fluorescent paint? We could hold a trial. I'd go first, and while the paint was drying . . ."

"This would be a lot funnier if your life weren't in danger," Harry said sharply.

"Spoilsport!" Meredith said.

"I know, but you're not thinking clearly."

"Clearly enough, Harry, to know that you're in far more danger than I," she replied, matching his tone, "but let's not wrangle. It's far too beautiful out here to spoil it."

"Are you changing your mind about the wilderness?"

"This much of it anyway, but I'm going on record as saying I don't think it's fair that only male fireflies' bottoms light up."

"Females do flash at males they wish to attract," Harry said, "but they usually don't fly."

"What's the point of having a really cool bottom and not being able to flaunt it?" Meredith protested.

"I wish I knew," Harry said.

Harry woke to find himself moving much less painfully than the night before. Pressing his luck, he went through the house opening windows and the front and back doors. A front had slipped down the peninsula in the night, announcing itself with a rumble of thunder and a brief bluster of wind. He had made the coffee by the time Meredith came into the kitchen, a towel wrapped around her head.

"Look at you!" she said, beaming. "I expected to be spooning gruel into you while you lay propped up."

"If I'd known," he said. "You actually look good in that towel, a little goofy, but if Elizabeth Taylor could get away with it . . ."

"Don't get carried away," she told him, plunking down and resting her forearms on the table. "I just used up a week's supply of morning good cheer in that greeting. Is the coffee ready?"

"Let's really start the day right," Harry said, putting a steaming mug in front of her. "Let's right away agree that you're leaving Avola, and nobody but Jim Snyder's going to know where you're going."

Meredith sipped the coffee, looked up him, and said flatly, "The coffee's good, the suggestion isn't. I've told you. I'm not leaving until your work is finished."

"What if I quit?"

"You won't, and if you did, I'd hire someone else."

"Meredith, you'd try the patience of a saint, and I'm not one of those."

"Maybe not, but you're working on it. Come on, sit down. Talk to me about this weird place you're living in."

Instead, he made breakfast from bacon to waffles with eggs in between. Then he sat down with her and described some of his adventures as a warden on the Hammock and in the Stickpen Preserve, the vast cypress swamp adjoining the Hammock.

"I liked the story about the red shoe best," she said as they were cleaning up. "It was a story, wasn't it?"

"Absolutely not!" he protested. "Everything I've told you is true."

"You want me to believe Tucker LaBeau has a talking mule

and a Spanish-speaking dog, Harry? Come on."

"A doubting Thomasina," Harry said, feeling good about having company for breakfast. "How long are you staying?"

She glanced at her watch and said, "Twenty-five minutes. God, that was a disastrous but delicious meal. Do you eat like this every day?"

"Half a banana and a cup of bran flakes," he replied and pulled a long face.

Her phone rang.

She looked at the number calling and jumped to her feet, her face brightening. "Got to take this," she said as she ran out of the kitchen and up the stairs.

Harry remained sitting until the expected sound of her bedroom door slamming confirmed his suspicions.

"Not her broker," he said, getting to his feet.

Bumping into blank walls wherever he turned, Harry decided to retrace some steps. Jonas Amstel was his first thought, but Amstel's recorded response was, "Out of town, be back sometime."

His second choice was Rycroft Tillman. Once again, Celine Tillman met him at the door and greeted him warmly. Seeing her again gave Harry genuine pleasure, and he realized, listening to her describe a run-in with a very large soft-shelled turtle that was determined to come into the house, that as long as she drew breath she would be delightful company.

"In the end," she said with a charming shrug, hands held palm up, "I decided to outwait him and, ending all communication, closed the door. Sometime in the night he decamped."

"Good," Harry said, "they are the reptilian version of a skunk. Irritated enough, they release a disgusting stench."

"Come up here, Brock," Tillman shouted down the stairs, "and stop carrying on with my wife."

"Spoilsport!" Celine called back. "It was I who was vamping him."

She touched Harry's arm lightly and said, "You may as well go, but please say goodbye before you leave."

"And what brings you out of the big city?" Tillman asked, sprawled as before in his swivel chair.

"I'm not sure but it wasn't for the pleasure of your company. Thanks for seeing me."

"Why haven't you told your boss to get her ass out of Avola?" Tillman demanded, sounding genuinely disgusted.

"I have talked myself hoarse telling her that, but she won't go."

"I know you're trying to pass yourself off as a gentleman, Brock, but there are times when a woman has to be told, not asked."

"I don't think they'd let me put her on a plane if I appeared at the boarding gate with her over my shoulder."

"Maybe not," Tillman said, finally grinning. "The bodies are piling up. You doing anything about it?"

"No, and it hurts to admit it. Whoever the killer is, he knows how to handle explosives and is connected somewhere because he knows who hired me—and he tried to kill me."

"I heard about that. Glad to see you're still with us. Have you gotten anywhere with your examination of Foster's outside activities?"

"No."

"Brock, you disappoint me. I handed you a good lead last time we talked, and you haven't followed it up."

Harry had to think hard before making a connection.

"Your hint that Foster had a mistress."

"That's right, only I doubt Cee would call *mistress* accurate."

"Another time, another culture?"

"Something like that."

"I don't think Foster's love life has much to do with what I'm investigating."

"You might try asking Jonas Amsel, to see what he thinks."

"Too late. He's left town."

"Nail this guy, Harry," Tillman said, more forcefully. "He won't miss twice."

Chapter 27

Harry left the Tillmans without feeling he had made any progress in his investigation, but one thing Tillman had said stuck with him, and it made Harry uncomfortable. Why would Tillman think that Foster's having an affair would be of any interest to him—aside from proving Tillman had spared him the damage that revealing it during their race would have done?

He had tried to clear his mind of the question and refocus on his investigation, but instead he suddenly conjured the expression on Meredith's face when she got the call that sent her running upstairs. That flash of recall was followed by an immediate recollection of Foster's uneasiness, bordering on hostility, at the beginning of their interview and the way in which it was slowly replaced by smug complaisance.

"Damned foolishness," Harry told himself and pulled onto Rattlesnake Drive with excessive speed that set his tires squealing.

By the time he reached the sheriff's department, he had calmed down and didn't put the locusts out of business by roaring into the parking lot. As a result, when he stepped out of the SUV and into the blazing heat of the day, he was greeted by their zinging fiddles.

"We've got a response from the Feds on the request for some background checks," Jim said, displaying some uneasiness as he sat behind his desk rubbing the top of his head with his right hand. He seemed to lose courage because he stopped rubbing his head and speaking at the same time.

"Captain," Hodges said encouragingly, "nobody knows about this but you and me and Harry here. So, you can go right on. Well, of course, Harry doesn't know about it yet, but since you brought up the subject . . ."

"Frank, enough!" Jim said loudly, "and don't interrupt."

Hodges turned and winked at Harry, who saw a chance to say nothing and took it.

"Now then," Jim went on after clearing his throat, "we sent in, as cloaked as possible . . ."

"The Captain chose the names," Hodges interrupted enthusiastically. "I typed up the paperwork, and he sent it all in from his computer, with a little help from me."

"Are you through, Sergeant?" Jim demanded, his face tomato red.

"Yes, and I wanted Harry to know what a good job you'd done to keep it secret."

Words apparently failed Jim because he sank back in his chair hard enough to bang it into the wall, which bore the scars and marks of many such encounters.

"Well done, Jim," Harry said quickly. "How long have you had to wait for a response? I've heard they're backed up pretty badly."

"A lot longer than I should have," Jim said sharply as if he'd found a safe subject on which to vent. "I don't think they've got everybody off typewriters."

"They must be harder up than we are," Hodges said. "Plus it's harder to get them to cooperate with another law enforcement department than it is to put a pig into a barrel."

"Why on earth would you want to?" Jim demanded.

"Well, suppose you did. Can you imagine the squealing and grunting, back-pedaling and switching ends you'd have on your hands?"

"I don't want to imagine anything about that pig, Frank," Jim shouted, all six and a half feet of him coming out of his chair. "Do you hear me?"

"I think if I'd been walking along Route 41, I'd of heard you," Hodges said, beaming.

"What have you found out, Jim?" Harry asked, seeking an exit.

"None of them except Lansbury has a prior," Jim said, "but in the eighties, O'Malley had connections with the IRA. How close is uncertain, but he was under scrutiny for the brief period he lived in Boston, suspected of running arms to the resistance."

"In the seventies and eighties half of South Boston was under scrutiny by somebody," Harry said. "In all the bars there were buckets prominently displayed for collecting contributions for the Provisional IRA."

"We came up nearly dry," Hodges said, trying to look gloomy.

"Why isn't Foster worried?" Harry asked.

"What makes you think he's not?" Jim asked.

"I've talked with him twice," Harry replied, "and whatever's troubling him—and I think something is—it's not being killed."

"There's probably a woman in the mix," Hodges said cheerfully. "There usually is."

"That's not helpful," Jim said, "but I agree with Frank anyway. Is he having woman troubles?"

"You two and Rycroft Tillman," Harry said. "He keeps telling me to look into Foster's love life. I can't seem to convince anyone around here that I'm trying to focus on these killings in hopes of finding out whether or not Amos Lansbury was murdered."

"You can't keep a thing like that a secret," Hodges said, apparently having gone on thinking about the possibility of Foster's having an affair. "Someone besides those two knows what's going on."

"Millard Jones and his people haven't got further than a snail could jump," Jim said, shaking his head.

"Did you two hear anything I just said?" Harry demanded.

"If you want to talk, Brock," the message said, "make it in soon or I'll be gone."

Harry shut off the electric kettle and called Amsel's number, guessing that like himself, the man was up before the sun.

"Come out," Amsel said. "We'll have breakfast and talk."

"What about your birds, Jonas?" Harry asked, having just cleaned his plate of the last of his fried eggs and grits, a southern addition to his diet he had learned to eat and not reject as pig slops, and risk restarting the Civil War.

"Sold them," Amsel said, refilling their coffee mugs. "The place will be cleared out by noon, chicks and all."

"Impressive," Harry said, "but that's not why you asked me out here, is it?"

"No. I'm going to vanish."

"You're really that worried about your safety?"

"Yes," Amsel said without hesitation. "I think my name's on the list."

"Whose list?" Harry asked.

"I don't know, but there's something I want to tell you because I think you will know what should and shouldn't be done with it."

"Think carefully, Jonas," Harry said. "There are things I can't keep to myself."

"Acknowledged," Amsel said. "What I'm going to tell you may or may not have something to do with the killings. If it proves out not to have anything to do with it, then I want you to keep it to yourself."

"I can't promise that until I hear what it is. Still want to tell me?"

"Yes. I trust you to do the right thing."

"Okay, I'm listening."

"Lansbury found out about a month before our last dive that Prentice Foster was screwing his wife, and had confronted Foster."

"How do you know?" Harry demanded, shaken and trying hard not to show it. *My God,* he thought, *Tillman was right*!

"O'Malley told me. All of us on the dive team knew it."

"How did O'Malley find out?"

"I don't know. I knew there was no use asking him."

"When did he tell you?"

"I'd guess it was about a week before our last dive."

"Did you and Lansbury talk about it?"

"No."

"Did any of you talk with him about it?"

"No," Amsel said forcefully as if he was offended. "Lansbury was a shit in many ways, but he didn't deserve to have that arrogant bastard Foster banging his wife. From everything any of us ever heard Amos say, he thought the world of her."

Harry restrained himself from commenting on that.

"I gather O'Malley didn't know then that Lansbury was playing a trick on him," Harry said.

"I don't know. As I've said before, he plays his cards pretty close to his chest."

"Did O'Malley ever say what he thought about Meredith having an affair with Foster?"

"Not to me," Amsel said, glancing at his watch.

"I've been slow to ask this, thinking it would come out, but it hasn't," Harry said quickly. "How did Lansbury learn about the affair?"

"I never heard."

"Was it you or Hornsby?"

"No, but Lansbury might have come on something himself."

"Any chance O'Malley made up the story to get even with Lansbury?" Harry asked.

He had wondered if Tillman might have been the source of the leak but dismissed the idea as unlikely. Tillman would never have exposed himself in that way.

"You'd have to ask him," Amsel said, getting to his feet, "but I wouldn't recommend it."

He came around the table to Harry and thrust out his hand. "Goodbye, Brock. My bags are in the car, and I'm leaving. I doubt we'll ever meet again so goodbye and good luck."

"The same to you," Harry told him, taking his hand. "I suppose you're not saying where you're going."

"No."

By the time he said that, Amsel was on the lanai. In the next moment the screen door slammed shut behind him, and he was striding across the yard toward his car. Harry, his mind filled with the news about Meredith and Foster, stood watching Amsel drive away, feeling strangely bereft.

With a sigh, he forced himself to take the step that would move him into a new and much less pleasing world. Amsel had driven out of the trees onto the berm. Harry, pushing open the screen door, gave the car a final glance, and in that moment it vanished in a ball of fire.

"What brought you out here?" Jim asked Harry after an hour's wait while the fire crew doused the flames and cooled the wreckage.

"Scraping around for information," Harry replied.

Harry and Jim were standing in the shade of the trees on the Hammock side of the wreckage, watching Jones's team in white coveralls slowly picking through and photographing the smoking remains of Amsel and his car, and carefully gathering whatever of Jonas Amsel's body hadn't been burned or obliterated. The smell of fried metal and exploded gasoline still hung in the air, tainted by the stench of torched flesh.

"You recorded the conversation?" Jim asked.

"I did."

"Learn anything that might explain this?" Jim asked, nodding at the wreckage.

"I'm not sure," Harry said, unwilling to say anything about Meredith and Foster, at least for the moment.

In fact, he was having trouble even thinking about it, a condition he attributed to having seen Amsel blown to smithereens, but at some level of his mind he knew it wasn't the answer.

"Ah," Jim said. "Millard is waving his arm. They're finished. Now the wrecker will take away the remains of the car. There's quite a hole been blown in the road. Want me to hold up the wrecker until you see if you can get through it?"

"The SUV will go through. I'm not so sure about myself."

CHAPTER 28

Jonas Amsel's death had shocked Harry deeply, no doubt in part because it was so unexpected and so violent. The news that Meredith and Prentice Foster were involved in a love affair had shaken him in a different and far more personal way, and more profoundly.

"But are you sure it's true?" Tucker asked.

"I have no proof beyond what Amsel told me. He was leaving. I see no reason for him to lie."

"Maybe O'Malley was lying," Tucker suggested. "Given what you know about him, does it seem a possibility?"

"I can't say no, but if you were going to kill someone, why would you go to the trouble of making up an elaborate lie—one that would harm people who have done nothing to hurt you?"

"I wouldn't, but I'm not Kevin O'Malley. Come on," Tucker said, getting off the seat by the citrus grove, "let's get this last coat of stain onto the bantam house and declare the project complete."

"The thing that troubles me most," Harry said as they began painting, "is not being able to make any connection between the killings and the affair. It was essentially the only thing Amsel wanted to tell me before leaving. Why did he think it was so important?"

"You're assuming there is any connection," Tucker said. "Why would O'Malley kill four men, only three of whom, presumably, knew about the affair?"

"That's assuming O'Malley is the killer," Harry said.

"True," Tucker replied with a chuckle, "and have you noticed that the Winters/Foster affair is another story?"

As they went side by side up the stairs together, Harry made conversation with the newly animated Raquel, but his heart wasn't in it. In fact, he was having to repeatedly swallow his heart, which was trying to exit by way of his throat.

"Harry!" Meredith said brightly, coming around her desk to greet him. She was wearing a peach-colored sun dress and her hair was pulled back. "I thought you'd decamped for Montana. I'm glad you haven't. Come, sit down."

I can't blame anyone for falling in love with this woman, he thought, the first positive thought he'd had since breakfast.

"Meredith," he said, "if what I'm going to broach with you didn't involve the deaths of four people, you wouldn't be hearing it from me because it would be none of my business."

That last bit about it not being any of his business was probably a mistake, but he'd said it, and there was no taking it back.

"Wait," she said. "I thought only three had been killed."

"This morning Jonas Amsel's car exploded with him in it. I saw it happen."

"Oh, God, Harry, how awful."

"I called him around six because I knew he was leaving, and I wanted to talk with him. We had breakfast together, and he told me he was leaving Avola for good, that he was afraid if he didn't he'd be killed. Then he said he had something to tell me he did not want to leave unsaid. Five minutes later, he drove out of his yard, went another fifty yards, and was blown to pieces. So he was right. Someone did want him dead."

"It's dreadful," she said, ashen-faced, "but I think you'd better tell me whatever it is this is leading to."

"All right, but there's no easy way to say it. He told me you've been having an affair with Prentice Foster, that your husband found out about it and confronted Foster. All the men in the diving group knew about the affair, and now, of that group, only O'Malley is still alive."

"And you believe the accusation is true," she said quietly, sitting very straight, her hands clasped on her lap, "and that whether or not it is, is none of your business."

"I'm going to set that last bit aside to say I dislike telling you this, Meredith," Harry said, "but it had to be done. If I know about it, there are at least four other people besides myself who know—Tillman, O'Malley, Foster, and you. Amsel didn't know how O'Malley found out or how Amos came to know."

"Well, Harry, you're right about the affair, but your timing is wrong. I told Amos a few weeks before he was killed that I'd had an affair with Prentice and that it was over. I found I didn't want him finding out about it from someone else. I don't know anything about his 'confronting' Prentice, if it happened."

"Then Amos knew the affair was over when he died?" Harry asked.

"Yes, Harry, and do you want to tell me that's none of your business either?" Her voice had become more and more pained.

"No, I don't, but I'm obliged to look at everything I learn about these deaths as objectively as I can."

"Are you angry with me?"

"I guess I'm angry that you haven't been honest with me," he told her quietly.

"Yes, I can understand that, but I didn't want you to think I slept around," she said, looking away from him and coloring a little.

"It never occurred to me to think that you slept around," Harry said, feeling himself slide a bit but ignoring the warning. "Your marriage was dead. Why shouldn't you look for love?"

"If I found it, I lost it," she responded ruefully, "not that it matters."

"Only if it matters to you," Harry responded. "The really pressing issue is what role has the affair played in what's been happening."

"I see that," she agreed. "I also see that it may be very dangerous knowledge. How in God's name did Rycroft Tillman find out?"

"I'm not sure he knows it was with you," Harry responded, "but indirectly, he kept telling me that Foster was having an affair. But more to the point, it has to mean Foster is somehow implicated, unless you're the one behind all the killings."

"Harry, that's not funny," Meredith said, suddenly looking frightened.

"No, nothing about the situation is funny. For example, how did whoever killed Jonas Amsel know he was back in town?"

"Perhaps whoever killed him didn't know he'd left," she said.

"Possibly, but there are two explanations for why things have happened that I don't hold in high esteem," Harry said, "luck and coincidence."

Harry had persuaded a reluctant Jim to call some of his people together to hear what he had to say. Harry, Jim, Hodges, Millard Jones, and three of his assistants were crowded into Jim's office and seated on folding metal chairs. Millard and his people had shed their jackets because the limping AC had lost the battle with the body heat being generated in the room.

"Sheriff Fisher has cut us loose," Jim told the group. "Harry has useful information. So, let's hear him."

"I just had a meeting with Senator Foster," Harry began. "Foster gave no indication of being concerned for his safety. In fact, when I suggested that he might be in danger, he dismissed my concern by saying he had done nothing to anyone but

Tillman that would warrant harming him and that he and Tillman were on good terms."

"Remind me why Senator Foster should feel threatened," Jones said.

"As you all know, Meredith Winters's life has been threatened," Harry said. "All of the lead people on Foster's election team are dead, as are three of the four members of the dive team. If I were Foster, I would be worried."

"I feel there's something we're missing, Harry," Jones said. "Joe Purcell wasn't a member of the dive group."

"Well, Jonas Amsel thought he was on the killer's list, and he was part of Tillman's team. Amsel was very concerned that he had been targeted. He never said he thought O'Malley was the killer, but he did say the killer was unhinged. I'm not certain he told me everything he knew about the situation, but he had sold up and was on his way out and would not tell me where he was going."

"Did Amsel have a name?" one of Jones's men asked.

"He said he didn't. But he turned out to be right about being on the list."

"Here's what troubles me most, Harry," Jones said, with more feeling in his voice than he usually displayed. "Speaking truthfully, it's probably impossible to prevent someone who's been targeted from being killed, no matter how well the person's guarded."

"Let me finish that thought, Lieutenant," Jim broke in. "You think Harry and Meredith Winters will be next."

"Do you want to add Foster's name?" Hodges asked.

Harry listened as the discussion shifted to strategies for intensifying the investigation, all the while wondering if he was doing the right thing in concealing Foster's affair with Meredith.

Since learning about their relationship, he had set his mind on not thinking about Meredith and Foster together. He tried especially hard to avoid asking himself if it troubled him. Sitting in the stifling room, voices rising and falling as the arguments over protection strategies then shifted away to finding the perpetrator and became more heated, Harry suddenly asked himself again why Tillman wanted him to learn about Foster's affair.

"Harry," Jim said, breaking into Harry's absorption with the question, "tell them why we should take Kevin O'Malley seriously as a suspect."

Harry ran quickly through the reasons he thought relevant, stressing O'Malley's losing money and his conviction that Foster's team were all in on the dirty trick.

"Despite those reasons, which I think are compelling," he added, "we should try to keep our minds open."

"Meaning what?" Hodges asked.

"In both meetings I've had with Rycroft Tillman," Harry replied, "he's urged me to look deeper into Foster's background but didn't elaborate. At first, I thought he was just looking for a way to get back at Foster for beating him in the election. Now, I'm beginning to change my mind."

"Why?" Jim asked.

"I'm not sure," Harry lied.

"Ha!" Hodges said loudly. "When you decide to tell us, we'll all listen."

That brought a general laugh and broke up the meeting. Harry remained behind to have a word alone with Jim, who was not happy with Jones's lack of progress.

"It's not that he and his people aren't trying," he said, disgust graveling his voice. "They've all been working hard, but there's nothing to work with. Beyond knowing the caliber of the gun that shot Hornsby and the one that shot Harkin Smith, the fact that the man who tried to kill you was wearing a hooded sweatshirt, and that Semtex was the explosive used to kill Purcell and Amsel, we haven't a single lead."

"I share your frustration," Harry said, having only half listened to Jim's complaint, still uncertain how much he should tell Jim.

"I'm going to tell you something that may or may not have anything to do with these deaths," he said, "but I've finally decided that Rycroft Tillman thinks it does. Everyone who's been killed with the possible exception of Joe Purcell knew about it."

"Let's hear it," Jim said.

"I'm not going to tell you how I know because it doesn't affect anything you might do. Up until a short time before the election, Foster was having an affair."

"Is that it?" Jim asked. "Because if it is, I can't see that it has any bearing at all on the killings."

"You've missed something I said earlier," Harry said quickly. "To the best of my knowledge, the only people who knew about the affair, other than Foster and his partner, were Lansbury, Amsel, O'Malley, and Hornsby. I can't say whether or not Purcell knew about it, but I intend to find out."

"The diving team knew, then," Jim said.

"That's right, and they're all dead but O'Malley. And it may be the reason Rycroft Tillman urged me to look hard, but I no longer think so."

"Who is the woman—if it is a woman we're talking about here," Jim asked, obviously not interested in the Tillman angle.

"I know, but I can't tell you."

"You're sure about this?"

"As sure as one can ever be about such things."

"Meaning?"

"Yes, I'm certain."

"All right," Jim said. "I can live with that, at least for now.

What does any of what you've just told me have to do with the killings?"

"Now we enter the land of speculation," Harry said, relieved that Jim hadn't pressed him for a name, "and I'll begin with an *if.* If Joe Purcell knew about the affair, then all the victims shared the same knowledge."

"I don't like where this is going," Jim said.

"I didn't think you would."

Having told Jim that he didn't know whether or not Joe Purcell knew about Foster's affair sent him straight to Clarissa Purcell.

"The room looks better than it did the last time you saw it," Clarissa said to Harry, leading him into the living room.

Harry was already smiling. He had half expected to see a woman who, by now, had internalized the full horror of what happened to her husband and was shattered by it. She had lost some weight, but that was the only outward sign of her loss. Her hair was brushed, her dark slacks were pressed and her red blouse looked freshly laundered.

"It looks great, and so do you. I hope you don't mind my saying so," he told her.

"Not at all and thank you," she said. "I probably look better than I feel—at least I hope I do. Please, sit down. Why do you want to see me?"

"Did your husband ever say anything to you about anyone in either campaign having an affair?"

"Yes, but I'm not going to talk about that."

"It was Prentice Foster," he said instantly.

She looked so startled that Harry had his answer.

"Don't worry," he said as though she was only confirming something he already knew. "I'm not going to broadcast it."

"I haven't said that," she told him sharply, having quickly regained her composure.

"We both know it's Foster, and the reason I'm asking is that it helps me to take another step closer to finding your husband's killer."

"Was Joe killed because he knew about the affair?" she asked, her eyes widening.

"I think so, but *thinking so* isn't enough."

Chapter 29

"Harry," Meredith said as though he'd lost his mind, "you can't be seriously suggesting that Amos died because he knew about my affair."

As usual, they were sitting in Meredith's study. What was unusual was her appearance. Searching for a word to describe it, *wasted* popped up in Harry's mind.

"Not yet, but it's the only thing they had in common," Harry said. "Are you feeling ill?"

"Bad night," she said, "very little sleep."

"Have you had another letter you weren't going to tell me about?"

"Well, yes," she said, lifting a wrinkled rectangle of yellow paper by a corner out of the center desk drawer and dropping it on the desk between them.

Harry leaned over the desk to read it. " 'You next,' " he said. "Pasted message. How did it arrive?"

"Same as before. Raquel wanted to call the police, but I didn't let her."

"Where is she? The maid let me in and sent me up on my own."

"She left."

"Did she quit?"

"Yes, I was a little harsh in my refusal to let her make the call."

"Meredith, get her back here. You need her."

"How am I supposed to do that?"

"For starters, tell her you're sorry. You know what needs saying."

"No. She's the one who's got to apologize. She was extremely rude, and she can whistle for a reference."

"Meredith, I'm on the verge of becoming very rude," Harry said. "You can have that effect on people."

"Nonsense."

"Stop pretending you're not to blame and that you're not frightened by the threat. Only an idiot could behave the way you're behaving and not know it."

Meredith rose. "You're fired!"

"Good," Harry said. "I'm wasting my time with you."

He had his hand on the doorknob before she folded.

"Harry," she said. "I'm sorry. I unfire you. I'll call Raquel and grovel, humiliating myself, then give her a raise. Will that satisfy you?"

"There's no such word as *unfire,*" he said. "As for the rest, it's a beginning."

"Don't think this gives you any additional privileges," Meredith said, struggling to regain some ground.

"Since I didn't have any to begin with, I don't care," he told her.

As he was speaking he walked back toward the desk just as she was approaching him, looking even more haggard.

"What am I going to do, Harry?" she asked him, standing in her wrinkled blue dress, giving a good impression of a lost soul.

"First a question, then a suggestion," he said, stopping when she did.

"Okay."

"What do you want to do?"

"Make all this stop," she said in a voice that wrung Harry's heart because he thought it was the most sincere answer she had ever given him.

His first impulse was to embrace her, but he blocked it, to do what he was sure was the more important thing.

"I wish I could do that for you," he told her, "but the closest you can come now to doing it is to get out of Avola as quickly as you can and not tell anyone where you're going. Throw away your cell phone and buy a prepaid phone. When you get where you're going, call Jim Snyder, to tell him where you are, but don't call anyone else until he tells you it's okay."

"No, Harry," she said. "I'm not leaving. My staying here is all that's keeping you alive."

Before Harry could respond, Meredith lost what little color she had in her face, said, "Oh," and, swaying slightly, mumbled, "It's pretty early in the morning . . . for me," then crumpled as if something had stolen her bones. Harry caught her under the arms, breaking her fall, and eased her shoulders and head onto the rug. Her eyes were closed, her breathing was shallow, and her face was the color of chalk.

"I'm Dr. Lepson. Are you the husband?" the slim, red-haired doctor asked Harry as if she was addressing a felon. Then, without waiting for an answer, she said, even more accusingly, "You might have put in a little more time making sure she was taking care of herself. I'm assuming it is your child."

"Yes, no!" Harry said.

"Hopeless. She's three months along, and why in hell have you let her get this far without seeking medical care?" She paused, waiting. "How much longer are you going to stand there with your mouth open?"

"I'm sorry," Harry said, having learned over time and marriages that when in this situation with a woman, the safest thing to do is to apologize.

"You should be," she said, sounding slightly mollified. "Now,

I'm going to give her some medication. See that she takes it and get her signed up with an OB as soon as possible, and don't take no for an answer."

"Right," Harry said.

"Good, I know she's not easy, but pregnancy takes some women this way." She grasped his arm and gave it a slight squeeze. "I'm going to check her vitals a couple of times," she told him, sounding almost friendly, "and if they stay positive, I'll cut her loose. Good luck, sport. I think you're going to need it."

"Can I see her?" Harry asked.

"No, she's resting—that's something else she hasn't had enough of, and she's slightly anemic—you wait here," she said, already turning away. "A nurse will fetch you when it's time."

Harry dropped onto the folding chair like a stone.

"Whoa!" he said, wild-eyed, to the empty room.

The nurse appeared as promised and led Harry to where Meredith was sitting in a wheelchair, looking like a thunder-cloud, except that she, Harry, and the young volunteer pushing the chair got to the sidewalk without a lightning bolt striking anyone.

"We will not be discussing this," were her first words, discounting the icy thank you flung at the young man once she was out of the chair.

"Have a nice day," the young man said.

"Oh, thanks, same to you," Harry said just in time to put himself between the smiling innocent and Meredith, whose blue eyes at that moment looked as if they had been chipped from a glacier.

"After what I went through getting you to the hospital," Harry said once they were driving out of the hospital grounds, "you don't get to tell me, 'we will not be discussing this.' We damned well are going to discuss it, starting with why you haven't been seeing a doctor."

"Simple," Meredith said, her head supported by the seat and her eyes closed, as if from frailty or disgust with what the world was offering her to look at. "I'm outraged over this. Outraged!"

For the second *"outraged"* she sat forward and turned, as fully as her seat belt allowed, toward Harry and shouted, "This can't be happening to me!"

"Is Foster the father?" Harry asked.

He had promised himself he wouldn't ask that question, but needing to know overrode discretion. He didn't stop to ask why.

"Is there a new star in the east?" she snapped.

"I don't think so."

"Then the answer's yes. Oh, joy!"

"You *are* angry, aren't you?" he said.

"You think?" she asked in her most dangerous voice.

"Okay, let's try something else. Is it that you don't want a child?"

"No, I don't want a child—at least not now, and I'm not thrilled by the idea of having my life scarfed by this ridiculous pregnancy, just when I was . . . never mind."

"Did you find out why you fainted?" Harry asked, changing directions.

"Low blood pressure, anemia, stress, hormone flood, body shifting into pregnancy gear, and a wish to be anywhere else other than where I am," she said in a rapid-fire delivery. "The doctor was not happy with my addition to her diagnosis."

"What did she say?"

"That I should be thankful I could have a child and have the means and intelligence to raise it properly. I asked her if this was so great, why wasn't she pregnant. That's when she walked out, leaving me to the tender mercies of the nurses."

Having delivered herself of that summary of her hospital stay, Meredith lay her head back against the seat and said, "Thank you Harry, for being there," closed her eyes, and instantly fell asleep.

Harry found Tucker sitting in his rocker. The older man did not get up to greet Harry but shook hands with him from his chair.

"Anything wrong?" Harry asked.

"I've felt better, but that's not what's keeping me in this chair," Tucker said, sounding irritated.

It was the middle of the morning and Harry could only recall one or two occasions in all the years he'd known the old farmer that he'd not found him working at this time of day.

"What is?" Harry asked, trying not to sound concerned.

"The doctor. Turns out my old heart trouble has reared up again, and he's put me on stronger medication that keeps me sleeping half the time and sitting two-thirds of the rest. I'm cutting back a little on the work until this nuisance is settled down again."

"Call on me," Harry said. "What can I do to help?"

"You can get that pitcher of lemonade out of the icebox, fill two glasses, and bring them out here. Then you can sit down and tell me how the investigation's going."

"Strange new developments," Harry said once he had put the ancient wooden milk bottle crate that Tucker used for an end table between them and set the mugs on it. "This is not for the legion of people on your phone line, by the way."

"You're telling the bees," Tucker said, picking up his icy mug that was already sweating, "and if I fall asleep, wake me."

"All right, but there hasn't been another death," Harry responded. "First, Meredith is pregnant, and she's mad as a wet cat. She keeled over while we were talking in her office—arguing is more what we were doing. She had fired Raquel and shouldn't have. So I persuaded her, none too gently, to call her and apologize. She'd no sooner agreed than she fainted. Cutting this short, when the doctor in the ER finished examining her, she told me Meredith was, in addition to being anemic, dehydrated and short on sleep, three months pregnant. Then she began reaming me for not taking better care of my wife."

"Did you tell her you hadn't yet had the pleasure of that promotion?" Tucker asked and had a good laugh at Harry's expense.

"Based on available evidence," Harry said a bit sourly, "Prentice Foster has first dibs on that honor."

"The father."

"So Meredith told me with no show of enthusiasm," Harry said, "but I have the feeling she tells me what she wants to tell me and no more."

"Has the snake appeared in Eden?"

"Maybe, but she said a very strange thing. I had asked her again to leave Avola—she's received another threatening letter. Her response was to say she couldn't because her being here was all that was keeping me alive."

"How is she doing that?" Tucker asked, suddenly a lot more alert.

"I don't know," Harry replied. "I didn't ask. At the time it sounded silly, and her fainting took my mind off it."

"Is she given to making silly remarks?" Tucker asked.

"No."

"I didn't think so," Tucker said, giving Harry a look that made him even more uncomfortable than he already felt.

CHAPTER 30

"The lab says this most recent letter was almost certainly not put together by the same person who sent the first one," Jim said, leaning back in his chair and rubbing his head vigorously.

"The Captain thinks, and I agree, you should tell Winters," Hodges said.

"Mrs. Winters, Sergeant," Jim said, frowning.

"Mrs. Winters," Hodges said, smiling agreeably.

"Tell me why I should believe it," Harry said, feeling the ground under him shift uncomfortably. "Why would two people be sending her threats?"

"That's why the Captain was rubbing his head while he gave you the news," Hodges said. "It's enough to make the cat go off mice."

"Does it make any kind of sense to you, Harry?" Jim asked, apparently forgetting he had been asked a question.

"It might if there were two people and not one behind these killings."

"We know you lean toward O'Malley," Hodges said. "Who's the second doer?"

"My first choice would be Prentice Foster," Harry said, "and just sit down, Jim, and hear me out."

Jim remained on his feet for a moment, his eyes wide, his face red, and his mouth open to protest. Instead, he choked back the words and eased himself into his chair.

"I can't believe I'm hearing this," he said finally in obvious disbelief.

"I can," Hodges said. "Let's hear what you've got to say, Harry."

"The only reason I could ever see for killing Joe Purcell was that he was present at the meeting in which O'Malley raised hell for having been suckered into thinking Tillman was going to win the election," Harry said, then paused. "The problem with that explanation was that Purcell had nothing to do with Lansbury's very impractical joke, and the only reason he came to the meeting was that O'Malley demanded he be there."

"So?" Jim asked.

"He knew about the affair. I checked with his wife."

"Are you saying Foster is using O'Malley to kill off all the people who knew about the affair?" Jim asked.

"I don't know that, but it's a possibility," Harry answered.

"I'm due in Sheriff Fisher's office in a few minutes," Jim said. "Have you got anything but speculation to support your accusation?"

"No, Jim, nothing but a gut feeling, fed, possibly, by desperation."

"For a start, that's sometimes enough," Hodges said, looking helpful.

"Stay away from the senator," Jim warned, frowning at Harry and getting to his feet. "I'm in enough trouble with Sheriff Fisher as it is."

"Jim," Harry said, "it's past time your people scoured O'Malley. Everything you've got points to him."

"I'll take it up with Sheriff Fisher," Jim said, looking grim as he pushed files into his briefcase.

"Can you find out why the lab people think someone other than the first sender put together this second letter?" Harry asked the sergeant as soon as Jim left the office.

"I'll give it a shot," Hodges said, "but I may just get my ass kicked."

"Maybe you'll be lucky," Harry said, trying to be hopeful. "What's he done to have Fisher angry with him?"

"Somebody ratted him out to Fisher about the background checks he signed off on," Hodges said, sounding disgusted.

"Politics?" Harry asked.

"Promotions," Hodges said, looking as if he'd bitten into a bad apple. "By the way, I hear Tucker's ill. Is that so?"

"Yes, his heart is acting up again. How did you know?"

"I've got a great-aunt who's in her eighties, she has a bunch of other oldies she talks with on the phone. They keep track of one another. I think she and Tucker might have had something going years back. She always gets her shoulders back a little when she's talking about him."

Harry left the sheriff's department in search of something to feel good about. Well, he had stopped wincing every time he stooped and groaning when he rolled over in bed. Oh, yes, he could take the coffee down from the shelf where it lived without gasping.

Then he thought about Holly and all the cheer he had garnered from his efforts was blown in an instant. The best way to deal with that iceberg resting on his diaphragm was to call her, which he did.

"I thought a 'gator had gotten you," she said, competing with the pick-up's engine and the thumping and banging sounds that gave the impression she was in a slow-motion head-on collision.

"Where . . . ?"

"Riding my fence line," she said. "There's a lot of prairie dog mounds in the area, and while that's good news, it makes what I'm doing fairly uncomfortable."

"You've mentioned them before. I thought prairie dogs were almost wiped out where you are," Harry said.

"They were a few years ago, but the ranchers finally got it through their heads that having prairie dogs meant we had a chance of restoring the black-footed ferrets, which eat a lot of mice, which eat a lot of seeds that never grow into grass, that cows eat to grow. So do coyotes, but that's a work in progress. You see where I'm going."

Before Harry could speak, Holly said, "Shit!" and cursed loudly and colorfully for the next several seconds.

"Sorry," she finally said. "I was avoiding a rattler, which also eats mice, and drove into a hole that nearly shook out the windshield. Where was I?"

"Ferrets and prairie dogs were the key words."

"Right. So we're learning to be glad we have prairie dogs and are trying to get into the Northern Cheyenne Reservation experiment, aimed at restoring the black-footed ferret to our ranges."

"Do you realize how much becoming a rancher has changed you?" Harry asked with a mixture of pleasure and a bad feeling of being left behind.

"Adapt or die," she said. "Hold on, I'm stopping. I need both hands to drive this pick-up and all my attention to check on the fence, dodge the really bad holes, and scan for stray calves. Cows are really dumb."

"Women lose their kids at the mall all the time," Harry said, grinning at her complaints.

"Would you like to have any more kids, Harry?" she asked, sounding slightly pensive.

"I might if the right woman suggested it," he said. "What about you?"

"The referee is counting, Harry," she replied.

"Whose time is running out, yours or mine?"

"Both."

"I would be on Social Security before any new kid of mine finished college," Harry said, hoping to dodge the bullet.

"How is your investigation going?" she asked.

Had he made her angry, hurt her feelings?

"It would help if I could see you while we talked," he said. "I might not make so many errors, such as mentioning retirement while you have babies on your mind."

"Well, if you weren't so cheap, we could."

"I would consider having a child," he said. "Would you?"

"With me?"

"Yes."

"How interested are you in having that happen?"

"As things stand, it would have to be done by artificial insemination," he said.

"Not funny, Harry."

"No, it's not."

Harry came away from that conversation feeling they had hit a new low in their relationship. He was sure that in mentioning the referee counting, she was talking about the relationship being on the canvas and in danger of not getting up. *And whose fault is that?* he asked himself.

For the first time since she'd left Avola, Harry couldn't say hers with any conviction. That he couldn't was another thorn in his flesh. This one forced him to stop thinking about what he and Holly were going to do to solve their dilemma.

Their exchanges over babies, however, had put Meredith's pregnancy solidly back in Harry's mind, leading him to consider how it might affect the investigation. He had no doubt that word of the pregnancy would circulate quickly among the groups to which she belonged, and no amount of effort on her part could prevent it.

He thought it best to take the problem directly to her.

"Thank you, Harry, for getting my job back," Raquel told him, having come out onto the steps to meet him. "Meredith said you twisted her arm. I almost told her you did the same to me but decided it would be better if I didn't."

"Glad I could help. Has she told you she's pregnant?"

"No, but I had more or less guessed she was. I feel I should wait and let her tell me before talking about it."

"Excellent idea. I don't think she's come to terms with her condition yet and is going to need extra space until she does."

Once they were inside, Harry shifted the conversation to her and asked how she was feeling. "You're looking great," he added.

"Thank you and I really think I'm going to be able to do this. It's beginning to feel good. I'm feeling better every day."

She knocked on the study door and then opened it and announced his arrival. Meredith was not working at her desk. She was sitting in front of the window that looked over the lawns toward the Seminole River and the sea.

"Come in, Harry," she said. "Sit over here."

She did not turn to look at him, only glancing at him when he sat down and said, "How are you, Meredith?"

The question prompted no answer. Instead, she remained sunk in her brown study. Harry thought it best to let her engage with him when she was ready and occupied himself by taking in her blue sundress and white sandals and her hair, caught back in the gold ring she favored. He took comfort from thinking she looked like her usual self.

"For a very long time, I've believed I was in charge of my life," she said, breaking her brooding silence. "I inherited wealth, and I have devoted time and energy to making sure it was properly managed and benefitted others as well as myself."

She fell silent again.

"I'm waiting for a 'but,' " Harry said quietly. "Is there one floating around somewhere?"

"How do you make sense of your life, Harry?" she asked, looking at him squarely for the first time. She appeared to be studying his face as though she'd never seen it before.

"I'm not sure I do," he replied. "What do you mean by *sense*?"

"Whatever allows you to get up in the morning with a modicum of confidence that you'll know who you are and what you're going to find in your day."

"I'm really not sure I can do what you're asking, so help me out here. What is causing you not to have that assurance?"

"Jesus, Harry!" she said. "I'm pregnant. How complicated is that?"

"Then being pregnant has made everything else in your life incomprehensible?"

"It's as though being pregnant has nudged everything else into another dimension and made it strange and stripped it of meaning."

"Are you frightened?"

"Probably. I don't really know."

"Are you angry?"

"Furious."

"Good. Hang onto it," he said. "Don't try to pretend you're not. If you're angry, embrace it. Study it. Find out all you can about it."

"Harry, I know you want to make me feel better, but cut out the bullshit."

"Try this, then," he said. "If you let yourself remain angry, sooner or later you'll have to find out who or what is making you angry."

"Idiot!" she said, raising her voice. "I'm angry because I'm knocked up. What the hell do you think I'm mad about?"

"Is it possible for you to do anything about your condition or has becoming pregnant robbed you of your decision-making capacities?"

She stared hard at him for a long moment, then said, "Are you suggesting I get an abortion?"

"No."

"It sounded that way to me."

"And because you thought that was what I suggested, you're angry with me. What's wrong with this picture?"

"All right! Jesus! I'm sorry! So I'm angry with myself."

"I forgive you for being angry with yourself. No doubt Jesus forgives you, but you'll probably have to take it on faith. Forging ahead: how long are you going to kick yourself around before you forgive yourself?"

She glared at him and said, "Not right away."

"Next question: when are you going to tell Foster?"

"At the conversion of the Jews."

"Good timing. Is this to reward or punish him?"

"He's got a wife and three kids, the oldest enters college in the fall."

"Speaking hypothetically, if you were to tell him, would he be pleased or not so?"

" 'Not so,' isn't sufficiently negative."

"Would killing you be negative enough?"

That brought her onto her feet. "That's not funny, Harry, and I don't like it."

"No," Harry said calmly, standing up to face her. "Neither do I. My name's on that list too."

"What do you mean?"

"Neither you nor I nor Joe Purcell had anything to do with Kevin O'Malley's being tricked into losing money on the senate race, but like the men who have been killed, including Purcell, they knew and we know about Foster's affair with you."

"I don't believe it. It's preposterous."

"Yes it is, but so is a camel."

"Harry, you must be mistaken," she insisted. "Prentice wasn't in love with me."

"I can't believe it. It would be very easy to love you. Why did you end it? I never asked."

Her shoulders sagged.

"I didn't, Harry. He did."

Chapter 31

What if she's right? Harry asked himself as he walked along the white sand road that ran from the humpbacked bridge to the northeast end of the Hammock. *What if Foster has nothing to do with the killings?*

He had stayed with Meredith for a while after she told him that Foster had ended their affair. He said nothing more about Foster's being involved in the killings but led her gradually onto safer ground by asking her where she would most like to go if she decided to leave Avola for a time. Once launched on the subject of travels, she revealed that she had never been to the Orient and had wanted to visit Vietnam ever since seeing two films, *The Lover* and *The Scent of Green Papaya.*

"I didn't guess you were a romantic," Harry said, hoping to make her laugh.

"I'm not sure *The Lover* is a romantic film," she said, managing a smile. "Have you seen it?"

"Both of them," Harry said. "I want to say two views of a world approaching a catastrophe."

"Yes, but what fine work, and it's true. I would like to believe it's the capacity to love that redeems us."

"But you don't?" Harry asked.

"Perhaps I do, but only if we have the courage to love and embrace the consequences."

"They can be dire," he replied.

"Am I hearing experience or ideology talking?"

"Experience."

"Would you do it over again?"

"Absolutely," Harry said with a firmness that startled him, "but I'd do it differently, and right now I'd probably be living in the Guatemalan mountains in a shack with a tin roof."

"I'm impressed," Meredith said and then laughed. "Then you'd agree the real tragedy was your turning down the offer of love?"

"Yes," he said, and for an instant the woman he was remembering was with him again and then vanished.

Standing on the edge of the road, staring down into the black water of Puc Puggy Creek, speckled with gold flecks of sunlight filtering through the leaves and dancing on the swirling surface, a sight that he found mesmerizing, Harry recalled the scene and what each of them had said, especially Meredith's assertion that love redeemed us only if we accepted its consequences and that denying love from fear of them was the greater tragedy.

"She might have said, 'the greater sin,' " Harry told the quietly murmuring stream, "because I think that is really what she meant."

He stood for a few more minutes, staring at the water, then turned away, feeling suddenly depressed and inexplicably dissatisfied with himself. The shadows were lengthening, and that special light of late afternoon was moving into the Hammock, bringing with it the lessening of the breeze, a softening of the bird calls, and the gradual decline in volume of the multitudinous fiddlers in the canopy.

Freed from his reverie, Harry glanced at his watch, gave the creek a final look, and strode away toward Tucker's farm, having found no satisfactory answer to his question of what he would do if he was wrong about Foster.

★ ★ ★ ★ ★

Harry had found Tucker pushing his wheelbarrow, loaded with mail-order trough feeders and bucket waterers. He was less than halfway between the barn and the bantam house and was already short of breath and making slow progress. Oh, Brother! and Sanchez were closely flanking him as if showing concern about what was happening.

"Let me take that," Harry said, hurrying forward. "Didn't the doctor say something about your taking it easy?"

"Well," Tucker said, dropping the wheelbarrow handles and pulling a blue bandanna from a back pocket of his overalls and mopping his face, which was dripping with sweat, "I thought this was light work." He sounded thoroughly disgusted with himself.

"Not if you've got a wonky heart," Harry said. "Let's get you out of this sun."

"Wheel this to the bantam house, then," Tucker said, still breathing heavily. "You can unload it while I do the heavy looking-on. Then we can sit down beside the citrus orchard."

They were closer to the orchard than the house, and Harry grasped the wheelbarrow's handles and got them underway.

"What brings you out here?" Tucker asked. "I hope you're not checking on me."

They were sitting on the split-log seat. Tucker was leaning back, his hat resting on one knee, and breathing without effort.

"No," Harry said, "I want to talk with you about some things and have the benefit of your input."

"When you use words like *input,*" Tucker said, regarding Harry closely, "I know you're only half thinking about what you're saying."

"All right, I'm thinking about you, out here alone, pushing a wheelbarrow in the heat of the day when you've been told to take care of yourself."

"I know you're being thoughtful, Harry, and I appreciate it," Tucker said quietly, "but I don't want you or anyone else worrying about me."

"You can't tell people not to worry when they find out you're not following your doctor's orders," Harry protested. "How smart is that?"

"From your point of view, not very," Tucker said calmly, "but from mine, entirely." He put his hat on and continued, sounding a little more forceful, "If you have the time, Harry, to listen, I'll tell you why."

Harry sensed that Tucker was doing more than just being stubborn and told him to go ahead.

"Unless a tree falls on me," he began, sounding pleased, "it will probably be my heart that carries me off by deciding to stop beating. No one can tell me when it will happen. It may be a day or three years. I've given it a lot of thought and decided that I have to make plans, although for the present I'm just going to go along as I have all these years, doing as many of the things as my strength will allow."

"But you were pushing a loaded wheelbarrow," Harry said, unable to just listen and not wanting to think of Tucker dropping dead hoeing his corn or tying up his tomato plants.

"If you hadn't come along, Harry," Tucker said, "I would have taken about three more steps and quit, and pushed it the rest of the way early tomorrow morning while it was cooler. My body will tell me what I can do. I'm not being foolish, just realistic."

"I can do those things you can't do, Tucker," Harry said, feeling suddenly wretched. "I understand what you're saying, but just promise me you'll be sensible and call on me whenever there's something you need help with."

"All right, but I have more to say," Tucker continued, fanning himself slowly with his hat. "I've known for some time, Harry, that it was unlikely I would live much beyond the place in time where I am now."

"Has the doctor told you what to expect?" Harry asked, wanting to believe Tucker was exaggerating the seriousness of the problem.

"Yes, I will gradually grow weaker as my heart has increasing difficulty in performing its task."

Tucker paused and appeared to be staring at something in the orchard. Harry followed his gaze but saw only the trees and the sunlight flickering in the leaves as the Gulf wind rustled them and set the branches swaying.

"And?" Harry said when his patience ran out. He really wanted to find out where Tucker was going with his explanation, if that's what it was.

"Yes, you know," Tucker said quietly, "I thought for a moment I'd seen Henrietta Yellen walking under the lemon trees, wearing a long dress and swinging a straw sunhat in her hand. I first saw her walking in an orchard. She was wearing a yellow gingham dress, caught in at the waist, and her long auburn hair was falling in waves down her back."

Tucker paused, laughed, and said, "Lord, she took my breath away and a good-sized piece of my heart with it. I'm not sure I ever did get it all back."

"Is there any chance of her being related to Frank Hodges?"

"Odd you should ask that. Yes, if I'm not mistaken, Henrietta was Frank's grandmother's sister. That would be on his mother's side of the family."

"What about you and Henrietta Yellen?" Harry asked, strangely pleased by what he'd just heard.

"We courted a while. Then I went away, and when I came back, she'd married one of the Ridley boys."

"Maybe you should have stayed and married her," Harry said.

"Should have, would have, could have," Tucker said, "don't count. *Did* is what matters."

"Okay," Harry said, amused, "I know when I've had my chain pulled. Finish what you started to tell me."

"I could have sworn I saw her walking there, swinging that hat . . . Oh well. Where was I?"

"Your heart was growing weaker."

"Right, it is. I'll make this brief. I've written out my advance medical directive, my will is with my lawyer, I have arranged for Oh, Brother! and Sanchez to go to a farm, and this place will be turned back to the state. Their plan is to open it to the public as a state historical farm site. Your place will either be torn down and trucked away or—and this is what I argued for—you will be allowed to stay where you are until you're done with it."

"Well," Harry said with a sigh, "I don't have enough money in it to matter. Looks like you've pretty well wrapped things up."

"That was my plan," Tucker said. "Now, Harry, there's one more thing to say and I'll be done. I don't want you worrying about me or coming over here trying to help me because when I can no longer maintain the place, I'm going into Gulf Shore, an assisted-living community in North Avola. I'm signed up and my entrance fee is paid. If I die first, it will be refunded, which I find comforting."

"Are you serious about anything?" Harry asked, but forced a smile.

"Not very, not anymore."

Harry and Frank Hodges were sitting alone in Jim's office, Jim having been called away to a county board of directors meeting.

"There goes his morning," Hodges had remarked when Jim had left. "He'll come back frothing at the mouth and ready to raise hell. I don't plan to be here. But what say we have coffee and some crullers, to give the coffee something to do? I saw Lieutenant Orwell bringing in a bag of supplies this morning. I'm still on her short list for extermination. So things can't get any worse."

Several minutes passed before Hodges hurried back in, carrying a battered aluminum tray freighted with coffee mugs and a paper plate stacked with crullers.

"Help yourself," he said. "How's Tucker getting along?"

Harry found he wanted to tell someone about Tucker and thought he would not find a better listener than Hodges. Having defied his better angel, he settled back in his chair with a mug in one hand and a fat, sugared cruller in the other and unburdened himself.

"Looks like you've been cut loose, Harry," Hodges said quietly, a sure sign he was feeling something strongly. "The man's got his mind made up. What do you think of it?"

"About being cut loose? I don't think I like it. It's bad enough that he's ill. To find out he's made his plans for leaving the farm has shaken me up. By the way, does the name Henrietta Yellen mean anything to you?"

"Lord, yes," Hodges said, smiling. "She was my grandmother's sister on my mother's side, said to be a beauty in her day."

"Did you know that she and Tucker 'courted' for a while?"

Hodges lost his smile.

"Yes, my mother knew about it. Sad story. Great Aunt Henrietta married Jack Ridley. It was a bad mistake. She and Ridley moved to North Carolina and made one another miserable for a while, and then she died. I don't know what happened to Ridley."

"Tucker didn't mention that," Harry said thoughtfully. "He said his going away broke their tie. I gather from what he said that he's never altogether gotten over her. I wonder why he told me about her? It's a departure for him."

"He might have wanted to tell you something by telling you the story."

"Possibly."

"Do you think the state will let you stay where you are if Tucker leaves?" Hodges asked, sounding concerned.

"Possibly. I'm still on their payroll, but the real question is whether or not I'd want to."

"I can see that. You'd soon have a lot more company, and the dust from that sand road . . . well, you know how that would be."

"I suppose they'd surface it."

"Sounds right. Where would you go?"

"It wasn't my plan to go anywhere," Harry said, experiencing a flash of anger mixed with some other emotion he quickly suppressed, then added with a confidence in his voice he did not feel, "Well, Tucker's had these sessions with his heart before. I'm guessing he'll recover."

Hodges had been watching Harry with a slight frown wrinkling his forehead, and he said, sounding doubtful, "It won't do any harm to hope."

Chapter 32

Having lost most of a night's sleep and wasted half a day worrying himself over Tucker's health and fighting off what had felt in the dawn hours like a major assault on his sense of security, Harry decided to go back to work. He'd begin with another talk with Prentice Foster, and to hell with Sheriff Fisher and Jim as well.

"I'm really busy, Brock," Foster said for openers, remaining standing behind his desk. "This will have to be brief."

"I'll try to be," Harry said. "You're about to be up to your ears in this investigation, and lying to me has only made the situation worse."

"Are you threatening me?" Foster demanded, his jaw jutting.

"Certainly not, I'm trying to get your attention. You and I both know the men who have been killed all shared the same information. Do you want to say what it is, or shall I?"

"I've got no idea what you're talking about," Foster said, making an effort to sound outraged.

"As far as I know, only you and I, Kevin O'Malley, Meredith Winters, and Rycroft Tillman are in possession of it," Harry countered, deliberately lying and ignoring the bluster. "Meredith has received another threat on her life, and someone tried to kill me. What conclusions would you draw from that?"

"How does this have anything to do with me?" Foster asked, speaking much more quietly.

"All right. You and Meredith Winters had an affair that you

terminated shortly before Lansbury died. And shortly after that, all the people who knew about the affair began dying."

"Did Meredith tell you?" Foster asked, turning pale.

"No. Jonas Amsel told me just before he died. I saw his car blow up."

"If this information reaches the media, my political career may survive, but my marriage will not," Foster said. "Is it money you want?"

"I have no intention of blackmailing you or revealing anything I know about you to the media. What I do want is cooperation from you in finding the killer. Is it Kevin O'Malley?"

Either relief or accumulated stress buckled Foster's knees, and he sat down hard in his chair.

"I have no idea," he said. "Why would he kill all these people over a bet gone wrong?"

"You're in a better position than I am to answer that question."

"Why?"

"Because you're the one who's actually benefitting from their deaths."

Foster had begun to recover from whatever the shock was that took him off his feet and had regained some of his color, but Harry's answer took it away again.

"Lord God, Brock," he began in a shaky voice, "you can't possibly think . . ."

"That you're responsible for the deaths of five people with two more under threat? I think I can make the case. Want to hear it?"

"I'll listen."

"In a nutshell, you allowed Lansbury to circulate the charge that Tillman had been screwing a girl under the legal age of consent. That indicates you were willing to inflict on Tillman whatever damage it took to win the election. You're on record as saying your next stop is the U.S. Senate. Word of your affair coming out now, especially if it results in a divorce, would shatter your 'sound family man' image and delay for a long time any hope of winning a conservative primary in this state. You thought you had scotched the snake when you killed Lansbury. Then you found out from O'Malley that he knew about the affair and that Lansbury had told some other people before he died."

"Hold on," Foster said, jumping to his feet. "Lansbury launched that lie about Tillman without my consent. I had two choices: refuse to acknowledge it or fire Lansbury and whoever else acted with him. That would have wrecked my campaign and lost me the election. I chose to win, but that doesn't make me a murderer."

"Why did you dump Winters?"

"I didn't 'dump' her. I had reached the place where I could no longer go on living a double life."

At least for the moment, Harry thought Foster might be telling him the truth. His hesitation gave Foster an opening. "And where is the evidence that I've had anything to do with the murders?"

"I think Kevin O'Malley has it," Harry said.

"If Sheriff Robert D. Fisher tries to have my license revoked," Harry told Jim, "I will go to Tallahassee and tell the Attorney General all the ways in which Fisher and the A.A.G. have acted to block a proper investigation of the murder of six Florida citizens in the employ of State Senator Prentice Foster. I wouldn't be surprised if they both went down."

"Lord, Harry!" Jim protested "Even if you won such a pissing contest, you'd never work in this state again. No police or sheriff's departments would ever give you the time of day."

The two men were standing in front of Jim's desk, and Jim

had just finished describing Fisher's response to the news that Harry had accused Foster of murder.

"Oh," Harry said, "I forgot to say that I will also give my report to *The Banner* and whichever TV stations want an interview. I think they'd particularly like to hear what Jonas Amsel told me."

Jim sat down on the front of his desk, bringing his line of sight more on a level with Harry's.

"You really mean this don't you, Harry?" he said quietly.

"You have gotten the message, Jim. Please share what I've said with Sheriff Fisher."

"I will," Jim said to Harry as he was leaving. Harry missed the wide grin spreading across the captain's face.

From Jim's office, Harry drove to Meredith's place. He was in an unfamiliar frame of mind and did not know quite what to make of it. It was, he reflected, what burning your bridges might feel like. So why would he want to burn his bridges? So that nothing could be sneaking up behind him, he decided. Somewhat cheered by that thought, he prepared himself—at least tried to prepare himself—for his encounter with Meredith.

"You did what?" she shouted, springing out of her desk chair like a jack-in-the-box.

"You heard me," he said, pretending she wasn't striding around the desk toward him like a Celtic wife with a sword in her hand, whose husband he had just killed.

"Did you tell him I'm pregnant?" she demanded, coming to a stop in front of him, eyes burning into his.

"No," Harry said. His newly acquired recklessness got out of hand, and he said, "When you're angry, you're really hot." She was wearing the blue sundress that thoroughly wakened the Old Adam in Harry.

"Cut out the crap," she said angrily, then paused, looked even harder at him and said, "You really think so?"

"I do. That blue dress really rattles my rafters."

"What if I took it off?"

"Please don't. My heart is not strong enough to cope with that."

"Come on," she said, grasping his arm and sliding hers under it, "we're going to sit down, and you're going tell me every last thing you two said."

Meredith listened very carefully, and when he was done, she said, "Harry, you are either brilliant or stark, raving mad. Which is it?"

"I think we're going to find out very soon."

"Prentice is going to have a talk with Kevin O'Malley," she said, looking thoughtful.

"I think that's a certainty."

"Then what's going to happen?" Meredith asked.

"If I'm right, nothing pleasant."

"If you're right about Prentice, you are in terrible danger," she told him.

"So are you. I want you to leave Avola this afternoon, and let me handle this."

"Prentice will not kill me. Neither will O'Malley," Meredith said confidently. "Prentice because he knows I don't want the affair broadcast any more than he does, O'Malley because he knows about the affair and that I stiffed Amos by sleeping with Prentice, which puts me on his side."

"The only way Foster can be safe," Harry insisted, "is with both of us dead. It's the same with O'Malley. He knows I put it all together and will keep pushing until the sheriff's department does something besides sit on their hands. Meredith, despite what you've said, if I'm right, you are in great danger."

She only smiled at him and said, "How about I take you to lunch?"

★ ★ ★ ★ ★

Harry had not persuaded Meredith to leave the city, but he called Hodges and told him enough of his exchange with Foster to convince him that Meredith was probably at heightened risk. Harry did this without any mention of Meredith's being pregnant or his having accused Foster of being implicated in the murders.

"I'll take care of it," Hodges said, and Harry knew he would.

For himself, on going to bed, he did nothing more than put his twelve-gauge shotgun and his 9mm CZ 75 handgun beside the bed in easy reach. The two weapons usually lived at night in their metal lock-away. Much of Harry's peace of mind came from his certainty that anyone driving onto the Hammock would hit the loose plank, which he had deliberately left unsecured, and its double clatter would tell him he had company.

Early in the evening, he had talked a second time with Hodges and was satisfied that Meredith's armed night shift would be watching very carefully. Then he called Holly and talked briefly with her, but she was driving a hundred miles for a cattleman's meeting following dinner. Their talk was brief but long enough to run into their wall, ending the conversation.

He went to bed far more concerned about Holly's intransigence over living in Montana, carefully avoiding the obvious parallel with his own stubbornness, than about the possibility that someone might be coming to try to kill him. Experience told him that he would hear nothing in the night but the swamp chorus and the occasional hooting of an owl.

He was awakened by the slam of the plank about two-fifteen. He slid out of bed, pulled on his black T-shirt and warm-up pants and running shoes, then strapped on his shoulder holster, holding the CZ. He picked up the shotgun and shoulder bag of shells and silently slipped out the back door of the house.

He could not hear the sound of an approaching vehicle, and

concluded that whoever was coming had abandoned it as soon as he heard the warning clatter and was continuing on foot. The sky was clear, and the quarter moon cast enough light to make anyone approaching through the open spaces on the road and the front of the house easily visible.

As always in these situations, Harry grew calmer and clearer-headed as the danger increased. Now, he stood between the house and the barn in the deep shadow of a big oak, looking out toward the white sand road as if he was staring at a moonlit stage.

To his surprise, he heard a car motor rev into life, and in the next moment the slam of the loose plank as the rear wheels went over it. Then, before the car could have gone more than fifty yards, the engine died and a car door slammed. Harry's jaw didn't drop, but he felt as though it should. He found himself almost feeling sorry for the idiot who was trying to kill him.

He had drawn the CZ then put it away and slipped the safety off the pump gun. If, he thought, it came to shooting somebody—and it looked as if it would—he might as well make a clean job of it. At the distance between him and the road, a charge of buckshot would settle things quickly if not cleanly. He sighed mentally. He did not like killing people, but unlike most people, he could.

He had raised the gun to his shoulder and had only to swing up the barrel, aim, and pull the trigger. No sooner had he readied himself than he saw the beam of what appeared to be a flashlight probing here and there on the narrow road as if the person holding the light had lost something and was looking for it.

"What in the world?" Harry whispered, thoroughly puzzled.

Then the person, wearing what looked like a warm-up outfit with its hood up and the long visor of a fisherman's cap shading his face, walking very slowly and apparently staring at the road, moved into the clearing. Harry raised the gun, hesitated, then lowered it, fascinated by what he was seeing. The figure turned the light on the sparse grass of the lawn and began moving slowly toward the house. Whoever it was gave almost all his attention to the ground in front of him and wasn't looking at the house at all.

Halfway across the lawn the person stopped and pointed the light at the house.

Harry moved around the oak, putting its trunk between him and the intruder. He lifted the barrel, pointed it at the person, and said, "Are you armed?"

"Yes, I am!" the person shouted.

"Oh, for Christ's sake," Harry said, pulling his head and shoulders behind the tree, just as whoever it was on the lawn dropped the flashlight and fired four rounds, three of which chunked into the tree. The fourth slapped into the side of the barn.

"Not bad," Harry called. "Now stop shooting, Meredith, before you hit one of my owls."

Chapter 33

"What were you doing with the flashlight?" Harry asked from the sideboard beside the sink where he was making coffee.

"I didn't want to step on a snake," she said defiantly.

She had shed her warm-ups and was sitting at the table, wearing a green and white striped tank top and a pair of green shorts. She was still wearing her fisherman's cap with the extended bill that made Harry grin every time he looked at her.

"That was probably smart," he told her, switching on the coffeemaker. "Now and then one of the Burmese pythons crawls onto the road because it stays warm from the sun."

"Are they poisonous?"

"No, but they're big."

"How big?"

"Anything up to seventeen feet, possibly longer."

"Oh, God," she said, looking terrified. "What if I had stepped on one?"

"I suppose you could have mistaken it for a log. But that's not likely."

Harry sat down beside her while she told him why it was important for him not to live in a place that seventeen-foot snakes called home. He lifted off her cap, allowing her hair to tumble in its heavy waves onto her shoulders.

"Did you really come out here to protect me?" he asked, studying her as he might stare at a beautiful painting.

"It's my fault you're in danger," she said, "and I decided I couldn't leave you out here alone."

"At two a.m.?" he asked.

"I couldn't sleep."

"I'm sorry you couldn't sleep, but I'm glad it was you who woke me up and shot one of my trees and my barn, which, I point out, had done nothing to offend you."

He succeeded in making her laugh, which erased all the worry lines in her face and raised his spirits, still buoyed by the adrenaline that their encounter had generated.

"Did you mean it, Harry, when you said I would be easy to fall in love with?"

"Yes, I did, do you doubt it?"

"Amos saw me as a meal ticket," she told him, "and Prentice . . . I'm not sure why he left me."

The coffeemaker announced that its work was done, but neither Harry nor Meredith seemed to notice.

"You're a beautiful, strong-willed woman, intelligent, hard-working, with a fine sense of humor," Harry assured her. "You've just had bad luck with a couple of men, who seem not to have known how lucky they were."

"Harry," she said, "get up."

"The coffee," he said, thinking he had made a mistake in criticizing her men.

"No," she said, standing up with him.

When he turned toward her, about to apologize, she lifted her arms and caught him around the neck, then kissed him, pressing herself against him as soon as their lips touched.

Perhaps it was the hour. Perhaps it was the pressure of her body against his. Perhaps it was the remains of the adrenaline, bubbling through his system, but it *was* because it was something he desperately wanted to do, and he wrapped her in his arms, tightened them around her, and gave himself completely to her and the moment.

"Believe me," she gasped when they surfaced for air, "now is the time, Harry."

"Right," he said, and with that he caught her up in his arms and carried her to the foot of the stairs and put her feet down. "Run," he whispered in her ear, having first licked it.

There was a brief scrimmage at the top of the stairs because she didn't know which way to turn, resolved when he swept her up again, briefly got stuck in the bedroom door, broke free and tossed her onto the bed. There was then a race to see who could get out of their clothes first. She won, but proved she wasn't selfish by peeling him out of his shorts and socks. Then, throwing her legs around his waist, she grasped his arms and rolled him onto the bed, coming to rest astride him.

From there, things progressed rapidly, getting them very quickly to where they wanted to be and kept on being where they wanted to be, as their cries and groans, interspersed with bursts of laughter, attested. With time-outs for rest and recuperation, this sort of shameless behavior went on until the sun peeked in the bedroom windows, ending their revels and soothing them into sleep.

Later that morning with bright, shining faces, Harry and Meredith left the house, talking and laughing as they crossed the lawn on the way to Meredith's car. They had stepped onto the white sand road and stopped to allow a gopher tortoise time to reach the creek bank without being hurried when the stillness of the morning was split by the flat slam of a high-powered rifle, and Harry was knocked sprawling as if a huge fist had struck him.

"I saw nothing, no one," Meredith insisted when she was questioned an hour later by Millard Jones in a requisitioned office in the Avola Community Hospital. "I think I heard a car drive away," she added, "but I was trying to stop the bleeding and get Harry to wake up, and dial 911—I couldn't . . ."

Then the tears came. It was questionable whether or not she should have been questioned at all just then, spattered and splotched as she was with Harry's blood and deep in shock, but as Hodges, the first officer from the sheriff's department to reach her, said—sitting in the road with her while two highway patrolmen were working on Harry, trying to staunch the bleeding and keep him alive until the EMS team reached him—"I know you're hurting bad, but you want to find whoever did this, so tell me all you can remember."

He didn't say the more she rested her mind from the sight of Harry being knocked off his feet, spraying blood as he fell, the better it would be for her. But Hodges sat in the road holding her, talking softly, keeping her talking as much as he could, shielding her from sight of the white-faced, blood-soaked Harry and the sound of his labored breathing. Later, he told Jim that he thought he'd never find a way to make her stop saying, over and over, "It's all my fault. I've killed him."

The ambulance team arrived and did their work with speed and efficiency, stabilized Harry, turned the collapsible gurney into a stretcher, carried him past Meredith's car, and secured him in the ambulance. Meredith insisted on riding in the ambulance with him, and Hodges seconded her demand because, as he said and the troopers confirmed, she was in no condition to drive a car.

The bullet nicked Harry's heart and passed through a lung, doing a lot of damage in its journey through his body. He had nearly bled out by the time the medics reached him, and the damage to his heart was serious enough to send him into cardiac arrest shortly after he reached the hospital. Once that was controlled, the ensuing surgery went well, and when it was finally over the heart was no longer bleeding and was beating strongly.

Meredith had stayed as close to Harry as the medics and the hospital staff would allow, and only when a shaken Raquel located her, still blood-spattered and trembling with cold, was Meredith persuaded to go home at least long enough to shower and change her clothes.

Several hours later, when Harry opened his eyes and knew what he was looking at, he remembered nothing after stepping onto the sand road. At first he had no idea why he was in the hospital or why Meredith had buried her face in the pillow beside his head and was weeping and repeating in a gasping, muffled voice that it was all her fault.

He tried to speak but managed only a croak. Two nurses finally lifted Meredith off the bed, plunked her none too gently in the chair, and set about doing what they had to do when a patient regains consciousness after surgery. Having stuffed a straw into his mouth and told him to drink from a plastic glass, the smiley nurse asked him his name and a few other questions he managed to answer a bit hesitantly. They conducted their examination cheerfully and briskly, and by the time they were finished, he was deeply asleep again. A moment after that, Millard Jones, Hodges, and Jim filed into the room.

"Mrs. Winters," Jones said. "We'll try not to tire the patient, but it's essential we talk with him. If you will please wait outside, we will talk with you when we're finished with Mr. Brock."

"Well, if you're not a sight for sore eyes," Hodges said to Harry loudly, a broad grin spreading across his face. "Whoops! He's gone again."

At that, Meredith, who had just gotten up to leave, turned on the three men and shouted, "Are you out of your fucking minds! Let him sleep!"

Of course, Harry stopped sleeping.

"Meredith," he said in a creaky voice, "it's okay. I'm fine."

"It's all my fault, Harry. All my fault," she cried.

Jones, speaking to her in a quiet voice, managed to lead her out of the room.

"Has any of the staff examined her?" Jim asked the young nurse who had run into the room, probably in response to Meredith's outburst.

"I don't know," she said, looking nonplussed.

"She needs attention," Hodges said sternly.

"I'll tell someone," she said and flounced out.

"I wouldn't count on it," Hodges said.

"That's supposed to be done by the doctor," Jim said.

"What's the doctor supposed to do?" a white-coated man, followed by two young men and a young woman, asked as they filed into the room. "I'm Dr. Cribbs. Who are you? Is my patient a felon?"

"Depends on who you ask," Hodges replied, unfazed by the stethoscope and the white coat, eliciting a snicker from one of the young men and a dark scowl from Cribbs.

"Captain James Snyder, Sheriff's Department," Jim said, stepping forward quickly to shake Cribbs's hand before Hodges could say anything more. "This is Lieutenant Millard Jones, and this is Sergeant Frank Hodges. No, Harry is certainly not a felon. A great support to all of us would be more like it. Have you or one of your colleagues had a word yet with Mrs. Winters, who's sitting out there in the hall? She's had a terrible experience. Now that I think of it, she's on your board of directors, if I'm not mistaken."

"Phelps," Cribbs said, "get out there. Sit down and very gently find out how she's feeling. Wait, did she witness . . . ?" He tilted his head toward the bed.

"Yes," Jim said.

"Come with me," Cribbs said and walked Phelps out of the room, talking earnestly and quietly as they went.

"How long you two been working here?" Hodges asked the

two young people remaining.

"Eight months," the young woman said.

"We're doing our internships," the young man said.

"You lost anybody yet?" Hodges asked.

"No," they answered together.

Fortunately, Cribbs came hurrying back, his face flushed. "Captain," he said, followed closely by Phelps, both puffing a little, "thank you for alerting me to Mrs. Winters's presence. She's in good hands. Now Celia, what are we looking at here?"

"Do you have to be on the board of directors before anyone pays any attention to you in this place?" Hodges asked in his medium-loud voice. "You and your interns walked right past her coming in here, and nobody did squat for her while she sat in here splashed with blood and in shock as anyone with half a brain could have seen."

"Sergeant . . ." Jim said, trying to step between Hodges and Cribbs, who looked as if he'd just bitten into a horse bun.

The interns were crowded together, their faces white as though they were witnessing a sacrilege unfolding.

"No, no, Captain," Cribbs managed to blurt out. "It's all right. The sergeant has a right to be angry. Things go wrong. Mistakes are made . . ."

"That would sound better," Hodges said, interrupting, "if you said, 'I make mistakes. My nurses make mistakes.' That way it would sound as if you might intend to do something about these mistakes."

This time Jim did step between the two men.

"Dr. Cribbs," he said, "Sergeant Hodges was the first officer to reach the scene of the shooting. He found Mrs. Winters with a finger stuck in the bullet hole in Harry's chest, keeping him from bleeding out, and there was a larger hole in his back to cope with. Between them, they kept him alive until the medics took over. Since then, he's been here."

"I have the picture, Captain," Cribbs said quietly and because he couldn't look over Hodges, he looked around him. "Sergeant," he said, more affirmatively, "I'm sorry Mrs. Winters went unattended, neglected, and I'm as much to blame as anyone."

At that point he turned to his three interns and said, "Absolute focus saves lives, but that's no excuse for losing peripheral focus. Call it context if you wish. Nothing happens outside its context. I and several others forgot that."

"I take it somebody shot me," Harry said suddenly. "Have I got that right?"

"You have, Harry, and it damned near killed you," Hodges said.

"Celia," Cribbs said in a chastened voice, "tell me where we are and what we do."

When the room cleared and Harry had slept again, he woke to find Meredith sitting beside the bed, her hair washed and brushed, wearing the orange sundress and a white cotton sweater over her shoulders, staring at the opposite wall, lost in thought.

"Hi," he said, making her jump.

"Oh!" she said, breaking into a smile. "Hi, how are you feeling?"

"I've felt better. What about you?"

"I think I'm higher than a kite," she said, still looking dreamy. "A while back, somebody gave me a shot and a couple of pills. I've been drifting in lotus land ever since."

"Good," Harry said. "I think you look very nice, but you keep going in and out of focus. You're wearing the orange sundress. I like that one the best but they all look fine. Thank you for saving my life. I'm sorry, but I don't remember any of that. I must have frightened you. Who did it?"

She said, "I don't know," but he was gone again.

"He's heavily sedated," Andrea, his dark-haired nurse, told her. "He probably won't remember much of this part of his recovery. You could drop in and out for a couple of days. I really think it would be better for you if you did."

"I'm staying," Meredith said defiantly.

Andrea sat down beside Meredith and took her hand. "Look, hon," she said, "you love him, right?"

It took Meredith a moment to unwrap that, but in the end she said, "Yes."

"Then do him a favor. He's not going to get up and walk away from this in a hurry, and if you're going to be looking after him, you'd better start getting in shape. You following me?"

"Only if I know where you're leading me," she said, suddenly feeling very affectionate toward Andrea.

"Okay, you're high. I get it," Andrea said, "but try to listen. For a while, you're going to be wiping this guy's butt. So go home. Do something fun. Then line up a load of stuff on your TV. Believe me, hon, you'll be glad you did."

"You're cute," Meredith said and gave Andrea a dazzling smile.

"So are you, sweetheart," Andrea said, standing up and patting Meredith's knee. "You'll be all right. Just don't drink tonight."

Meredith didn't seem to notice that Andrea had left because she went on smiling. A moment or two later, Harry said, "What's funny?"

"I am," Meredith said. "I just hit on Andrea. I told her she was cute."

"How did she take it?"

"She patted my knee. Do you think we'll get together?"

"If that's what you really want, I hope you do."

"Will I really be wiping your butt?"

"Probably not."

"Maybe I'll get Raquel to do it. Would you like that?"

Fortunately, Harry didn't have to answer because Meredith leaned back in the chair, closed her eyes, and was gone for the next ninety minutes.

Chapter 34

When Harry was released from the hospital, he entered Rigby, an extended-care facility in Riverside, a section of Avola popular with young executives and their families, where, thanks to grueling weeks of physical therapy, he gradually regained full use of his body and was finally released with Dr. Cribbs's blessing. Jim and Hodges visited him at least once a week, but carefully steered clear of any discussion of his shooting or their search for the shooter.

Raquel made flying visits, usually when she was running an errand for Meredith, but Meredith came every day, keeping him supplied with chocolate and scotch, to the degree that he became the first place nurses and patients came for counseling.

"Come and stay with me," she said on the day before his release. "There's everything you need there, and Raquel and I and a nurse if you need one will make sure you're cared for properly."

It was odd but a fact that they didn't talk about their night of love-making until nearly the end of his stay at Rigby. For at least the first third of the time he was there, Harry had little space in his mind to devote to sexual encounters. His medication lessened but did not eradicate his pain, and most of his waking hours were filled with either exercising or recovering from it. His meetings with Meredith had been brief and quickly erased by what was happening next and how uncomfortable it was going to be.

Quite possibly she had taken his silence on the subject to mean he did not want to talk about it or explore its significance in their relationship. Were they going to move forward into a deeper exploration of their physical attraction for one another or not? It was likely she thought the answer to that question was *not.*

Or, possibly, she was as ambivalent about what had happened as he was.

Whatever the answer, when Meredith suggested his coming to stay with her, his first response was to say, "I haven't forgotten what happened between us the night before I was shot. Has what came after cleared it right out of your memory?"

They were sitting in the sunroom. It being south Florida, a translucent beige curtain was drawn across the entire expanse of glass, robbing the blazing light of most of its force.

"My God, Harry," she cried. "I thought you'd forgotten it. Cribbs told me you might lose as much as a week of memories from before the shooting."

"No, I remember everything up to the event itself."

"Is it a pleasant memory?" she asked.

"Very."

"Me too, and that was a starter kit. Imagine what we could do with practice," she said, beaming. " 'Come live with me and be my love.' "

"It's tempting but not now," he told her. "Whoever shot me will be coming back. He'll be figuring that the third time never fails, and he'll be up close this time, to make sure he finishes the job."

"You're trying to protect me, aren't you, Harry?" she said angrily. Without waiting for him to answer, she said, "Have you noticed he didn't kill me at the same time he shot you. Get it through your head, Harry, he doesn't want me dead."

"There may be two people who want you dead for quite different reasons," Harry said. "Actually, I'm acting very selfishly. If we're together when the next attempt comes, I'll be thinking of you instead of focusing on saving my own skin. And that's a sure way to buy the one-way ticket. So, no, I'm not coming to live with you, tempting as the offer is."

"It's Holly, isn't it?" she said.

Harry hesitated and the pause said more than any explanation. Meredith's gaze dropped away from his, and her shoulders slumped.

"That's not why I'm not going home with you, Meredith," Harry said quietly. "What I told you is true. Also, I want to be in my own home again. I miss it. Also, I want to be able to look in on Tucker. He's not well."

"Stop, Harry," she said in a resigned but still friendly voice. "Let's forget it and move on. But I hope you're not going to go to work right away."

"One step at a time," he said.

"You lie like a fisherman, Harry," she said with a wry smile.

"You going to be all right on your own?" Hodges asked, helping Harry out of the police cruiser onto the thin grass of his lawn.

Hodges was not happy about leaving Harry alone on the Hammock, but his efforts to persuade him to stay on at the extended-care facility having failed, he let Harry have his way.

"It won't be pretty, but I can drive," Harry said, already buoyed just by feeling the Hammock under his feet. "I'll be fine."

"You're pretty exposed out here," Hodges said, looking around at the barn and the house and the dark forest beyond.

"Frank, I'm exposed everywhere," Harry said, dropping a hand on Hodges's shoulder. "Thanks for the ride. Has Millard talked with O'Malley again?"

"Yes, but like always, there's no evidence to hook him to your shooting," Hodges said gloomily. "The crime scene people have combed his house, his office, his car, and come up empty. If he's the shooter, he's a master at covering his tracks."

"If he's the shooter," Harry added.

"You're still thinking Foster," Hodges said.

"Just not forgetting him," Harry said. "Now, I'm going to start getting my life back. Thanks again for the ride."

"Good luck," Hodges said, wringing Harry's hand, "and watch your back."

"I'll do that," Harry replied, burying his crushed hand in his pocket to stop himself from shaking it.

Harry waited until he heard the loose plank bang before crossing the lawn to his house. The mockingbird began singing in the wisteria vine at the south end of the lanai. And Harry, feeling better by the moment, decided he was being welcomed home.

Hodges had returned to close up the house once he was sure Harry was stable and likely to live. Because he'd shut down everything in the house except the refrigerator, the house had been storing heat, and Harry's first task was to go through the place opening windows, to let the breeze, warm as it was, chase out the hot, stale air.

To his dismay, he found the stairs a challenge and had to pause twice to let the pain subside before making it to the second-floor landing. His next task was to get the mail, and, against his better judgment, he decided to walk to the mailbox. In payment, before he got back to the house, his right side and shoulder were aching like a bad tooth.

He had just finished sorting his mail when the phone rang.

"Mr. Brock?" the caller asked.

"Yes."

"Good. My name is Everett Hackaway. I'm Tucker LaBeau's

lawyer. He might have mentioned my name."

Harry felt a sudden chill pass through him. "Yes, I recognize the name."

"Is this a good time for you to talk?"

Harry had gone into the kitchen to answer the phone, and now he pulled a chair out from the table and sat down. "I think so."

"I know you're just out of the hospital, so I'll get right to the point."

"How bad is the news you're bringing?"

There was a pause, and then Hackaway said, "I'm not sure. I gather you and Tucker are old friends."

"That's right."

"Well, I'm calling you because he's not up to it—at least at present. About ten days ago he checked into Gulf Shore. That's an extended-care facility in town."

"Tucker mentioned it," Harry responded. "How ill is he?"

"It's difficult to know. It's his heart, and its principal symptom is that he's very weak. He held out on the farm as long as he could. About two weeks after you were hospitalized, he called me to say he could no longer care for himself and the farm and was going into Gulf Shore."

"Have you been in touch with him since then?"

"Oh, yes. I've talked with him once or twice a week. You and he have very unusual property arrangements with the state government. Very unusual. I've found it most interesting."

"Is he relinquishing the farm?" Harry demanded, the chill that hadn't left him deepening.

"That's one of the things I've called you to discuss. As you know, what happens to your property arrangements depends, to an unspecified degree, on what happens to Tucker's farm."

"That's right," Harry said. "If the farm reverts to the state, I may or may not have to leave this place."

"Right, but Tucker has charged me with intervening with the state on your behalf."

"What about the animals?" Harry said, alarmed that he hadn't thought of them until that moment.

"The mule and the dog have been taken to a farm up the state a ways. I believe it's a cattle spread in the La Belle area. The hens have been moved to another relative's place, and for the moment, the beehives are on their own. I'm negotiating with a professional beekeeper in Port Charlotte, who, I'm hoping, will take them."

"Then Tucker's move is permanent," Harry said.

"Not necessarily, but he was insistent that the animals be placed where, if necessary, they can remain," Hackaway responded.

Not liking how that answer made him feel, Harry shifted his mind back to the farm. "All of his tools and equipment?" he asked.

"If he surrenders the farm, the Division of Recreation and Parks is poised to take charge of the entire property and everything on it. They did not want the animals. The person I talked with said the division will stock the farm when the time comes."

"Are they also going forward with plans to turn it into a farm museum and open it to the public?"

"They're being close-mouthed about exactly what's going to happen, but it will be something very close to what you've described."

"What's my situation as of today?" Harry asked, bracing himself.

"Undecided, but if I were to guess, I'd say you'll be allowed to go on living where you are as long as you continue in your warden's posting. These plans for establishing a farm museum will go through several permutations, but in the end the division will do whatever it intends to do. By the way, one of the people I've been talking with said they would be 'contacting' you soon."

"Then it's really a done deal, and you're trying to let me down easily."

"I can't be sure one way or the other. Tucker may rally and return home, but if he does, he will almost certainly have to give up his farm work. By the way, he talks about you as if you were his son."

"I guess it would be fair to say he and I have grown close over the years. I can't seem to believe he's actually done this."

"I'm sorry, but I suspect Gulf Shore or another facility will be where he ends his days. If you're up to it, I urge you to see him. He's very anxious to talk with you."

"Yes," Harry said, thinking it would be one of the most painful conversations he would ever have, but it had to be done.

An hour later, Meredith called.

"Why didn't you tell me you were being discharged?" she demanded as soon as he answered.

"Hodges was there and offered to give me a ride. I took it."

"What's wrong?" she asked, her voice climbing.

"Tucker's left the farm, sent Sanchez and Oh, Brother! to live on a ranch in the La Belle area, and checked himself into the Gulf Shore extended-care facility."

"Oh, Harry, I'm sorry. Is it his heart?"

"Yes, his lawyer Everett Hackaway called me and gave me the news. I knew this was coming but not so soon."

"I suppose I can't persuade you to come and stay with me for a while, for as long as you want?"

"No, Meredith. It's very generous of you, but I can't."

"We're not going to try to make a life together, are we, Harry?"

She sounded defeated, and Harry forced himself to be honest though he hated having to do it.

"I don't think so, Meredith," he said quietly, "but I'm not really in any state of mind to know what I want."

"I think you do know, but it's kind of you to pretend otherwise. I guess I've known for a while that you don't love me. It hurts, but it's not your fault. Are you going to be all right there alone?"

"Yes, I'll be fine."

"I'm going to be out of town for a few days. One of the companies whose board I'm on is holding a director's meeting in New York, followed by a tour of their new plant in Charlotte, and a second meeting in the new facilities. I hate not being here for you, but I feel I can't just skip these meetings."

"Go, I'll be all right. I've got a ton of paperwork to catch up on."

"Harry, promise me you'll be careful."

"I promise. Don't worry about me, and have a good time."

"Goodbye, Harry," she said, her voice breaking, and hung up.

Rather than wonder if he had made a terrible mistake, he called Jim.

Jim had known Tucker as long as Harry but not as well. Nevertheless, he listened to Harry's account of Tucker's move to the Gulf Shore facility and his fear that Tucker would not recover enough to return home. Harry also told him about Everett Hackaway's call and the uncertainty of what was to be done with his house.

When they had finished saying to one another those things that were intended to make them feel better but didn't, Jim abruptly changed the subject and said, "I'm putting constables out there nights. They'll be on a rota. I can't give you cover long, but at least until you're fully on your feet."

What he really meant was until Harry was moving freely and able to handle a gun.

"A week should do it and thanks," Harry said. "Any new developments?"

"No. Somebody walked in there the morning of the shooting, but the sand in the road won't hold a real print. There was no spent shell that Millard's people could find."

"Frustrating," Harry said.

"You've noticed," Jim said.

There were voices in the background and Jim said, "Got to go."

There ought to be three men doing that job, Harry thought, putting down the phone. He stood without moving for a moment, listening, and could hear nothing. The crickets were not fiddling. The mockingbird in the wisteria had fallen silent. The barn swallows that had been diving low over the lawn for the past half hour had vanished.

He went on standing, knowing that a large animal, particularly a predator, moving through a forest or a field, for that matter, moves in a zone of silence that closes behind him and opens before him like a snail carrying his house with him. Harry was trying to determine in which direction whoever or whatever was moving out there was going. It was still early enough in the day for Harry to have all the windows and doors open.

It's at the back of the house, Harry thought. *The question being, will it keep going?* At this point he had not bothered himself much over the identity of the critter. Then he heard a scuffing sound from the rear of the house and knew what was happening.

Moving as quickly as he could, he stripped off his shoulder holster and shoved the CZ into the sling, cradling his right arm. Then he flung the holster through the door onto the lanai, pulled the chair around the table until it faced the dining room door, grabbed his coffee mug off the sideboard, set it on the table and put the coffee pot beside it, and sat down, facing the rear of the house, with his mug in front of him.

There was a faint squeak, which Harry knew was the screen door being opened very slowly. He drew the pistol out of his sling and rested it in his lap, the safety off. He was pouring coffee into his mug when a large man holding a handgun stepped into the kitchen.

"You're a hard man to kill," Kevin O'Malley said with a lopsided grin cracking the otherwise harsh expression on his broad, red face.

"It doesn't feel that way," Harry said.

"No, I don't suppose it does. Get up."

"Are you sure you want to do this?"

"Oh, yes."

"I thought you would kill Meredith first."

"No. You, her, and then the senator. I want him to know she's dead before I remove him from office. Get up."

Harry should have gotten up then, everything in the man's voice said so, but curiosity was too strong in him, and he went on sitting.

"Just one more question. Why have you killed all these people?"

O'Malley threw back his head and laughed.

Harry fired through the table and shot O'Malley through the heart.

Kicking the man's gun out of reach, Harry satisfied himself that O'Malley was dead. Then, still holding the CZ, he went back to his chair and sat down, resting his gun in his lap, and waited.

Fifteen minutes later by the kitchen clock, Harry got up and called Foster's office. His office manager answered.

"I'm sorry, Mr. Brock," she told him. "The senator is in Tallahassee and probably won't be back for at least a week. If this is urgent, I'll give you the office number."

Harry thanked her, then punched in the number. One of the senator's interns answered and told him Senator Foster was out of town for a few days.

"Is he going to New York and then Charlotte?" Harry asked.

"Just a minute, his itinerary is here somewhere. Yes, here it is, and you're right, New York and then Charlotte. Can I convey a message?"

"If he calls, tell him Kevin O'Malley is dead."

"Oh, my God!" the young man said. "How did it happen?"

"I shot him," Harry said and hung up.

Chapter 35

"Did you have to tell that poor kid you'd shot O'Malley?" Jim asked. "He did everything but try to raise a *posse comitatus* and go after you himself."

"The devil made me do it," Harry said.

"I'm glad he did," Hodges said. "You ought to get something out of the encounter."

"He did," Jim said sternly. "He's alive."

"I suppose that's something," Hodges acknowledged grudgingly.

"The thing that bothers me most," Harry said, "is not waiting to see if he was going to tell me why he'd been on such a killing spree."

"My guess," Jim said, leaning forward to rest his forearms on his desk, "is that he would have shot you as soon as he stopped laughing."

Hodges countered with, "I think he was enjoying himself too much to have ended it there."

"Well," Jim put in, "one thing is certain. He's not going to tell us now."

It took Harry another two days to finish with Millard Jones and the court work, establishing that he had shot O'Malley defending his own life. Once that was out of the way, and it was established that O'Malley's Browning 9mm had been used in Hornsby's death, Harry went to see Tucker.

Harry found the hospital wing of Gulf Shore was much like the real thing, smelling of disinfectants and ominously quiet, especially the patients' rooms. Wendy Hoffman, the woman who had taken his call, met him at the main entrance, shook his hand, and steered him to the registration desk.

"Our guests as well as our residents sign in and out," she said with no trace of apology in either her voice or her manner. "One of the principal responsibilities of a facility like Gulf Shore is knowing who's in and who's out. You might be surprised, Mr. Brock, to learn how difficult it is to be sure we do know."

Making an effort, he braced himself to see Tucker in a hospital bed. By now he and Hoffman were approaching the end of the black-and-white tiled corridor. Hoffman stopped short of the last door and turned to Harry.

"I think I should warn you," she said softly, "that Mr. La-Beau may or may not be communicative. He's mildly sedated and may be asleep. His cardiac team at ACH stabilized him, and we're keeping him comfortable."

"All right," Harry said, but found that it wasn't at all right.

"Oh," she said, pausing again, "one of the nurses may come in while you're with him. He's being carefully watched. He or she will not disturb you beyond being in the room, checking the numbers. You'll see what I mean when you go in."

The tiny figure in the bed scarcely lifted the sheet pulled over him, and the head on the face staring up from the pillow was pale as snow. Stopping beside the bed, Harry looked down at Tucker, whose breathing was scarcely perceptible. Feeling suddenly panicked, Harry sat down on the chair pulled up to the bed, forced himself to breathe, and took a firm grip on his emotions.

"Tucker," he said, "it's Harry. Can you hear me?"

Tucker's eyes popped open.

"Hello, Harry," he said, putting out his hand. "I won't try to get up. When I do, the good-looking nurses get into a snit."

"What about the others?" Harry asked, grinning in relief.

"They are all lovely. The sight of a beautiful woman is one of the things, no, the *only* thing that makes me wish I was young."

"How are you feeling?"

"Surprisingly, fine. I find being looked after is a pleasant experience."

"Is there anything I can do for you here or at the farm?"

"I left in a hurry. You might go over and see if there's anything you think needs redding up."

"Gladly," Harry said. "How long are you going to be in here?"

Tucker left the question unanswered.

"You know," he said, "I sent Oh, Brother! and Sanchez to a nephew's ranch?"

"Yes, Hackaway told me."

"They'll be well cared for and have a new world to explore. I was sorry to have them go, but I ran out of alternatives."

Harry considered saying he could have looked after them, but something stopped him. Possibly it was knowing that if Tucker had wanted that to happen, he would have asked him when he was making his decisions.

A young blonde nurse appeared on the other side of the bed. She picked up Tucker's right hand and, eyeing her wristwatch, took his pulse.

"Is it still there?" Tucker asked.

"Yes," she said, "and it's a bit stronger than yesterday. Are you comfortable? Is there anything I can get you?"

"Just come back soon. I'd much rather look at you than the ceiling."

"That's not much of a compliment," she said and grinned.

"While you're away, I'll think of a better one."

"I can see why you like being here," Harry said when she was gone.

Tucker made no response because he had fallen asleep. Harry stayed with him a few more minutes then left.

In the hall he met the nurse who had taken Tucker's pulse. "Did he fall asleep?" she asked.

"Yes, did you expect it?"

"Yes, he's had a lot of company today," she said. "He has a lot of relatives. Are you a relative?"

"No, an old friend and neighbor. Is he going to get better?"

"Not quickly," she said with a smile, "but if things go well he'll make at least a partial recovery."

"*Are* they going to go well?"

"We hope so, but you shouldn't be expecting miracles. He's not in any pain. There are no signs of agitation. Stay here as long as you want. He probably won't surface again, but he might."

Harry left, tried to believe he would.

As he was signing himself out, Wendy Hoffman came out of her office.

"I'll punch in the exit code for you," she said as they walked toward the door. "Were you able to speak with him?"

"Yes, then he fell asleep. The nurse said he'd had a lot of visitors today."

"Yes," she said, punching a number into the wall pad beside the double glass door, both fitted with panic bars.

"Is he going to recover?" Harry asked.

"There's no predicting these things, Mr. Brock, but much will depend on whether he wants to or not."

He pushed open the door, paused, and turning to her again said, "Thank you for taking such good care of him."

"He makes it very easy for us," she answered with a quiet smile.

Once out of the building, Harry called Everett Hackaway.

When he was put through to the lawyer, he asked, "If Tucker remains at Gulf Shores, how long before the state moves to reclaim the farm?"

"That's not clear in the agreement," Hackaway said, "but Tucker has told me that if he's not home in two months, he will be staying in Gulf Shores permanently."

"He seemed pretty contented when I spoke with him."

"I think that's true. He's tired."

"Something I never expected," Harry said.

"His being tired?"

"No, his being contented in a bed. In the past, when he's had to go into the hospital, he was a bearcat until they released him."

"I guess time changes everything," Hackaway said.

"It looks that way. Has he arranged to be cremated?"

"Yes, and the ashes scattered on the farm."

"That sounds right."

Once away from Gulf Shores, Harry's pain and disorientation from finding Tucker so weakened and, despite that, at ease, began to be replaced by resignation, and he found he took increasing comfort and an unexpected sense of release from knowing Tucker had made his plans so carefully. He was especially pleased that Tucker's ashes would be spread on the farm.

He could not, however, shake off his sense of loss. It was not confined to Tucker's situation but was much more general, as though it encompassed his whole life. He thought at first it came from his confronting the possibility that Tucker was unlikely ever to be able to live on his own again. But he also began to see that whatever the outcome of Tucker's illness, something of great importance in his own life was drawing to a close.

For relief from that thought, Harry turned to the matter of

Meredith and Foster away on trips to the same cities. It, too, was an uncomfortable fact, and he was not sure he fully understood why he had made the call that revealed it.

He had turned onto the humpbacked bridge when his phone rang. He stopped and answered the call.

"I've just learned you were shot, Harry," Holly said at once. "How are you?"

"Sore but okay. There's some bad news. Tucker is very ill. Sanchez and Oh, Brother! have been moved to a farm north of here. I should have called you, but I kept hearing myself say, 'Hi, Holly, I've been shot,' and lost my courage. It's good to hear your voice."

"Were you planning to tell me you were wounded? No! Cancel that. I'm sorry about Tucker and the animals. Are you very upset?"

"Yes, I would have told you once I was sure it was behind me. As for the second question, I guess I have to answer yes."

He started to say he had finished the investigation then found he couldn't trust himself to speak.

"Tell me about the shooting," she said quickly.

Harry gave her a sanitized version of what had happened, omitting the sequel in which he shot O'Malley.

"I'd urge you to come out here to recoup, but I know I'd be wasting my breath," she said.

"You're giving up pretty easily," he said, hoping to make her laugh.

"Good try, Brock," she told him, "but we are not amused."

"No," Harry said, feeling his spirits plummet, "there's not a lot to laugh about."

There was a long moment of silence.

"The case is nearly closed," he told her.

"What's going to happen?" she asked. "Will you lose your house?"

"Not any time soon, given the glacial speed with which the state moves in these matters, but Hackaway, Tucker's lawyer, said the agreement between Tucker and the state is now in play. Even so, I'm not thinking about that. I've got a little more work left on the case to do."

"And I've got this spread to run. So I'd better get at it. It's a big place, big enough for both of us. Think about it. I love you, Harry. Think about that too."

That evening Harry answered his phone and a nearly jubilant Prentice Foster began shouting in his ear.

"You've done it, Harry," he said. "I've just picked up my messages. Congratulations! How did you figure it out?"

"He did it for me," Harry said, thinking the bastard was trying to game him. "He had another go at shooting me. I turned the tables on him. Are you and Meredith spending some quality time together?" He failed to keep some of his bitterness from seeping into the question.

"Yes," Foster responded almost gaily, either indifferent to Harry's tone or unaware of it. "How did you know? Hang on. Meredith wants to speak with you."

"How are you, Harry?" she asked.

"Mending," he said. "Is there something you want to tell me?"

"I'm limited in what I can say but the gist of it is that Prentice met me in New York, and after my commitments were met and we were on the way here, we came to an agreement. By now his lawyer will have made a preliminary filing for divorce on his behalf, and when that has worked its way through to completion, we're going to be married."

"When exactly was it decided?" he asked.

"Shortly before he got word that you shot O'Malley."

"Then I wish you both well," Harry said, surprised to find he was relieved to know that Foster could not have been involved in the killings. "I think my job is finished."

"Thank you, Harry," she said. "It might have ended differently."

"Yes, it might," he said. He wondered whether she meant they might have been together or that he might have been killed, and as quickly decided not to ask.

"By the way," he said, "you were wrong about one thing. O'Malley was planning to shoot both of you."

"Harry, are you trying to be funny?" she demanded, her voice rising.

"Honor bright, he said you first, then Prentice. I'm glad he didn't do it. Goodbye, Meredith."

After the best night's sleep he'd had in weeks, Harry called Wendy Hoffman and asked after Tucker.

"He's responding when spoken to, eating a little, and is pretty much the way he was with you yesterday. This is going to be a long process, Harry. We'll know more in a few days than we do now. Visit him all you want."

Harry went that afternoon and found Tucker awake and without visitors.

"Don't you have a living to make?" Tucker asked in a moderately firm voice.

"All work and no play," Harry responded. "How are you feeling?"

"I don't hurt anywhere, and nobody's asking me to dance," Tucker replied. "Believe it or not, I'm enjoying this much more than I expected."

"That's very good news. Want to hear about the Lansbury case?"

"Go ahead, but I won't promise not to fall asleep."

Harry gave a quick summary of what had happened.

"Well done," Tucker said. "I'm glad Meredith and Prentice weren't involved. Looks like the pregnancy can go forward with two happy parents. Thanks for telling me."

He closed his eyes for a moment, and Harry thought he had dropped off. But he opened them again and said, "Listening tires me, Harry, and I want to rest. Before I shut down for a while, however, I want to say something to you. It's time you cut yourself loose, Harry, from me, from the Hammock, everything. I will get better or I won't, and there's nothing you can do about it. Give me your hand."

Harry took his old friend's hand.

"I owe my life to you, Tucker," he said.

"You've repaid the debt ten times over, my young friend. The rest of your life awaits you."

Harry held Tucker's hand until he was sure Tucker was asleep, then left and drove back to the Hammock.

Once home he felt a restlessness and need to do something that took him outside again and turned his feet toward Tucker's farm. The midday heat was dissipating, the shadows lengthening. Harry pulled off his sandals, to feel the soft, white sand under his feet as he walked, his mind slowing and emptying in the coolness of the intermittent breeze redolent with the damp, enticing scents of the forest.

As he followed the winding, white road, vaguely aware of the dark water murmuring as it flowed beside him, Harry began recalling his early responses to this strange world he had wandered into and the painfully slow falling-away of the misery that had driven him here. He recalled his first meetings with Tucker and the man's unwavering kindness, patience, and encouragement while helping Harry to struggle out from under his burdens of guilt, anger, and hatred of the world from which he had fled.

Coming to Tucker's farm road, Harry paused to put on his

sandals. He experienced a brief but intense regret that Oh, Brother! and Sanchez were no longer there to greet him. But that feeling lifted and, moving more quickly, he walked into the farm clearing, the vegetable gardens to his right, the bantam house and the orchard to his left, the barn in front of him and beyond the barn the chicken house and the hives, then the house beyond them.

He stood for a moment, taking in the sun-drenched scene, silent in the somnolence of late afternoon. Harry had braced himself for a drenching flood of sorrow and loss because Tucker was no longer present and, he could now admit, probably never would be. To his astonishment, it didn't come. The farm lay quiet, peaceful but without emotional charge.

Puzzled, even troubled, by its absence, he walked along the familiar path past the barn and on to the house. He did not ask himself why he was here or what he was searching for. He went forward because doing so assuaged that need to do something he had experienced so strongly.

When he reached the back of the house, he stepped onto the stoop and stopped. The two bentwood rockers stood in their places, the upended milk crate between them. He had intended to go into the house, but now he hesitated. He no longer feared the slam of grief in finding it empty, but now he feared going in and not being hit with it.

Trying to work out what it meant that so far nothing had created pain, he turned his back to the door and stared at the narrow strip of grass where Oh, Brother! had grazed so many times while he and Tucker sat talking over mugs of cider, waiting for a chicken or a ham to come out of the oven.

Nothing. His focus shifted to the white oleander, under which Sanchez usually lay, but he was not there. Still nothing. In desperation, Harry spun around, dug the house key out of the brown jug sitting in the corner, unlocked the door, and charged into the house, coming to a halt in the center of the kitchen.

The room had that dry, airless smell that comes so quickly to a house with no one in it. The gingham curtains, usually billowing gently in the breeze coming through the screens, hung motionless. Finding he was holding his breath, Harry released it and breathed hard for a moment.

Gradually growing calmer, he began trying to find something, anything, that would tell him this was Tucker's home. Then he did sense something. It was the house itself, only the house, silent, still, indifferent. A sudden puff of wind rattled the damper in the wood stove's chimney, causing Harry's heart to race then slow again in the returning silence.

He had not found what he had expected and quickly went out, locked the door, put the key in the jug, and walked back the way he had come. When he reached the stripped garden, he paused and looked back. He might have been looking at any deserted farm. Facing forward, he turned down the farm road. As he walked, a weight he had not known he was carrying began lifting off him, and he walked more quickly. When he reached the white sand road, he picked up his pace and strode away.

Jim slowly laid the letter beside its envelope and ran a hand over his head, his face somber.

"Is it from Harry?" Hodges asked.

"Yes," Jim said, picking up his pen and beginning to click it.

"Well?" Hodges asked, getting up from his creaking chair.

"He's gone."

"Gone where?"

"Montana."

ABOUT THE AUTHOR

Kinley Roby lives in Southwest Florida with his wife, author and editor Mary Linn Roby. *An Anecdotal Death* is his tenth Harry Brock novel.